ANGEL'S PROMISE

ALEATHA ROMIG

NEW YORK TIMES BESTSELLING AUTHOR

New York Times, Wall Street Journal, and USA Today bestselling author of the Consequences, Infidelity, and Sparrow Web series: Web of Sin, Tangled Web, Web of Desire, and Dangerous Web

COPYRIGHT AND LICENSE INFORMATION

ANGEL'S PROMISE

ANGEL'S PROMISE

Everett Ramses came into my life like a hurricane on a dark New Orleans night. With a deep voice and penetrating gaze, his mere presence tingled my nerves and twisted my insides much like the city's legendary stories of spirits and ghosts.

As the ruler of New Orleans, Everett Ramses lives life hard and takes what he wants without apology.

He wants me to be his queen.

I am not an unwilling capture or a damsel in distress.

No, I, Emma North, willingly fell for the man who proclaims himself the devil.

Do I follow through on the promise I made to Rett, or do I listen to my own instincts and run before it's too late?

The future of New Orleans is now in my hands.

Have you been Aleatha'd?

#enemiestolovers #arrangedmarriage #age-gap-romance #dangerousromance

*From New York Times bestselling author Aleatha Romig comes a new romantic suspense duet set in the dark and mysterious world of New Orleans. This full-length novel is the conclusion of the *Devil's Series Duet* that begins with the prequel "Fate's Demand", continues in *DEVIL'S DEAL*, and concludes in *ANGEL'S PROMISE*.

PROLOGUE

The conclusion of DEVIL'S DEAL

Emma

*A*s the solid doors to the house opened and we all progressed toward Rett's front office, the soft music and Miss Guidry's excitement mixed with loud voices coming from down the hall. Rett's and Ian's posture changed, our steps staggered, and Miss Guidry reached for my hand.

"Oh no," she said, "Mrs. Ramses, come with me."

Judge McBride seemed confused.

"You too, Judge McBride," Miss Guidry said, trying to lead us back to from where we'd come.

I tried to make sense of what could be happening as the mixture of concern and anger radiated from my husband's being.

The voices were close, near the grand staircase in the foyer.

It didn't make any sense.

Who would be in Rett's home—our home?

Henri, one of Rett's men, came around the stairs. "Mr. Ramses, I'm sorry. They demanded to wait for you. They have been checked and are free of weapons."

They?

Weapons?

"Ramses." The loud call came from beyond our view.

Rett turned to me. "Emma, go with Miss Guidry. She'll take you upstairs another way." He looked at Judge McBride. "This won't take long."

I reached for Rett's arm. "Will you be safe?"

"Yes, and so will you. Go."

Miss Guidry seized my hand and tugged me back toward the courtyard. Before we could get another step, the loud voice called again.

"Ramses. Where is she? Your man is telling the truth, we're not armed. Come meet me like a man."

My fingers flew to my lips as I pulled away from Miss Guidry. I knew that voice. I'd grown up with that voice. For eighteen years we'd lived under the same roof until he left for college.

"He's really alive."

"Emma, go," Rett commanded.

"No. Kyle said he isn't armed. You won't let him hurt me." I didn't even consider he was now going by a different name or what his men had done. He was my brother, Kyle O'Brien.

Rett seized my arm. "Not like this, Emma. Go."

I pulled my arm away. "I may be your wife, but I can make my own decision."

We both pivoted near the end of the staircase. In the large foyer, staring back at us were two men. No introduction was necessary for either. One was the man I'd thought was my brother. The other was the brother of the man in the picture Rett showed me when I first arrived. While his brother Greyson had died, by the evidence before us, Liam Ingalls was very much alive.

I sucked in my breath as my eyes opened wide.

"Fuck, Emma," Kyle said, "tell me you didn't marry him."

My tongue faltered, forgetting how to speak as I stared at my brother. This was New Orleans; maybe he was a ghost or one of Miss Guidry's spirits. However, I knew he wasn't, and neither was the boy-turned-man beside him who'd taken my heart. Liam Ingalls had taken more than that. It was then I realized Rett had a pistol in his hand pointed at the two men.

With the large light shining down in the foyer, I scanned them both. With the same color hair and eyes as me, I again questioned if Kyle and I were biologically related. Liam was Kyle's polar opposite. Where Kyle was golden blond like me, Liam's hair was dark like Rett's. Kyle's eyes and mine were both blue. Liam's were a mesmerizing green. I'd seen those eyes in my dreams and nightmares. After my family's death, images of his eyes brought on tears with the memory of how Liam told me he was leaving and that there was no future for us.

"Emma, go the fuck upstairs," Rett growled as he lifted his pistol.

He wasn't the only one holding a gun. Ian and Henri both had barrels pointed at Kyle and Liam and in the distance, I heard others coming.

Kyle lifted his hands above his head. "I told your man I'm not armed, Ramses, and neither is Ingalls. There's no need to kill us like you did Greyson."

Rett took a step forward. "Unarmed, it will make it easier to kill you both."

"No." I had found my voice.

"Emma, upstairs."

"You married him?" Liam asked.

"Why are you here?" I asked as memories of my abduction came back. "Leave. Listen to Rett and get out."

Kyle spoke with his hands now on top of his head. "Em, I came to tell you what's happening and to free you from...him."

Free.

"I'm not captive, Kyle. I live here." The lies I'd lived with for too long gave me strength. "Furthermore, why would I go with you? I'm Rett's wife. You lied to me. God, Kyle, you're alive. You let me think...let me mourn...."

The male image of me took a step closer, but stilled his steps as all the guns lifted, still pointed his direction.

Kyle shook his head. "I'm sorry I couldn't tell you before now. I didn't mean to hurt you, Em. I meant to include you. That's why I hired Underwood to watch you and get you here to New Orleans."

My gaze went to Rett and back to Kyle. "You hired Ross?" I lifted my hands to the side of my head. "I can't believe you, Kyle." I looked to Rett and shook my head. "I'll ask Ross."

"Sis, he's dead," Kyle said. "Your husband had Underwood killed. Ramses not only had him killed, he had Underwood's death ruled a suicide."

"What?"

"He's lying, Emma," Rett replied. The volume of his voice rose. "Now get the fuck out of this house."

"Are you going to slaughter me in front of my sister?"

"You know she isn't your sister."

"Is it true?" I asked Rett in disbelief. "Is Ross dead?"

More men had gathered, coming from where I wasn't certain. In a mere matter of minutes, they outnumbered Kyle and Liam by at least eight to two and also eight firearms to none.

"Get them out of here," Rett ordered.

As a large man I didn't know gathered Kyle's arms behind his back and my brother struggled, he said, "Em, you look just like her and so do I. There's so much you need to know. Ramses is a liar and a murderer. Come with us."

There were too many things going through my head. "Where have you been for four years?"

"It's a long story."

I took a step toward him. "You talk about Rett. What about you and your men? Did you know what your men did to me?" Tears infiltrated my words. "You let them hurt me. Get out of this house and out of New Orleans."

"Get him out," Rett yelled.

Kyle's head shook back and forth as he was dragged toward the door. "I don't know what you're talking about. I've been trying to find you. It was the court filing this afternoon for the marriage license that tipped us off."

"Your men," I said, explaining, "the ones who took me."

"No, Em." Kyle's expression was puzzled. "My men would never touch you. I wouldn't allow it." His blue eyes went to Rett and back to me. "Listen to me, don't stay here. Come with us and learn the truth."

As I tried to grasp what Kyle was saying, Rett's men surrounded him and Liam, pushing them through the double front doors out into the yard and driveway. As the volume rose, the air filled with Rett's orders.

If Kyle's men didn't take me, who did those men work for?

My stomach lurched at the only other possibility— one I couldn't bear to entertain.

Rett stood in the doorway. Turning, he looked back my direction. "Emma, remember what you said."

My expression must have asked for clarification.

His dark stare bore down on me. "You said you'd trust me."

There was too much.

I needed clarification.

I hurried past Rett and yelled to the outside for Kyle. "Who is *us*? Who should I listen to, you and Liam?"

Kyle turned my way.

"You've both lied to me."

Kyle's voice came over the dull roar of the commotion. "Em, I'm sorry. I'll tell you the truth. Us doesn't mean Liam. You should listen to our mother."

"She died," I reminded him.

He fought as he was being pushed into the back seat of an SUV.

"Kyle," I called one last time.

"Jezebel, Em. She's alive and I swear, she can explain."

As Kyle disappeared into the SUV, I stepped back and back, into the foyer. My heart beat in overtime against my breastbone as the bodice of the dress grew tighter. Breathing became difficult as too many thoughts clouded my mind and I sank to the stairs, sitting on the bottom step. Beyond the double doors, Rett's men disappeared, taking away my brother and my first love.

When Rett stepped back inside, he closed the double doors. With a deep breath, he ran his hand over his hair, pushing it back from where it had become disheveled. I looked up, wondering who was telling me the truth.

Rett offered me his hand. "Come, we need to sign the marriage certificate."

I didn't budge. "Jezebel is alive?"

He nodded. "I never said otherwise."

I shot to my feet. "So you lied by omission?"

"Miss Guidry told you. She speaks of Jezebel in the present tense." He reached for my hand.

I pulled it away. "She speaks of your mother in present tense too."

Rett continued to offer his hand.

Refusing to reach for it, I held the banister and stared back up to his gaze. "Tell me who took me."

"I have their names if you want to see them. Their identities are irrelevant, Emma. I won't allow them or anyone else to harm you. They're dead."

Just like Greyson and now Ross.

The finality of his statement cooled my skin. "Who hired them?"

"Emma." Rett took another step closer, his presence dwarfing me as his timbre slowed. "Come with me, now."

Applying pressure to my teeth, I stared at the man before me.

Had Rett told me the truth?

Was he truly the devil?

The earlier noise from all the commotion was gone; a new blistering silence rang in its place as Rett's nearly black eyes narrowed. "Now, Emma. You agreed to this deal with me."

I had, and yet as my grip tightened on the top of the banister, I was unable to move forward.

The doorway to the room right off the foyer caught my attention. The tall doors were opened. The room within glowed with golden light from a large chandelier above. The furnishings were like something out of a museum or a palace. Standing guard were more of Rett's men. Ian was within, speaking with Judge McBride.

Miss Guidry was also there, her head shaking as she added to their conversation.

As my presence lingered, it was as if I were one of her ghosts, present, but unable to affect the world around me.

Rett's voice lowered, piercing the fog of illusion. "Emma."

My chin snapped toward him, yet my lips didn't move.

His earlier emotion was gone. In its place was Rett's usual demeanor, one of superiority and power. It was as if the world was once again in his control. For a moment that dominance had been in jeopardy but no longer. His firm lips curled in victory as his arm wrapped around my waist and tugged me toward the room with the others.

With Rett's warm breath near my ear, to others his attention might have appeared gentlemanly. However, as goose bumps coated my skin, I heard what others couldn't: the underlying growl and warning.

"Remember my rule."

My feet began to move in unison as we neared the room.

"You promised, angel. Judge McBride is waiting with our marriage certificate, and you will sign."

EMMA

*R*ett's grip of my waist tightened as we continued our walk into the room with the golden glow, the one they'd referred to as his front office. This room wasn't anything like the office I'd been taken to after my abduction, the one hidden within the bowels of this mansion. This room was as if, upon leaving the foyer, we'd stepped out of current time and traveled back to the days of kings and queens, exemplified by lavish castles filled with riches.

It was a sitting room fit for royalty.

Inhaling deeply, I turned to the man at my side. In that split second, I saw only the pressed white shirt from beneath his custom tuxedo jacket covering his wide chest. I dared not to look higher, beyond the bow tie, to see his dark gaze upon me or invoke his deep tenor that would remind me again of the promise I'd made. Instead, I turned back to the room, gaping at the opulence, not as a would-be queen but perhaps as a peasant who had been mistaken for royalty.

I couldn't help but wonder how this was suddenly partly mine.

Standing by the entry and also in the far corners, similar to guards on sentry, were more of Rett's men. They didn't wear the uniforms and tall hats of the guards at Buckingham Palace, but rather dark suits, grim expressions, and beneath their suit coats, undoubtedly the firearms that had moments earlier been aimed at my brother and...Liam.

In the time that I'd been living within this dwelling, never had I seen so many of Rett's men in one place. Then again, the night had brought many unusual sightings. Trying to ignore them—or more likely seeking a diversion from them—I took in the luxury around us.

While polished to perfection, the wood floor showed a bit of the age of Rett's home.

How many people had stood in this room?

My attention was quickly diverted elsewhere. Beyond the fifteen-foot windows accented with heavy drapes, streetlights glowed. Their radiance created starbursts glimmering within the panes. And above us, the twenty-foot ceiling was covered in detailed murals surrounded with intricate trim and crown molding. In the center of the room, a large chandelier shimmered, sending light in prisms that flickered around the room and onto the extravagant furnishings.

Judge McBride, Ian, and Miss Guidry were gathered near an antique console table beautifully adorned with golden legs and a marble top. The judge's eyes were wide, and Miss Guidry wrung her hands as we approached.

Despite Rett's pressure moving me forward, each step I took was smaller than the last.

Earlier in the night, Judge McBride had asked me if I was marrying Everett Ramses without misgivings. In that moment, under the twinkling lights and standing before the fountain upon the pebblestone walkway that made up the Ramses family crest, I'd answered honestly.

That moment, maybe thirty minutes earlier—maybe an hour—now seemed like a lifetime ago.

The shutting of the large double doors behind us caused me to startle.

Rett tightened his grip, adding a little more pressure for me to move forward.

My first thought was to run, but run where and to whom?

"I believe," Judge McBride said as he lifted a long fountain pen our direction, "that despite the interruption, all that is left to be done is to sign the certificate."

Where was his question now?

How would I answer it if posed?

"It's customary," the judge continued, seemingly unaware of my new inner struggle, "for this certificate to come later from the courthouse; however, per our agreement earlier today, Mr. Ramses, tonight we'll complete all the legal documentation. Mr. Knolls and Miss Guidry have already signed as witnesses. Once the two of you sign, I'll add my signature and you two will legally be Mr. and Mrs. Everett Ramses."

When I didn't reach for the pen, Rett did. Releasing me, he stepped to the table and by the movement of the long pen, signed his name. It was then he turned to me, doing as the judge had done and extending the pen. "Emma."

My breaths pushed against the fitted bodice as I tried to comprehend what had transpired.

Judge McBride called it an interruption. That seemed too simple of an assessment of what had occurred. An interruption was a blip of time, a sidetrack, or maybe an intermission. Kyle and Liam's appearance wasn't the intermission but rather the unexpected second act.

"Emma," Rett repeated.

"Rett," I said, finding my voice. "I don't want to delay Judge McBride any longer than necessary, but before I sign, I need to speak with you" —I looked around the room— "in private."

I would have had to have been blind to not see Rett's jaw clenching, the tendons pulling taut in his neck, or his gaze darkening. While my experience with this man was limited by the length of our acquaintance, I had witnessed a full range of his emotions. Currently, he was not pleased. If I were one of his men, I might fear his next reaction.

To be honest with myself, I did have fear of his reaction. I simply refused to give it power.

Rett stepped closer with the pen in hand, then closer still, until I was craning my neck upward.

"You will sign." His declaration came from between clenched teeth.

Swallowing, I took a step back and walked to the double doors. Another of Rett's men was standing there. My neck straightened as I approached. "Open the door."

The man's stare darted from me to Rett.

Before anyone could speak, I turned to the room. "I am Mrs. Everett Ramses in every way with the exception of a signature. Do I or do I not have the power that accompanies that title?" I turned my blue stare toward Rett. "I would assume you're the one to answer that."

For a moment in time, the room took a collective breath. All eyes were on the man in command, the self-proclaimed king of New Orleans.

"Out," Rett bellowed as he turned to the man at the door and back to others around the room. "Give us five minutes. And then everyone will return." His gaze met the judge's as Rett offered the slightest of a bow. "Thank you for your patience."

My confidence built as one by one, the room emptied. The guard in the far corner was the last to move. It wasn't until Rett assured him that we wouldn't be long that the man finally joined the others. Once Rett and I were alone and the doors closed, I let out a breath.

It was a misjudgment on my part.

Before I could inhale, the man who was nearly my husband had me captive. With one arm around my waist and the other hand holding tightly to my chin, I was pinned against his solid body. Inclining his face toward mine, with our noses nearly touching, Rett's tone rumbled through me with the ferocity of a lion's growl, leaving goose bumps scattering in its wake.

"Never again." His nostrils flared with each deep breath as darkness swirled in his almost-black orbs. "I am in charge in all things, Emma. Don't forget that. That will be the last time you overstep your position."

If I were a sane person, I would retreat, perhaps apologize, and accept where fate had brought me. It seemed that based upon the evidence at hand—Rett in a tuxedo, me in his mother's wedding dress, and our marriage certificate upon the console—sanity wasn't my forte.

My neck and back straightened as my shoulders squared. "What is that position?"

"My wife."

I shook my head as much as his grip would allow as my eyes narrowed. "That isn't the only title you offered." His grip of my chin lessened. "You told me I would be your queen. A queen has her own power." I smiled. "If this were a game of chess, it would be my job to protect you."

"It's not a fucking game." Rett tilted his head toward the table. "You will sign the certificate."

"First, I want you to answer two questions."

Rett's arm around my waist pulled me closer. "Never again, Emma. Not in front of my men, household staff, or *anyone*..." He allowed that word to hang in the air. "Never will you make a public spectacle of contradicting or questioning me. If you choose to take that risk in private, that is your choice, but never again will anything like what just took place happen. Are we clear?"

"I asked to speak to you in—"

Rett's grip of my chin shifted to a finger upon my lips, stopping the rest of my sentence.

"Fucking say, 'Yes, Rett.'" He glared down at me. "That is all that needs to come from those beautiful lips."

As he slowly removed his finger, I acquiesced—sort of. "Yes, Rett, but that isn't all I'm going to say now."

Letting go of me, he exhaled and stepped away, heading toward the far side of the room. "Of course it isn't."

"Where are Kyle and Liam?" I asked. "What's happening to them?"

Rett spun my direction. "They're currently taking a ride with a few of my men. If you're asking me if I plan to kill them, the answer is yes."

I sucked in a breath.

"Don't give me that fucking wide-eyed-doe look, Emma. I've told you that was my goal since the first night at Broussard's. Isaiah or Kyle, I don't give a fuck what name he uses, lied to you." Rett gestured toward the doors. "He lied right out there in my—our—home. He lied about your abduction. He's lied to you for four years. What do you think would have happened if you'd gone with him?"

I wrapped my arms around my midsection as I allowed myself to think beyond what had occurred earlier in the foyer. It was the pearl-studded bodice that reminded me that this was my wedding. A half hour ago I was happy and now...

I wasn't certain where the new emotion came from.

Bewilderment and anger melted away as a sense of abandonment and sadness infiltrated my words. A rogue tear escaped my eye as I blinked away the moisture. "Maybe I'd meet my mother."

Rett's fingers combed through his dark hair. The styled gel from before had given way to his wavy mane. "It would be better if you didn't."

This time I went to him, the skirt of the wedding dress brushing the floor as the train followed in my wake. "You don't have any say in who I see."

"You're wrong, Emma. I have total control of who you see and what you do."

I wanted to argue that point, but based on the last month, I was without any solid evidence for an adequate defense. Instead, I asked the question Kyle's announcement had prompted. "Why didn't you tell me that Jezebel North is alive?"

"I never said she wasn't."

My lips pursed as I shook my head. "Stop it. I'm not stupid. You purposely misled me."

"We can discuss this matter of interpretation later. Judge McBride has plans."

"Life or death isn't an interpretation."

"You're right. They are a matter of being and if you left this house with him, your life would be over."

I laid my hand on Rett's sleeve. As I did, the rings upon my fourth finger caught my attention. Exhaling, I offered a deal. "Rett, I'll sign the marriage certificate.

Hell, I'll even work on what I say or don't say in front of others, but I need some promises from you too."

His dark orbs turned back to me. "Emma, that isn't how I work."

"You're not working with me. This isn't a business deal. This is a marriage. Remember what you said out in the courtyard?" I didn't give Rett a chance to answer. "You said that Miss Marilyn told you that anyone could propose. It's a simple question." A grin threatened my expression. "I believe you offered three proposals this afternoon." The muscles of his jaw loosened as I spoke. "She also told you that marriage wasn't easy. It required commitment. You asked me to believe that you, that we, are worth the effort. Do you still want that?"

Rett lifted my left hand and turned it ever so slightly, watching as the light from the chandelier reflected off the large diamond. His shoulders straightened as his stare met mine. "What promises do you want?"

It wasn't an answer to my question, and yet it was.

"Don't kill Kyle...or Liam, not yet."

"You don't understand what you're asking. If it's them or you, they will die."

I knew better than to do more than make the request. I continued, "The other promise that I want from you is the promise that if I do as you want and hold my tongue while in the presence of others, you will give me the chance to discuss anything—anything at all —in private. I can wait, and I will wait, as long as I know I'll have my chance."

"I can't promise *anything*. There are things you don't

need to know, things that would be safer for you not to know."

"Legally? Is this back to me making a statement?"

Rett's chest inflated as he inhaled. "Yes and no."

"No." My head shook. "The deal you offered wasn't for me to only be your wife but also your queen. I can't be a queen if I don't know what's happening. I'm not saying I need a report every night."

Rett curled the ends of his lips in amusement. "That's good because I have a long list of much better things for us to do each night than recite reports."

I wanted to deny how with a simple change in Rett's voice, his timbre and his pitch, that my body responded. He hadn't even been direct, yet his innuendo had my insides twisting and warmth pooling between my legs. I wanted to hate that he had that kind of effect, but then again, it was part of his allure. Over the last month, I'd become addicted to Everett Ramses and what he was capable of doing.

Trying to ignore the rise in temperature, I clarified my request, "I'm saying that if I have a question, you'll answer me honestly."

Rett lifted my left hand to his lips and planted a soft kiss to my knuckles. "I can do that...in private."

"Tonight I asked to speak to you in private. That needs to mean something too."

Rett nodded. "We both have work to do, Emma." With my hand in his, he confessed, "I have many dealings, irons in the fire. My first reaction may not always be what you want to hear, but this" —he tenderly squeezed my hand— "is why you, Emma Ramses, are fit to be a queen. I'll work on being patient with you if you'll give me the same honor."

I nodded. "And Kyle?"

"He'll be spared tonight."

My last request was the hardest one for me to make, to ask for leniency for someone who hurt me and left me without considering my needs. "Liam?"

Rett's dark eyes narrowed. His face tilted as if he understood my quandary—he couldn't and yet his response seemed as if he did. "What is the queen's request?"

My stomach twisted. "They both live, for now."

His lips landed upon the top of my head, just in front of the crown. "You will sign now."

It wasn't a question, but that inclination defined the essence of the man I'd agreed to marry—one who didn't ask but rather who proclaimed his wishes.

"I will sign."

EMMA

"Open the door," Rett said with a tilt of his chin as he retrieved his phone from his inside suit pocket.

Instead of doing as he said, I stilled, trying to read his expression as he looked down at the screen. Dread twisted my stomach as my pulse sounded in my ears. "It's not too late, is it?" I was asking about Kyle and Liam.

"No." His head shook as he sent a text message.

I wanted more information than one word, but I knew I wouldn't be getting it now. *No* was enough. Kyle and Liam would make it another day. Stopping at the double doors, I turned back as Rett slipped his phone into the breast pocket of his tuxedo jacket. "When you saved me..."

"Emma, Kyle lied. You know that in your heart. You know I wouldn't..." His head shook. "You know that isn't possible. Look inside your heart."

My heart.

Seeing Kyle and Liam, looking at Rett, I wondered what my heart believed and what my mind believed. Liam had been the last man I'd given my heart to. He was also the first. I shared more than my heart with him. We were young and I'd believed that we were in love, sneaking around so Kyle and Greyson wouldn't know. After all, Liam was the oldest, and I was the little sister.

Sister.

Kyle said *our* mother when he referred to Jezebel.

My heart was as confused as my head.

"Emma," Rett was now beside me. His palms came to my cheeks and his lips brushed my forehead. "Tell me that you trust me."

"I want to, Rett."

"Then open the door. Sign your name and be my wife. We'll work the rest out." His tone lowered. "They will both live another day because of you. One day, I won't spare them. His men took you. They..." The cords in his neck grew taut. "The people responsible at all levels for that will pay. Just not today."

"I have so many unanswered questions."

"Do you trust me? I trust you with my name and to sleep beside me."

Swallowing, I nodded. "At this moment, yes."

Reaching for the doorknobs, I made the decision to believe the handsome man at my side. Liam had left me when I needed him. Kyle lied about being dead. As I stared up into Rett's dark gaze, I knew I wanted to trust him, to believe him, to fulfill my promise to him.

When I opened the doors, Judge McBride, Ian, and

Miss Guidry were front and center. "I apologize for the delay," I said as I motioned for them to join Rett and me. "I'm ready to sign the certificate."

"Praise be," Miss Guidry exclaimed as she clasped her hands together.

The judge, our witnesses, and the man about to be my husband followed me to the antique console table as I reached for the pen. Rett's other men continued to enter, taking their respective places. I stared down at the document. Under the title of bride read my name, the one I'd always used: Emma Leigh O'Brien. Gripping the pen, I hesitated. "Do I sign my maiden name?"

"Once you sign as Emma Ramses, your marriage is official," Judge McBride said.

For a moment I considered what I'd said earlier to Rett, that maybe I wouldn't change my name. It took only a glance at the man watching me with his intense stare to know that the battle to retain O'Brien or take on North wasn't one I was willing to fight at this juncture. There were too many other matters at hand.

As I formed the letters, the swirl at the top of my E and an eloquent L, I realized I'd never written the name Ramses. It was an odd thought, but one that hit me, nonetheless. I forced my hand to keep moving, spelling out my new last name.

When I was younger, much like other girls my age, I would doodle names, such as mine with other last names. I'd spent many years imagining that I'd leave O'Brien behind and become Ingalls. Never before this moment had I considered that my name would change to something altogether different.

Placing the pen next to the document, Judge McBride came forward and added his signature as the officiant. He turned to the room. "Congratulations, Mr. and Mrs. Ramses." He looked to Rett. "I will file this first thing in the morning with the court; however, not to worry" —he removed his phone from his inner coat pocket and clicked a picture of the document— "for I'll send this via email to my secretary, and as of" —he read the time stamp— "this evening at 8:14 p.m., you are officially and legally married." He folded the certificate and placed it in his inside breast pocket.

Rett offered the judge his hand. "Thank you, Raymond. The dinner offer still stands."

The judge shook his head. "I believe you've had enough visitors for one night."

With my hand in my husband's, we escorted the judge to the front door. "Thank you again," I said as he stepped through the threshold onto the front steps.

"It was very nice to meet you, Mrs. Ramses."

Hearing my new title from his lips caused my cheeks to rise. Despite the turmoil, Rett and I were married.

"Everett, could I have a word?" the judge asked.

Rett released my hand. "I'll be a minute." He stepped out onto the front steps, closing the large doors behind them.

When I turned back to the foyer, I stood for a moment staring at my surroundings. I'd lived in this home for over a month, and yet I was seeing much of it for the first time. My gaze went up the grand staircase to the stained-glass window at the landing. There were so many unanswered questions swirling through my mind as I stared at the Ramses family crest. It was as Miss Guidry appeared that I realized we were alone. Rett's men had disappeared.

Where did they go?

"Mrs. Ramses," Miss Guidry said with a smile, refocusing my attention. "Mr. Ramses asked for your dinner to be served in the courtyard."

"Will you and Ian join us?" I wasn't sure what prompted the question, but since they'd both been involved in the wedding, it seemed appropriate.

"Oh no, ma'am, that wouldn't be right. Tonight is about celebrating."

I let out a long breath. "Is it? Did we do the right thing?"

Miss Guidry reached for my hands as her hazel gaze came my way. "Mrs. Ramses—"

"Emma," I interrupted.

"Miss Emma," she said with a nod, "you must believe in your heart you did what was right, always believe that."

It didn't go unnoticed that Rett and Miss Guidry both mentioned my heart when Rett and I had specifically stated this wasn't about love.

"Being Mrs. Ramses," she continued, "comes with responsibilities. Miss Marilyn didn't fully understand the weight of her responsibility. I believe that was because Mr. Abraham chose to keep things to himself. Mr. Ramses, your Mr. Ramses..."

My Mr. Ramses.

"...didn't marry a woman like Miss Marilyn."

"Is that bad?"

"No, child, it's the answer to prayers." Miss Guidry squeezed my fingers as she looked down at the rings and back up. "Times were different back then. Mr. Abraham had Mr. Boudreau to carry some of the load that is New Orleans. Their relationship wasn't always contentious." She shook her head and peered back up. "I've watched Mr. Ramses through the years, how he now carries that same burden alone. Don't think that he'll include you in his plans, but that's no never mind. You are included. You are here for a reason." She grinned. "The spirits are rejoicing. You see, you are the combination of your momma and your father."

Rett had said that I was the daughter of a king and a whore.

"I want to meet her."

Miss Guidry stood taller—her whole five feet nothing—as her smile faded. "She wants that, Miss Emma. She does, never doubt that. But first, I'd be right pleased and so would Miss Marilyn if you'd concentrate on him." She lifted her chin toward the front doors. Rett's silhouette showed through the leaded glass. "He needs you more than you know, more than he knows. Prayers from the spirits brought you here to us and to him. Not only those of Miss Marilyn, but Miss Delphine also. You see, it took them some time to find common ground, but in you, they have it. You are the answer to their prayers, and they know you won't let them down."

"Miss Delphine?" I questioned, having never heard the name before.

"She would be Mr. Ramses's grandmother."

"Miss Marilyn's mother?"

"No, her mother-in-law."

I nodded, remembering Miss Guidry mentioning her earlier, just not by her first name.

"I don't understand what they want from me."

"They want what they aren't able to accomplish. They believe in your promise."

"My promise?"

Miss Guidry grinned, small lines appearing at the edge of her hazel eyes. "Miss Emma, they have entrusted you with their most cherished treasure."

I looked down at my hand as my mind went through the different pieces of jewelry that had come my way over the last month: the rings on my fingers, diamonds in my ears, and the ruby and diamond necklace.

She lifted my hands. "No, Miss Emma. Their treasure isn't a piece of jewelry, money in the bank, or even this home. What they treasure above everything is now yours to keep safe."

The door to our side clicked as the doorknob moved.

"Do you mean Rett?"

Miss Guidry nodded.

"And what does my mother want?" I asked.

Before Miss Guidry could answer, the door opened and Rett entered, his brown orbs moving from me to Miss Guidry and back. Instead of addressing our conversation, he offered his arm to me. "Dinner, Mrs. Ramses."

Miss Guidry released my hands as I laid one on Rett's arm and together we walked beyond the staircase back out to the courtyard. Two of the men who had disappeared earlier, reappeared at the threshold, opening the doors as we stepped back under the lights and stars. As we continued along the pebblestone walkway, I asked, "Are there guards at each entrance?"

Rett patted my hand. "Neither Kyle nor his men will ever enter this house again. You can take my word. I promised you that you would be safe. You are."

I was.

Was I also captive?

It wasn't a thought I wanted to entertain on the evening of my wedding, but it was there.

As Rett pulled back the chair at the table near the fountain, he lowered his lips to my ear. "You're striking tonight, the most beautiful of brides."

His compliment returned warmth to my skin as I tucked the long skirt around me and sat. His next statement made me grin.

"I can't wait to get you out of that dress."

He took the seat across from me.

"Is everything all right with the judge?" I asked.

Rett shook his head. "That isn't your concern."

I looked from side to side and leaned forward. "We're alone, Rett. You promised."

"Yes, my dear, everything is all right. I assured him that nothing he witnessed was factual. He asked if tomorrow he'd be questioned regarding the unexpected meeting."

"Why—?"

The word barely left my lips before I knew the answer: Kyle and Liam.

"And you said...?"

"I told him the same as I promised you, Emma. They will live to see tomorrow."

We turned at the sound of doors opening and a cart coming our direction. Ian and Miss Guidry were both present, complete with a silver ice bucket and a bottle of champagne. Once two glasses were poured, Rett lifted his to mine. "To fulfilling promises."

That shouldn't be a daunting toast, but I couldn't help but think about the conversation I'd only recently had with the older lady still at our side. My gaze went to her and back to Rett as I too lifted my glass.

As the bubbling liquid glistened under the lights of the courtyard, I realized that the toast Rett had offered wasn't only for me. The handsome man staring now, focused solely on me, also had made promises.

Our glasses clinked. "To promises."

RETT

*A*s Emma and I reached the door to her suite, the one connected to mine, there were messages multiplying upon my phone. I'd felt the vibrations throughout our dinner. There may even be missed phone calls. Henri had made a terrible mistake allowing Isaiah Boudreau II and William Ingalls into my house. He would be dealt with in time. Most recently, I'd sent the message to my men currently transporting our unexpected visitors. Their lives would be spared, but not without a ride they wouldn't soon forget.

I gave no explanation for my change in orders. That wasn't necessary. My word was law. Nevertheless, sparing their lives didn't mean the night would be without terror.

My men were taking Boudreau and Ingalls on a tour of the Louisiana bayou. Maurepas Swamp wasn't far. The marshland took up nearly one hundred square miles, encircling three sides of Lake Maurepas and was located about twenty-five miles west of New Orleans.

Boudreau and Ingalls would be taken out on an old wooden boat with oars, deep into the cypress swampland on this nearly moonless night. It was a ride few lived to describe. Though theirs would be different.

There were old roads, not known by many, where tonight my men would be retrieved before leaving the two unwanted visitors afloat with bindings that with some perseverance would come undone.

My word to my wife would remain true.

Neither man would meet a bullet tonight. However, their survival skills would be tested as they tried to make their way out of the vast wetland.

The area in question was home to many creatures including raccoons, white-tailed deer, and alligators. The latter was known as a nocturnal feeder. It would be up to the two men to remain off the menu.

Their adventure, at best, would take them out onto Lake Maurepas where once daylight broke, they may possibly meet up with tour guides or locals. At worst, they would descend deeper into the bog and learn what other creatures lurked in the canopied undergrowth. Rumors swirl about the possibilities.

Either outcome worked for me and allowed me to keep my word to both Emma and Judge McBride.

Before opening the suite door, I stopped and releasing Emma's hand, whisked her off her feet, cradling her against my chest.

Her giggle was sweeter than the blues and jazz I enjoyed listening to.

"Rett, put me down."

Reaching beyond the layers of the dress's skirt, I

found the door handle. "I'm carrying you over the threshold."

Once inside, I gently placed her feet upon the floor and closed the door behind us. Without a word, I circled her, once and then again. "I've given those buttons some thought," I said, talking about the long line of pearls going down her back. "I think the best answer is to simply rip the lace. Anything else would take too long."

"Oh no you don't. This dress was your mother's, and Miss Guidry would not be happy if it was ruined."

Facing Emma, I stared for a moment at the crown secured in her golden locks. Before our dinner, the veil had been disconnected, making the crown freestanding. "You deserve a crown, Emma. You're my queen, the queen of New Orleans. Soon, the world will know that." I ran my finger from behind her ear to her collarbone and then to the V of her cleavage.

Emma's breasts heaved against the bodice. A grin curled my lips as I leaned down and kissed the round mounds peering over her neckline.

Her fingers wove through my hair as Emma's mews filled the air.

Fuck, the sounds she made were stronger than any blue pill.

My cock was like steel from the moment I carried her into this room. All the times we'd fucked, when I'd taken her, we had been in my suite. We were now married, and it was time to christen both rooms.

I led her toward the bed and brushed a kiss over her lips. The crown glistened in the light from above, emphasizing her position. Emma Ramses was regal not only as my wife but as the daughter of a king. She deserved to be worshiped and adored.

She was also the daughter of a whore.

My plan was for her to embrace both.

Step by step, I walked around to Emma's back and slowly began undoing the tiny buttons. One by one. Beneath each button was a small latch. Whoever designed this dress should die a slow and tedious death, one filled with a daunting, seemingly endless task. With each successful release of a button and a hook, I added a kiss or a nip to her neck.

As more and more of her flawless skin was revealed, my kisses went lower.

Goose bumps peppered her flesh as her neck swayed from side to side as if her thoughts filled with lust made it too heavy to hold upright.

The more I unfastened, the harder my erection became.

Each bump of her spine became visible.

By the design of the dress, I could tell Emma wasn't wearing a bra. It was as I undid the final buttons that the indentation above her perfectly round ass told me that she hadn't tried to secure panties by some other means. My hands went to her shoulders, pushing the lace and pearl-studded material down her arms. Her perfect breasts showed above the fallen fabric. She winced as I tweaked one nipple and then the other as the dress pooled around her ankles.

Standing in nothing but the crown and the shoes, I offered her my hand, helping her step beyond the dress.

As Emma moved, I was able to see the deepening red of her areolas, the hardness of her nipples, and the glistening light reflecting off her own essence present on her inner thighs. Once she was beyond the dress, I grinned and said, "I could look at you for hours on end and never tire."

Her small hands came to my jacket. "I believe we have a playing field to level."

Allowing her to remove my jacket, I then stopped her hands as she reached for my belt. "It's not level, Emma. Don't fool yourself."

Deep shades of blue swirled in her eyes as she stared up at me. "I'm not under any illusions, Rett. It was you who has called me your queen." Her gaze scanned lower, stopping at my obvious erection. Her pink tongue darted to her lips and back. "I want you as exposed as I am."

"Why, Emma? I could carry you to that bed and make you come without freeing my cock. I could work you all night with my tongue and hands. You know I could."

She nodded. "I do, but I want you to come too. I want to feel you inside me."

"Why?"

"Is it wrong to want my husband to find pleasure?"

"No, but if that's your goal" —she yelped as I lifted her from the floor and dropped her upon her bed— "I find pleasure in watching you come."

With her weight back on her elbows, she watched as I pulled her ass and her pretty pink pussy to the edge of the bed. Next, I lifted each one of her feet, still in the heels, to the bed. Slowly, I applied pressure to her inner thighs, pressing her knees back. Each manipulation gave me a better view of what was mine.

"Lift your hands over your head." Her head fell back to the soft bedspread as she obeyed. Each arm moved above her head and her round breasts pushed upward.

Emma was a fucking goddess lying there.

The reality hit me.

She was my wife.

We'd married.

"You're mine," I growled as a memory of her abduction tried to infiltrate my thoughts. Splaying my hand and fingers over her flat stomach, I slid two and then three fingers inside her. Emma bucked as I curled and moved them. She was so damn receptive. "This pussy is mine." Leaning over her, I sucked one nipple and then the other, still working her.

Emma's moans wafted through the air.

Applying my thumb to her clit as I pressed and circled the tight bud of nerves resulted in her calling out my name. Her pleas echoed throughout our suites.

"Rett, please."

With a quick undoing of my belt and zipper, I pushed down my silk boxers. There were times in our future that I would deny Emma. It could be a denial of my permission or her freedom, but with the way my cock ached in my grasp, denying her tonight wasn't in my plans.

"Tell me your name," I demanded as I stepped closer, pressing the tip of my rock-hard cock against her folds.

"Emma..." Her blue eyes disappeared as her eyelids fluttered.

I pulled away and the blue reappeared. "Your last name."

"Ramses."

Her answer was rewarded as I held tightly to her knees and pressed deep inside her.

The way her back arched as her body hugged me, we fit together like two pieces of a puzzle.

In and out, I drove faster and harder. Our bodies slapped against one another as I kept her knees captive and thrust over and over inside her. Since the first night I took her completely, I couldn't stop. Even a simple thought of this woman throughout my day rerouted my circulation.

I wasn't certain how fate had been so right about two strangers, but without a doubt, Emma was meant for me and I for her. Her legs tensed beneath my touch as her pussy tightened.

Without warning I pulled out, my fist going up and down my cock, smearing her essence as she stared up at me.

"Why did you stop?"

Taking a deep breath, I pushed my cock back into the constraints of the boxer briefs. "You married a busy man."

Her weight returned to her elbows. "Too busy to finish fucking his wife?"

"No." I zipped my fly and latched my belt. "I could fuck you all night long. However, our interruption from before is still an issue. My damn phone won't stop vibrating."

"You don't think..." Her blue eyes grew round as saucers. "They didn't...kill them?"

"Would that ruin your wedding night? Would it be so awful that the men who'd lied to you and allowed you to be...*hurt* were dead?" I had other descriptions on the tip of my tongue, but as much as I blamed Emma for the abduction, I wouldn't facilitate her reliving it.

Emma kicked her feet from the bed, now sitting on the edge of the mattress. "It would ruin my wedding night to learn that my husband's word was useless."

Offering her my hand as she stood, I marveled at the red marks upon her alabaster flesh caused by my touch. She wasn't marred. I wouldn't do that. No, Emma was marked in ways that would soon fade.

It wasn't enough.

I wanted her to carry my mark for the world to see. I lifted her left hand. "You know that this ring tells the world you're mine."

"I want you to wear one, too."

Ignoring her comment, I went back to what she'd said moments ago. "You can trust that my word is true. I will give you another of my promises. I will go downstairs and put out whatever fires currently seem to be raging, and when I return, we will spend the rest of the night—"

"Making love," she said with a tilt of her head.

"We will see where the night takes us." I lifted both of her hands and held them together. "While I'm gone, I have one rule."

"And what would that be?"

Unbending her fingers, I kissed the tips of each one. "These fingers must not touch your pussy. I know you were close, Emma. You were on the edge. I want you close. I want you teetering on the precipice so that your mind is so consumed with wanton need that nothing else matters." Within her eyes, I saw the taming of a ravaged sea. Her thoughts were going where I led. "And when I return, if you can answer me honestly that you didn't please yourself in my absence, I promise you a night you won't forget." My cheeks rose as a grin formed. "Will you follow that rule?"

Emma nodded as she peered down at our hands. "You know, if you wouldn't have said anything...I wouldn't be thinking about it."

"Good. Think about it. Think about me inside you. Think about our bodies entwined as the sheets become tangled around us. Think about screaming my name as orgasm after orgasm leaves you painfully weary. Imagine what it will be like when you believe you're too spent to come again and yet you do..." I kissed her forehead. "Think about that."

After reaching for my jacket, it was as I started to walk away that I heard her.

"You won't know."

"I will, Emma, because I'll ask and you won't lie to me."

"And if I don't follow your rule?"

I reached for the doorknob. "Do you really want to find that answer out on our wedding night?"

RETT

*I*t was my fucking wedding night and I wasn't where I wanted to be. I wanted to be upstairs with my bride. The tap of my shoes upon the hardwood announced my arrival seconds before I entered the room outside of my inner office. Truly, the cameras in the hallway should have warned my men I was coming—that and the text message I sent for them to meet me here.

"Boss..." Leon said as I entered.

The lifting of my hand and a shake of my head was all I could manage at the moment. I'd purposely put off this conversation for as long as I could. Emma deserved a damn candlelit dinner after her wedding. What she didn't deserve was the reason I was here now. As two of my most trusted men, Noah and Leon were both present. I would have included Ian, but he was upstairs making certain Mrs. Ramses was not disturbed again.

Henri, the man who'd allowed Boudreau and Ingalls entry into my home was currently on a drive with

Carter, another of my men. The question at hand was where that drive would end.

Leon pushed the button. We all turned expectantly as the bookcase slid behind the wall, creating the entry to my inner office. The men waited as I led the way, taking my place behind my desk. Before sitting, I removed my phone from my pocket, then removed the tuxedo jacket, placing it on the back of my chair. Once everyone was within, I sat and closed the door from the control on my desk.

I gestured toward the two chairs opposite my desk. "Sit."

Silence prevailed as I loosened the bow tie. "I don't fucking want to be here," I confessed. "Tell me what's happened, is happening, and why. I need to decide if Henri's service to Ramses is over."

Leon and Noah exchanged a look before Leon took the floor. "Henri fucked up. He knew he did the moment Ingalls pushed into the front door."

"It was because of McBride," Noah added. "Henri didn't want a commotion with the good judge present."

"If that was his goal, he fucking failed," I said, standing. "My wife is waiting upstairs." Looking from Noah to Leon, I walked around the desk. Crossing my arms, I leaned against the large wooden monstrosity. "Henri's worked for me for over five years. He knows things, too many things. I watched the surveillance video. He fucked up by not recognizing Ingalls. As soon as he saw Boudreau, he called for backup. Henri did everything right up until and immediately after he fucked up." I waited before adding, "He still fucked up."

"If you put him back on the streets," Leon said, "he's vulnerable."

I nodded. "That's not one of my options. He stays put or he's gone. I can't risk him giving shit up to Boudreau because he's upset that he was demoted." It was a genuine issue with my trusted capos. There was no unknowing the secrets they learned working in close proximity to me. They either succeeded or died.

"Boss," Leon said, "Henri knows he fucked up. He knows that right now you're making the decision on whether he comes back from that drive with Carter. Fuck, Carter knows what may go down. Ain't nobody happy about it. I for one am pissed." He stood and walked to the bookcase and back. "I also have known Henri for some time, and I think he deserves another chance."

Letting out a breath, I turned to Noah. "You?"

These two men understood the significance of their presence. The final judgment would be my call. I'd make it. I'd live with it and own it. I wouldn't pass the fucking buck on to anyone else. However, a lesson I learned in my family journals was that not every decision had to be made alone. Get trusted advisors and utilize them.

It worked on multiple levels.

My confidence in these men was evident in their presence and in my asking their advice. With that confidence came responsibility. By trusting their opinions, it raised their position in my ranks and worked to ensure their loyalty. That in turn increased their stake in the Ramses name and cause.

Noah leaned back, placing one ankle on his knee.

"Comfortable?" I asked, more than a bit put off.

"He fucked up, boss. But I think we can look at this for what it really was."

"And what the fuck was that besides nearly a shoot-out in my foyer?"

"You watched the surveillance?"

"I did." I watched it in fast motion. I had this little issue of a wedding this evening and a sexy wife I wanted to fuck.

Noah placed his foot on the floor and turned to Leon. "We have some thoughts."

"About Henri?" I asked.

"About Boudreau," Noah said. "I've watched the video about four times. Leon mentioned he had the gut feeling Boudreau was nothing more than a mouthpiece for someone else. Fuck, boss, I'm not sure why we didn't pursue this in the past. I know all the evidence, even the ranks we've infiltrated, led to Boudreau, but after watching Ingalls and him tonight..." Noah shook his head. "There's no way he's the fucking brains in this operation."

"It's her," I said. "I've suspected it since I spoke to Michelson yesterday. It's like she wants us to know. She's fucking giving clues. I've got men working on the cryptocurrency, but it was the numerical code that was her calling card. Mrs. Ramses wants to see her mother." I shook my head. "That isn't fucking happening. It's Jezebel, she's the money and the brains."

"No one has seen her in years," Leon said. "We suspected she was alive, but where?"

"She's here in New Orleans," I answered. "Fuck, I

think Ruth talks to her somehow. Then again, I never know if what comes out of Ruth's mouth is fabricated or authentic."

"Ruth thinks it's real," Leon said with a grin.

"Do you trust Ruth?" Noah asked.

I walked around the desk and sat again in the chair. Removing my cufflinks, I rolled my sleeves halfway up my arm as I thought about Ruth Guidry. "My mother did. She trusted Ruth implicitly."

"That's not what Noah asked, boss."

"I don't trust her to keep her mouth shut around Emma. I do trust her when it comes to Ramses. She's devoted her life to this family."

"Then we need to find out if she's really talking to Jezebel," Leon said. "Boudreau confirmed while he was here that he's in touch with her. It fucking makes sense. I'll have Ruth's phone records scanned."

My lips came together. "Fuck, I pay her bill. Do that."

"It won't be that easy," Leon said. "Jezebel North has been planning this for too long to fail."

"You know," Noah said, "if we're right and Jezebel is the brains behind this, it answers other questions, such as where Kyle O'Brien was for two and a half years before resurfacing in New Orleans."

My fingers splayed over the desk before I looked up. "I could have fucking killed Boudreau tonight and it wouldn't have ended the coup." I was voicing my realization.

"If she sent them here, it was a test," Noah said.

"For them or us?" I asked.

"Probably both," Leon answered.

My questions continued. "How have we missed this?"

"Because she wanted us to," Leon said. "I used to know her, back when she ran her business."

"I don't want to know how well," I replied with a bit of a grin.

"No, it wasn't like that." Leon's lips came together. "She was always beautiful, striking even, enticing. It could be said she was bewitching."

"Is this a conversation you should be having with your wife?" I teased.

"Maybe your priest," Noah added.

"No, like I said, it wasn't like that. Neither of you knew her?"

"Not well," I said. Although, the description Leon had just given of Jezebel—striking and enticing—reminded me of her daughter, the one waiting for me upstairs. "Fuck, here's where your age gives you a better understanding. I was young when everything went down between her and Boudreau. Over the years, Jezebel North has become more of a legend than reality."

Leon paced behind the chair where he'd been seated. His brow furrowed as he began to talk. "Jezebel North made a name for herself because she refused to go away quietly. Society fucked her over and she made it her goal to return the favor. She worked hard to learn things. Ain't no better way to learn secrets than from a man about to come. Hell, he'll say anything."

Speaking of which...

I looked down at my wristwatch. "I have a bride

upstairs and this conversation will wait." I turned to Leon. "I want you to think on this. You've been around these parts and have connections. There isn't a square inch of the seventeen wards you don't know. If Jezebel is here, where is she hiding?" I spoke to both of them. "Keep tails on Boudreau and Ingalls after they make it out of the bayou. Maybe they'll take us to her. Check Ruth's phone records and the house phone. Leon, I also want to hear all you have to say about Jezebel, just not now." I thought for a moment. "Miss Guidry won't tell me anything about her; my concern is that she'll tell Emma. Fuck. We've wasted time concentrating on Kyle when who we should have been trying to find was her. We only have ourselves to blame."

"We weren't expecting a woman," Noah said.

"She ain't no ordinary woman," Leon said wistfully.

After checking the camera in the outer room, I hit the button to open the door. The bookcase moved. I stood and began walking that way.

"Boss," Noah said, "Henri?"

"It's my fucking wedding night. I'm feeling generous. Besides his fuck-up gave us some needed information. Warn him. If he does it again, he's done. And as for this house, I want the guards doubled. No one is getting in who isn't approved. Is that clear?"

Both men nodded as they followed me from the office.

EMMA

*T*oo many emotions fought for dominance as I stared into the courtyard two stories below. The Ramses family crest changed color as bubbles floated to the top of my champagne flute. Ian had brought up the bottle only to learn Rett had left. Maybe because it was my wedding and I was the bride, or because my new husband had left to tend to fires, or perhaps it was learning that my business partner who I would begrudgingly call my friend was deceased, I couldn't say for sure what exactly prompted my drinking spree. I just knew that I wasn't a big drinker and the more of the champagne I consumed, the less I thought about all the reasons to drink.

Instead, I focused on what had occurred near that fountain, the vows Rett and I had spoken. Knowing that neither of us had rehearsed somehow made the vows even more special, as if there hadn't been time to build our feelings up into something that society deemed appropriate. The words we spoke were simply honest thoughts given from one to another without the fanfare of a large church or hundreds of onlookers.

Rett and I both admitted to our shortcomings as husband and wife. Those weren't meant as an excuse for future behavior or a negative assessment of what was to come. Our admissions were a reminder that this relationship and the deal we'd made would take time.

As I swirled the remaining golden liquid, I told myself that repeatedly: time.

It was one thing I had in abundance.

Truly, to look around at the house, I had many things. It didn't occur to me until after Rett was gone that we didn't sign a prenuptial agreement. It was one of the many questions I had waiting for the right time.

There it was again: time.

Another check of the computer's corner clock told me the time was nearing midnight. If Rett didn't return soon, our wedding day would be over.

As I sipped the champagne, I shook my head at the man I'd married. I'd already told myself he was a master at manipulation. His rule upon leaving was another example. I'd be lying if I didn't admit that his forbiddance was a seed of thought that sprouted within my mind. Yes, I'd considered defying him, not to learn the penalty but to relieve the pent-up frustration he left behind. It was as I was washing the makeup from my face and combing out my long hair that I saw his command for what it was—a diversion.

By thinking about the sexual need he'd left unattended, I wasn't thinking about what took place following our private ceremony. I wasn't rehashing my brother's words about Ross or his plea for me to speak to Jezebel, the woman he called the mother of both of us.

Sadly, with time my thoughts did drift from away my physical needs to revisit what happened.

I was left wondering who I should believe and who warranted my anger: Rett or Kyle and Liam. The question boiled down to who was telling me the truth. Call me naïve but I wanted to believe the man I'd just married. I couldn't bear to imagine that Rett was responsible for my abduction and the degrading way I'd awakened. I also knew without a doubt that he was the one who saved me, who covered me with his shirt—literally off his back—and carried me to safety.

As the last five weeks rewound through my mind, I couldn't come up with a single time Rett had lied unless omission counted—Ross's death.

I recalled times Rett hadn't answered my questions and instances where I'd pushed for more, but never had I caught him in a lie. When it came to Kyle, I could go back a decade and make a long list of lies or untruths. Of course, those didn't really count. They were fabrications spoken between siblings. The world dubbed them "white" lies as if those were better than other options.

I recalled the time Kyle had eaten the last brownie and blamed me and the instance when he purposely recorded over my favorite show and blamed it on equipment malfunction. Neither of those occurrences were earth shattering, and yet they were both untruths.

And none of them—not one—compared to the

biggest lie of all, making me believe that he was deceased, letting me mourn, and presumably watching as I tried to survive without my family.

Liam wasn't any better—my heart told me he was worse.

Had Liam's lies began when we first confronted our feelings?

The lies he told didn't have the innocence of sibling rivalry. No, Liam's untruths were the most heartbreaking, the promises of forever, the one that seduced a girl into believing she was a woman and taking her most prized possession. Yes, he'd taken my virginity—or more accurately, I'd given it—but that wasn't what I missed; the severing of a membrane wasn't as important as the object he took.

As the doorknob to the hallway clicked, I felt the void of what I'd given Liam long ago—a hole within my chest, the place where my heart should be.

Maybe if it wasn't gone, I could consider giving it to Rett, my husband.

I turned toward the door, watching it move inward.

A smile came to my lips as Rett stepped beyond it. His hair had lost its gelled perfection. His tuxedo coat was missing, his tie loosened, and his sleeves rolled up to below his elbows. Even though he'd shaved before our evening wedding, sprouts of dark hair growth were beginning to show on his cheeks and chiseled jaw. However, it was what was between his mussed locks and stubbly chin that had my attention.

Rett's dark gaze came my way as his steps brought him closer.

He tugged at the opening of my robe and ran the sash through his fingers. "When I left you, this robe wasn't present."

My body turned toward him. In my bare feet, he was significantly taller, yet we fit together—he and I. Rett was a magnet I couldn't repel as our hips touched. If I weren't leaning back to see him clearer, my breasts would be against his solid chest. "When you left was a long time ago."

His palms framed my cheeks. "I'd like to tell you that it won't be like this, that work and fires won't take me away." Kisses came to my hair as he tilted my face down. When our gazes again met, he went on, "I can't tell you that, Emma. I can't help that there will be times I must be gone. But believe me when I say that never before have I wanted to get away from a meeting like I did tonight." He stepped back and tugged at the sash until the tie released. A grin curled his lips as the sides hung open, revealing what I'd hidden beneath. His dark orbs came back to my eyes. "Tell me."

"What, Rett?"

"My rule."

I'd followed it to the letter and having him close twisted my core tighter, almost painfully so, but I was curious. "If I broke it, what would happen?"

"I'd walk away...to my suite."

"And tell me to follow?"

"And leave you while I take care of myself in an ice-cold shower."

"So, my punishment would be..." I left it open.

Rett lifted my chin, bringing my lips to his. "You

didn't break my rule, Emma. I see it in your beautiful eyes. I can smell your desire. It's hanging around you like the most enticing perfume. I know that you waited. Tell me why? Were you worried about what would happen?"

My head shook. "I wasn't. You don't scare me, Everett Ramses." I laid my hand on his white shirt and splayed my fingers, feeling his heartbeat. "I wasn't worried. The truth is that I didn't want some sort of relief. I'm your wife. You're my husband. We have a lot to work on in this marriage, but granting sexual pleasure isn't one of them. I waited, not because I couldn't ease the tension on my own, but because I didn't want that. I want what only you can give me, what only I can give you. I want it both ways. I want you, Everett Ramses, more than I've ever wanted any man in my life."

His eyes closed and opened as he inhaled and exhaled.

"What?" I asked.

"I have questions I want you to answer."

He had questions. I had a damn journal full. Instead of saying that, I swallowed my comment and nodded. "Not tonight, Rett. Tonight is us. Tonight is our wedding." I turned toward the computer, unable to see the small numbers in the corner. "What is left of it is about us."

My feet left the ground as he reached down, cradling me in his arms and carrying me away from my suite. It was silly, but I didn't enter his suite when he was away. The rooms were intimidating to say the least. And yet when I was with Rett, his presence made them welcoming.

Through the dark hallway we traveled and into his dark suite.

He gently placed me on his sofa and went to the giant fireplace. With the dim light from the windows, I watched as he moved, majestic and proud. There was a grace to his step that could never be interpreted as unmanly. As he leaned down and brought the fireplace to life, I saw for a moment the man others saw, the one who commanded others and ruled with an iron fist.

Rett Ramses wasn't the king of New Orleans simply because he took the position. There was regality in his blood that couldn't be hidden, even in our private suites.

Flames roared to life within the giant enclosure, flickering and sizzling. It was as Rett turned in the fire's light that I saw the same inferno within his dark eyes. This wasn't a reflection of what he'd just started but a manifestation of what had been growing since the night at the restaurant.

That night, he'd told me I would be his wife.

He'd proclaimed it would happen, and as I peered momentarily at my left hand, I knew that the man walking toward me was more than the king of New Orleans. He was more than a prophet of fate's demand. Everett Ramses was capable of changing my stars.

A tap of his phone and the room filled with music.

Rett's hand was before me.

I stood; the warmth from the flames reminded me that he'd loosened my robe. I reached for the sash.

"No, leave it."

My breath stilled as I stared into his gaze. There was one thing I wanted to say—three simple words that were on the tip of my tongue—and yet I wouldn't lie. I wouldn't proclaim emotions that I couldn't share even if on our wedding night it seemed right.

Rett's large hands pushed the robe from my shoulders, leaving me naked in the firelight. He gently moved my long blonde hair behind me as he scanned my body from my toes to my hair. "Emma, you're perfection."

I took a small step and stopped. "Now, may I even our playing ground?" I reached for the loosened bow tie. When Rett didn't respond, I pulled it free. Next, I began undoing each button down his wide chest. Then, I pulled the tails free and unbuckled his belt. As I worked lower, I knelt down. It wasn't planned. I hadn't given my actions that much thought. Nevertheless, soon I was on my knees in front of my equally nude husband.

I peered up. "I want to be everything you want in a wife." His erection was right in front of me. Rett wanted submission. I didn't move, staring upward as his chest inflated and deflated with each deep breath.

"Tell me what you want, Emma."

"I want to please you. I'm not submissive, yet when you're here and I'm here, I want you to want me."

His hand came my way.

I placed my palm in his larger one and stood. The music was still playing. The flames were still flickering. He wrapped one arm around me and took my other hand. In seconds, we were dancing, both nude in front of his fireplace.

It was like nothing I'd imagined ever in my life.

It was perfect in every way.

When the song stopped, Rett's arms encircled me as his forehead came to mine. "I never gave it any thought, not before now."

"What?" I asked.

"What I wanted in a wife. I honestly never imagined marrying, and if I did, it was strictly for power and influence."

"Is that what you get marrying me?"

His hands skirted my arms as they came up to my cheeks. "So fucking much more, Emma. You never need to worry that you're enough or right or if I want you. Banish those thoughts away tonight. We will argue. There are things we need to discuss, but at this moment, you were right. Tonight, I want you to know that you are everything I never knew I wanted and more. You are Mrs. Emma Ramses."

I smiled at the use of my first name. "And Mrs. Everett Ramses," I added.

"We have some battles to fight, Emma. What we need to decide is if we'll fight them together or against one another. I want you on my side."

"The Ramses side."

Rett nodded. "It's your name now."

I too had many thoughts. There were the things Miss Guidry had said and questions I'd conjured up before our wedding and since. Nevertheless, at this moment, I wanted to be on Rett's side. I took a step toward his bed and our fingers intertwined. "Come show me."

His lips curled upward. "What do you want to see, Mrs. Ramses?"

"Not see. You promised me a night of lovemaking, of so many orgasms I'd lose count. I have trusted you, Rett. Don't let this be where you let me down."

As he threw back the covers and exposed the soft sheets, I had no concerns about his inability. Whether making love or the simple brush of his lips on my hair, there was a pull and a connection that I wouldn't deny. Tonight would be a culmination of the intimacy we'd shared, all brought together with the knowledge that now we were married.

I kept count of the number of times he brought me to ecstasy until I couldn't, until my body was awash on the shore of satiation. We'd both found our mountains and our cliffs. Hand in hand, we'd climbed together only to jump as one. Together we'd found bliss and gone back for more. At some point, I believe I slept in his arms only to awaken to the rhythm of his thrusts. No longer forceful, we had progressed to the part of the night that was what songwriters meant when they spoke of making love. It was the slow and meaningful cadence of two people who simply don't want to disconnect but rather to stay as one.

When my eyes finally opened, and my body was used, sore, and oh so satisfied, I was alone in Rett's suite. The sun shone through the tall windows and on the table near the fireplace was a silver-domed dish and a vase with a single red rose. On Rett's dresser the clock told me that it was almost noon. It appeared that I'd slept blissfully through the night and into half the day.

As I pulled the sheets around me, I realized Rett had done exactly what he'd promised. He'd made love to me throughout the night. We both had questions to be answered and things to share, but last night had not been the time.

My muscles ached as I moved. It was as my feet hit the floor from way up high upon his large bed that I saw the note near the domed plate.

Mrs. Ramses was scrolled on the outer fold. Opening the paper, I read:

"I could spend every night like last night.

Eat, shower, and come to my office. Ian will show you the way. We need to talk.

-Rett"

RETT

*T*he icon on the monitor on my desk signaled that people were entering the outer offices. A quick hit of a few keys on my keyboard and the image of them appeared. While there were two, it was only one of the occupants who had my attention. The one who I'd left asleep earlier this morning after a night fit for the record books. If this was what it was like to be married, I should have done it a long time ago.

I turned to Leon, sitting across the desk from me. "Do you believe everything you just said?"

He nodded. "I decided you should know. I can't explain it, the pull she had. I thought I'd broken free. I haven't seen her or talked to her in nearly ten years." He stood. "I know I'm not the only one. She never promised exclusivity. Hell, legends like Jezebel aren't contrived by one man."

Leon took a deep breath as he leaned forward, holding the arms of the chair. "I'm a lot of things, boss. I'm not a man who cheats on his wife, not readily."

His dark expression showed more pain than I'd ever seen in him. This was a man who had helped me take over New Orleans. He carried out executions and stopped for a Po' boy twenty minutes later. What Leon had been describing over the last hour had tortured his soul in a way the life we chose never would.

"And even after all this time," he said, "talking about Jezebel yesterday, I can't shake the thoughts of her, the memories...the desire to find her."

In the pop-up in the corner of my computer monitor, I saw that Ian and Emma were waiting. Before they entered, I needed a few more answers from Leon.

"We do need to find her," I said, "if she's out there."

He nodded. "She is. I know it in my bones."

"You never had a physical relationship?" I exhaled and stood, stretching my legs. "Fuck, Leon. That's none of my damn business. I'm hardly in a place to exert moral superiority. I'm just trying to understand how one shunned woman is as powerful as people say."

"Once, I slipped. Tara knows. She forgave me. Maybe one day I can forgive myself. Thing is...I ain't proud of it. That night was a symptom of my disease, not a cure to it."

"Disease?"

"Obsession. Hell, Jezebel was a drug more addicting than cocaine. The high came in her presence. Sex was the pinnacle, but it wasn't enough." He shook his head as he stood. "I'm being honest, boss. Thoughts of Jezebel began slipping back into my mind when you brought Miss North here. I reasoned that she looks similar, but she ain't Jezebel. Then like I said, after talking about Jezebel yesterday, I couldn't stop thinking about her. Even a decade later, she has a power that I've never known in any other woman." He looked toward the bookcase and back. "Do you want to know the God's truth?"

"Yes."

"He hurt her, Boudreau. He thought he could stop her, bring her down and shame her." A smile split Leon's face in half. "Not her. Fuck no. Jezebel would have walked down Bourbon Street stark naked without blinking an eye. She didn't give a fuck about what people thought they knew because she made it a point to know more. She set her mind to one thing, revenge. In that pursuit, she did her best to learn secrets.

"You see, it isn't the wealthiest who hold the power; it's the people with the most knowledge. Like that old saying—knowledge is power. Jezebel knew how to bring any man to his knees. She shared those secrets with her girls. From what I heard, they were good but not as good as the mistress herself.

"You know who has knowledge, boss?"

"You're going to tell me."

"Sometimes it's the powerful, like Boudreau and your daddy, but it's the others, their employees, butlers, groundskeepers, maintenance. They see what is happening every day inside the big houses. They know secrets from behind closed doors that others can't imagine.

"I said yesterday, a man about ready to come can't lie. There'd be few families around these parts whose secrets she didn't know, things the fancy ladies don't discuss, Jezebel had it all. And then, before you took control, she disappeared.

"But her power ain't gone. If my granny were here, she'd call Jezebel a sorceress. Whatever power Jezebel had, she knew how to use it. Still does, I'd imagine."

"We need to find her," I said. "Hell, if she's in New Orleans, she's been living like a hermit."

"No, I'd say if she's still in these parts, which is a possibility, Miss Jezebel North is living exactly how she wants to live." He tilted his chin toward the bookcase. "I know you need to talk to Mrs. Ramses about Underwood. If she has half the bewitching power of her mother, be careful."

A grin came to my lips. "You're the second person to warn me that Emma is possibly dangerous."

"You can laugh it off," Leon said, "but it's the way a woman like her momma could get under your skin. Those secrets she learned? She didn't need to push. Men offered them like sacrifices for a moment in her presence." He stood taller, straightening his shoulders. "I think I'm going to follow up on a few things on the street. I'll send in a report, but tonight, I'm going home and gonna take my wife out for an expensive dinner. Remind us both that even though she married a fool, he knows good when he's got it. Tara is good, boss."

I nodded. "Sounds like a plan, man."

I hit the button to move the bookcase. Leon nodded to Ian as they passed one another. Ian stopped, allowing Emma to enter. My gaze met Ian's as I stood. "I'll text you when Mrs. Ramses is ready to be escorted back upstairs."

Emma's blue gaze went from me to Ian. Her neck straightened, yet not a word was uttered. Not until the bookcase closed and we were alone.

"When will I not need an escort?" she asked.

A grin came to my lips. "See, that wasn't difficult."

"What?" she asked as she dropped her arms to her side.

Emma Ramses was a fucking vision. Her damp hair and makeup-free face gave her an appearance of innocence, one I knew from only a few weeks of intimacy was deceiving.

Was she bewitching?

Prior to her learning of her adoption, Emma never knew the name Jezebel North. Prior to her coming to me, she didn't know anything about the woman who bore her. As Leon's words rambled around in my thoughts, I doubted that Emma knew what she was—innocent or bewitching—or what she was capable of doing with that knowledge.

I came to a stop merely a foot away, entering a soft, floral-scented cloud surrounding my wife. My gaze scanned from Emma's rhinestone-studded sandals, to her sexy ankles, and the long gauze skirt—not much different than the one she wore the first night—and up over her white blouse. My attention went to the way her blouse stopped an inch above her skirt allowing a small strip of her midsection to show and up further to the scooped neckline.

Emma's long hair was plaited into a long braid that went down the center of her back. Though everything about her was casual, I sensed what Leon warned me about. Emma emanated power that I would be better served if she never realized she possessed.

I answered her earlier question. "You waited until we were alone to question me. It wasn't difficult, was it?"

Emma's arms crossed over her breasts as she exhaled. "I'm trying, Rett. Give me something in return."

"I think I've misled you. It wasn't intentional."

"What do you mean?"

"I don't make concessions or deals that involve my authority, Emma. You're my wife now. That position has its benefits, its own clout, but don't forget: that power never supersedes mine nor is over me."

Emma looked around the office and back to me. "Why am I here?"

"I have a few reasons." I took a step closer until her chin rose, continuing our eye contact. "Tell me. Am I interrupting your busy day?"

"Well, you see, my day was already cut short because I didn't get a lot of sleep."

"Get used to it, Mrs. Ramses."

Her smile grew.

"One reason I called you down to me was because I knew if I went upstairs, my agenda would be lost."

"And why would that be?"

My hands went to her waist, my fingers splaying on her soft, exposed skin. "Because seeing you, knowing you're mine, not only because of fate but legally ordained by the State of Louisiana, I can't keep my hands off of you." The blue of her eyes swirled with emotions as her nostrils flared and her breaths deepened.

This wasn't why I called her down. It was why I didn't go upstairs, but that was what Emma did to me. It was what Leon warned about.

I tilted my head as I pulled her hips to mine. "Do you regret it?"

"You need to be more specific."

"Marrying me, Emma. I told you the first night we met what your requirement would be. You said *I do* and signed the marriage certificate...now you have an obligation to fulfill. Do you regret any of that?"

"You said I'd be your queen. That's hardly something to regret."

"I promised you the world at your feet and every desire to be indulged, with one task. Tell me you remember that task."

Her breasts heaved with my words. The soft material of her blouse tented as her nipples hardened. It was impossible not to notice.

"I remember," she said, her words coming in a breathy gust.

"Tell me."

Emma's eyelids fluttered as she seemed to be fighting her own battle, the one where she wanted the influence that came with being my wife, the power she displayed last night in the front office, but was still unsure about the rest.

With one finger, I lifted her chin. "Don't make me wait, Emma. I don't like waiting."

"You said my task was to be ready for you no matter what you ask."

"There's a word you're missing."

"Obey," she said, her gaze locked on mine.

"Good girl." I took a step and another, leading her toward the conference table. Each of my steps forward caused her to take one backward. Never did our eyes leave one another's.

"What are you going to do?" she asked.

"Are you ready? Did you come down here ready to obey?"

RETT

"Your note said we had things to discuss. This" —Emma gestured toward my growing erection— "isn't talking. I have questions too."

She was right. It wasn't.

The mental list of things I wanted to talk about or even her questions paled next to what was now forefront in my mind. I pulled a chair away from the conference table and spun Emma's shoulders until she was facing the table. "Kick off your shoes, Emma."

She craned her neck my direction.

My tone changed. "Don't make me repeat myself."

Turning away, she pushed one off one sandal and then the other.

I leaned close to her ear, purposely exhaling on her soft, sensitive skin as I gently kicked her feet farther apart. "Pull up your skirt and then I want you up on your toes, leaning over the table until your perfect ass is at my disposal."

"Rett—"

"Now isn't the time to speak or I'll find something else to occupy those pretty lips."

From behind her, I pulled down the front of her blouse, exposing her perfect round breasts. Even from my angle, I saw the way her nipples hardened in the cool air. Next, my fingers splayed between her shoulder blades and I pressed her forward until those soft breasts flattened against the hard surface. Before she could say a word, I lifted the back hem of her skirt, pulling it up until her bare ass was before me.

I leaned my weight over Emma, pressing my growing erection against her and covering her to remind her of who was in charge. A tug of the braid caused her chin to rise. I wrapped her long hair around my fist, while also maintaining the pressure between her shoulders. Her whimper confirmed the discomfort of the position. My words came in a menacing whisper. "The next time you're told to do this, Mrs. Ramses, you won't hesitate. If you do, instead of fucking this tight pussy..."

I plunged two fingers inside her warm, slick haven, eliciting a whimper.

"...I'll spank this perfect ass, turning it bright red." Leaving her pussy unattended, I lightly swatted one side of her ass and then the other, bringing a blush of red to each cheek. My whisper deepened to a growl. "It won't be like that, Emma. I'll enjoy watching my handprints rise. When I'm done, sitting won't be on your agenda." I brought my hand up higher, poised to demonstrate. "Do you want a sample?"

Her head shook as much as possible between my hold of her braid and her placement on the table.

"Rett, don't."

I could barely hear her request between her whisper and my pounding pulse.

A quick unlatching of my belt and unzipping of my pants and my rock-hard cock was free from my boxers. "Reach back and grab your ass on both sides, Mrs. Ramses. Show me my options."

Beneath my grasp, Emma's body tensed.

"Please. You don't mean this."

She was wrong. While *this* hadn't been my plan, I did mean it.

It was what needed to happen.

I was as much at blame as the woman before me, the woman I'd married.

From the first night, I'd been too soft on Emma, too lenient. I should have punished her after she put herself in danger. I should have quelled her show of power last night.

I didn't.

I'd allowed her to do to me what Leon described. I was bewitched by Emma's beauty, taken with her company, enthralled with her conversation, and completely spellbound by her body.

The power she had over me was my doing.

It was time for that to end.

This afternoon would remind Emma of her boundaries.

Her toes strained as she slowly obeyed, one hand and then the other. Her weight was balanced on the hard table, her breasts flattened, as her fingers grasped her own flesh, revealing both of her holes.

I refused to acknowledge the tears pooling on the table's surface or the way she gasped for breath. This wasn't a time to concede. Instead of recognizing her discomfort, using my fingers, I swiped Emma's essence up and around her tight ring.

She flinched, but with no place for her to go, she was a captive to my ministrations.

A grin came to my lips as I repeated the exercise one more time, applying a bit more pressure. Hell, her pussy was tight, but her ass would be like a vise to my cock. Her breathing shuddered and more tears fell. Using my thumb, I pressed a little harder.

Emma's fingers blanched as she maintained her position.

As much as I would enjoy pushing myself through that tight barrier, today wouldn't be the first time I took her ass. Today's lesson was in hierarchy, not as a cause to justify my wife's hatred. She'd have enough reasons for that as the years passed.

"Where should I fuck you?" I dipped my fingers into her pussy and then ran them around the ring again. "Last night you were ready to exercise your newfound power as Mrs. Ramses. Tell me now, who decides where my cock goes?"

"Why are you doing this?"

Releasing her hair, I pressed upon her lower back and brought my cock to her ass.

Emma gasped as I applied pressure.

"Answer me," I growled.

From Emma's position, I was able to see only one side of her face. Her blue eye peered back as best it could. Instead of fear or submission, the blue swirled with determination and anger. "Do it, Rett." Her tone grew stronger with each word. "If this is some macho display because I threatened your manhood last night, fine, fuck me. Take my ass. Show me what a big man you are. Congratulations, you can overpower a woman, one you vowed to marry. Do it." More tears fell as her eye closed.

Fuck.

"Move your hands back to the table, Emma."

"You're a dick."

I had the urge to laugh at her assessment. The impulse was totally out of place, but it was there. I whispered close to her ear. "Yes, sweetheart, it's my dick you're going to get." I moved each of her hands to the table's edge. "Now, hold on."

If Emma didn't do as I instructed and grip the table, her hips would bruise on the table's edge. Marking her in that way wasn't my goal. I enjoyed the perfection of her skin. My objective was to mark her in places unseen, deep in her psyche so she obeyed without hesitation and submitted when it went against her every instinct.

As soon as Emma gripped the edge of the table, I slid inside her—her pussy. It was fucking heaven. The friction grew as I lifted her hips and continued my surge.

With each thrust, I concentrated on the way her core tightened around me.

I'd fucked up, but I wasn't going to stop until she

came apart. Emma needed to learn that I was in control of all things, including her orgasms. She'd learn to obey and in return, I would lead her to pleasure like she'd never known. And when she didn't do as I said, she'd be punished.

Her eyes closed as she lay unmoving, taking everything I gave.

Even with our short history, we'd been together too many times for me not to recognize her current ploy.

"Don't fucking fight it, Emma."

"Go to hell."

Pulling out, I spun her around. Her obstinate expression glared my way, but before Emma could verbally argue, I lifted her ass to the table and roughly spread her thighs. In seconds, I was on my knees as my tongue took the same trip my cock had enjoyed. My chin was quickly covered in her essence as I buried my face. Her mind could fight me, but her body wouldn't.

I didn't let up, lapping her juices and teasing her clit.

Emma tried to resist. The battle was in the air, metaphoric shots whizzing by and exploding around us.

My tongue delved deeper as I nipped her clit. When I peered upward, I witnessed her perfection. Emma's head wobbled and her eyes were veiled by her lashes as she bit tightly to her lip. The way her legs quivered despite her attempt to be impervious to my attention, she was on the edge.

Standing, I stepped between her knees as our eyes again met.

Hers still glistened with defiance, its presence churning within a chaotic sea of lust.

Reaching for Emma's chin, I brought my mouth to hers. Despite her lack of response, my tongue pushed through the seam of her lips until it met with hers. When I pulled away, I asked, "Do you taste yourself?"

She didn't respond.

"You can fight me, Emma, but your body is mine." I leaned down to her breasts, sucking each nipple and leaving the wetness from my chin on her skin. Our eyes met again. "We're not stopping until you come."

I showed no mercy as I pierced her, taking what was mine by fate and now by law. In one full thrust, I was completely buried.

Her moans filled my ears as I lifted her ass from the table. The choice before her was to hold on or fall back. Either way, I wasn't stopping or slowing.

Emma's decision was to hold on.

Her petite hands came to my shoulders and her legs wrapped around my torso. I stepped away from the table. By the time we made it to the bookcases, her entire body tensed. Pressing her into the shelves, I thrust in and out.

It was the greatest workout these old shelves had seen maybe ever.

Grunts.

Heavy breaths and whimpers.

Moans and hums.

Shouts and curses.

My office filled with our noises.

They weren't the sounds made by two people making love.

This was a battle and we were both in it to win.

Finally, Emma's goal changed as her pussy quivered, she clung to my neck, and her body tensed. I didn't slow until her tension gave way to convulsions, ripples of nerves sparking from her head to her toes. I held her tight against me as she lost control, quaking in my arms.

Emma's grip of my neck tightened as I too gave in to the pull this woman had on me, filling her as my cock throbbed within her. "You're mine."

When she looked up, she replied, "You didn't have me sign a prenuptial agreement."

It wasn't a reply to my comment and was an odd time for her to mention this, but it wasn't a subject I hadn't thought through.

I leaned my face closer to hers until our noses touched. "We don't need one."

"But you have so much."

"I told you, Emma, there's only one way this marriage ends...and it isn't in divorce." Her eyes widened as I repeated, "Until death us do part. Rest assured, that too will be at my doing."

Emma closed her eyes. Still in my arms, with her skirt bunched between us, her breasts still exposed, and my cock buried inside her, Emma laid her head on my shoulder, exhaling in defeat.

What this stunning woman didn't know and what I couldn't tell her was that she'd already won.

Lifting Emma off me, I eased her feet to the floor as her skirt cascaded down her legs and she adjusted the top of her blouse.

When my wife looked up, I saw the kaleidoscope of

emotions swirling amid more questions in the turbulent blue sea of her eyes.

I wasn't completely out of touch.

Mentally, I knew what Emma wanted to hear.

Now would be the perfect time to admit she was right and I'd been a dick, or to apologize for what had just transpired, or maybe tell her that I cared what she thought of me and admit that I was affected by everything about her, or that she was already so buried in my psyche that I was more of a subject of hers than the other way around.

I couldn't form any of those words. Or maybe I wouldn't.

Instead, I tilted my head toward a door beyond the table. "There's a bathroom through there. Go clean yourself and we'll talk." When she didn't move, I added, "Unless, of course, you enjoy my come dripping down your legs."

Her eyes blazed as if napalm was exploding before me. Her palm came to my cheek with an unexpected slap. "Don't be crude. It doesn't become you." The sting came a millisecond later than the strike, in tune with her words.

The shock of her slap outweighed any pain she'd inflicted.

Seizing Emma's wrist, I held it tight as we both stared at one another.

EMMA

My body quaked with emotions I didn't welcome—pent-up rage combined with disappointment—as Rett's grip of my wrist tightened. This was another of those moments when sanity was forgotten. Unwilling to budge or look away, I continued my stare. "My answer is yes." It hadn't been when I'd committed to this marriage or even earlier when Rett had asked, but after what had just happened, I was confident.

"Yes?" he asked, his eyes narrowing.

"Release me, Rett, unless you have more to prove."

His grip lessened, but my wrist was still not free. "Yes to what?"

"Do I regret marrying you? I've changed my answer to yes."

Exhaling, he loosened his grip further, his attention going to the faint white line around my wrist. For a moment, his dark stare met mine and then he dropped his hold and tilted his chin toward the door he'd indicated earlier. At the same time a buzzing sound filled the room. Its tinny quality reminded me of the sound coming from an old-fashioned intercom.

Leaving me standing barefooted where I was, Rett began walking toward his desk. With each step, he did as I had done, adjusting himself. While my breasts were now covered, his cock was once again hidden beneath his boxer shorts, his pants were fastened, and his belt buckled. In a matter of the seconds it took him to make the journey from me to his desk, Rett looked nearly as put together as he had when I entered the office.

I said *nearly* because his longish hair was disheveled. Once Rett reached his destination, he ran his long fingers through the waves. By the focus of his stare, his attention was now on one of the large monitors on his desk.

I watched as he hit a button.

It must have been a speaker because Rett began speaking to someone not present. "What happened? I thought you had plans."

"Boss."

I tried to place the voice, but one word wasn't a lot to work with. I was sure that it was coming from one of Rett's men. I just wasn't sure which one. The only one I could eliminate from contention was Ian.

"This news shouldn't come in a report. You should hear it from me."

Rett's dark stare came my way. "Go clean up."

I crossed my arms over my breasts as I kept my lips together.

In the course of three strides or maybe less, Rett's long legs had him back to my side of the office. He scooped up my sandals and pulling a handkerchief from his pocket, he wiped the evidence of our encounter from the table. Shoving the handkerchief back in his pocket, he returned the chair he'd moved earlier to its proper place. Next, Rett handed me the sandals. "Put these on. Our talk can wait."

Exhaling, I reached for the sandals. "Call Ian. I want to leave."

He tilted his head toward the bathroom again.

"Go to hell, Rett. I'm going upstairs and soaking in a hot shower. I know that's the opposite of what they tell you to do after an assault, but you see, my options are limited, and besides, I have no problem identifying the assailant." My wedding rings caught my attention as I held the sandals. Pulling both rings from the fourth finger of my left hand, I tossed them onto the cleaned table.

The tendons in my husband's neck came to life as he clenched his chiseled jaw. Retrieving the rings from the table, he handed them my way and said, "Fucking Christ, Emma. You weren't assaulted."

Not taking the rings, I dropped the sandals to the floor. "Call Ian, or when you let whoever that is in the outer office inside, I'm leaving."

"You won't make it out of this house."

Easing each foot into its respective sandal, I shook my head. The crude comment Rett had made was now happening—with each movement, my thighs slid one over the other. However, I refused to acknowledge it, obstinately denying Rett the satisfaction.

My thoughts went to the hot shower and perhaps I'd follow that with a bath.

I stared up at him. "Leaving the house wasn't my plan. I believe I can find my way back to my suite."

Rett took a step back, pushing the rings into the pocket of his pants. "Fine. We'll talk later."

With my arms again crossed over my breasts, I stood there, waiting as Rett pulled his phone from his other pocket and appeared to send a text message. When he was done, he went to his desk and did whatever needed to be done for the bookcase to move. The man waiting to enter was the same one who was present when I arrived. Dressed in a dark gray suit, he was tall with rich dark skin. By the sparse gray in his black hair, I would assess he was older than Rett, but I couldn't judge by how much.

As the man stepped into the office, I remembered him from the time Rett brought me here to describe my abduction.

"Mrs. Ramses," the man said with a nod.

"Emma," Rett said, "I don't know if you remember Leon Trahan. He was here the first time you came to this office."

It seemed as though my husband had the ability to be polite in the presence of others. I could do the same.

Stepping closer to Leon Trahan, I offered my hand. "Nice to see you again, Mr. Trahan." I turned back to the man across the desk, my tone unconsciously cooling. "I assume you texted Ian. I'll wait for him in the outer office." As I started to walk away toward the still-open passageway, I paused and made an effort to consciously contain my disgust or at least keep it from infiltrating my words. "If that is all right with you, Everett?"

"Don't leave without him."

What could I reply?

The response that was on the tip of my tongue was closer to *fuck you* than *yes, dear*. I chose the third option, a simple nod.

"Boss," Mr. Trahan said, "this information concerns" —he turned his eyes to me— "you too, Mrs. Ramses."

Rett gestured to the chairs before his desk, successfully thwarting my escape.

As I complied, I wished that I'd taken the time to go into the bathroom. Instead, I feigned a placid expression and took a seat, thankful that the skirt had a silk lining.

"What is it, Leon?" Rett asked.

"I told you I was going to check on a few things. Before I got far...my brother called."

Rett sat in his throne-like chair and leaned back. "How does this concern Mrs. Ramses?"

My eyes quickly went to Rett, wondering if this was about the statement he'd mentioned I may be asked to make. Before either of us could ask anything more, Mr. Trahan went on.

"They ain't releasing the information yet. No one's supposed to know."

My husband leaned forward, his interest piqued.

Mr. Trahan turned to me. "Ma'am, my brother, he's a detective with the New Orleans Police Department." He nodded. "Just so you know, this is coming from a reliable source. He wouldn't tell me if it weren't true."

Rett's eyes narrowed. "Or he wanted to know what you know."

"What did your brother tell you," I asked.

Mr. Trahan sat in the chair to my side, his body stiff as he began sharing his information. "Judge McBride, he didn't show up to the courthouse today. According to my brother, the judge had a full docket starting at eleven. He says the judge usually shows up about seven or eight in the morning to go through his schedule and read the briefs for the day's cases. His assistant said she was concerned, but it wasn't until she realized it was ten in the morning and he wasn't there that she started making calls." His head shook. "She said it just wasn't like him."

My pulse sped up, racing through me as I leaned forward. "Did they find him? Is he all right?"

Mr. Trahan's lips came together. "Well, yes and no, ma'am. They found him. When the judge didn't answer no one's calls, they sent a patrol car to his house. The two officers found him in his running car in the garage. He was dead. They're suspecting it's carbon monoxide poisoning. Of course, that ain't official until all the tests come back. Visually, there ain't no signs of foul play." His head moved again as he hummed. "Says it looks clean, like he just fell asleep. Thing is, it was near seventy degrees by nine this morning. Ain't no reason he'd be warming up his car in a garage. The police don't want no news people snooping about. So, right now, ain't nobody supposed to know."

My mind raced with brief memories of the man who was here last night, the man who married us. "Does he have family?" I asked. "Are they okay?"

Mr. Trahan nodded. "His kids are grown; one's here in New Orleans. Mrs. McBride's a teacher over in the Fifth Ward. She was already gone to work." He turned back to Rett. "My brother asked why he was here last night. They found your name on his calendar."

"There's nothing illegal about a wedding," Rett said. "We filed the application yesterday afternoon. There's a paper trail." His gaze narrowed. "Did he expect to get something else out of you?"

"No, boss, 'cept here's the thing. The application is on file, but the marriage certificate is gone."

"What?" Rett and I asked at the same time.

"The judge," Mr. Trahan explained, "he emailed a picture of it to his personal assistant. She was planning on filing it first thing this morning. Then the judge didn't show and now there's no sign of a certificate. Without the actual signed paper, it seems your marriage is in question."

"That's ridiculous," Rett said as he stood. "The certificate is somewhere."

"When I told Noel" —Mr. Trahan looked my way— "that's my brother's name. Our momma was funny like that. When I told him that Judge McBride performed a wedding, he followed up with the judge's office. That all checks out. The police went through everything inside the judge's car, including his pockets and briefcase. Now, they're waiting on a search warrant to go through his house.

"Anyway, so far, there ain't no marriage certificate anywhere. Nothing else is missing. Noel said the judge had a couple hundred in cash in his wallet and some more bills in a money clip. He also had plenty of credit cards. It's all there. Judge McBride had other files in his briefcase. No marriage certificate for Mr. Ramses and Miss O'Brien."

Rett's brown orbs turned to me. "We'll sign another one if we have to. I'll get my attorneys on this. Don't worry, Emma, we'll get it settled."

Did I want it settled?

Utilizing my recently proclaimed obedience to remaining silent in the presence of others, I relished the fact that I didn't need to make that question known. Instead, it was definitely something to ponder.

As Rett finished speaking, Ian appeared at the passageway. "Mrs. Ramses?"

Standing, I gave Rett my sincerest smile and turned to Ian. "It seems that it may be back to Miss O'Brien...or let's say North for the sake of argument."

"Emma." Rett's address cut through the air.

I didn't turn; instead, I began walking toward Ian.

My forward progress barely allowed me a few steps before my upper arm was seized and I was spun back, dark brown eyes filling my vision. "Emma. We're married. This will get worked out."

"Or it won't." I shrugged. "Of course, seeing as we're in the presence of others, I'll refrain from further discussion until it's appropriate...Rett. In the meantime, perhaps I've been given a second chance to decide my fate. That doesn't often happen." I feigned a grin. "Could it be a sign? Maybe, I should engage the services of an attorney as well." I pulled my arm away from Rett's grasp. "Now, if it pleases your highness, I'll take my leave. My busy day awaits."

"Kyle is still out there, Emma. You're not leaving this house."

With a nod, I walked away through the passage and into the outer office as Ian followed. I didn't slow to let Ian lead. I knew the way to the suites. I'd paid attention last night and again today.

It wasn't until we were climbing the front stairs that Ian spoke. "I heard Leon when I entered. I'm sorry about the judge, Mrs. Ramses."

"It is sad." It was. I could acknowledge that, but this also changed everything from a few minutes before. The marriage I'd decided to regret was now in jeopardy. The future course that only minutes ago had named death as my sole means of escape had been rerouted, now offering alternatives.

Rett was right; Kyle was out in the world.

Was he the only person I should avoid for my safety?

The moisture between my legs was my answer.

Rett was here in this house. I had choices to make and as Ian and I climbed the stairs, I decided that this wasn't the time to make a rash decision.

I needed my questions answered and time to think.

When Ian and I arrived at the door to my suite, I turned to him. "Ian, I'd like to move some of my things to the third floor. I believe I'll spend some time upstairs." Something else occurred to me. "I will also need someone to help me with the handle and lock on the third-floor suite. Can you help me?"

RETT

The pressure I applied to my teeth endangered their survival, threatening to splinter each one as I watched Emma walk away. No one spoke as she led Ian through the outer office. If I pushed a few keys on the keyboard, I could watch longer, seeing the way Emma kept her head high, her voice measured. She was a fucking queen. It didn't take marrying me to prove that. After all, she too had the ancestry to prove her regal heritage.

"Fuck," I grumbled under my breath.

"Boss, if you call Michelson or Clark, what are you going to say? Word isn't out on the judge's death. No one knows the certificate is gone."

I had an idea. "Who is Judge McBride's assistant, the one he emailed the picture of the certificate to?"

Leon pulled out his phone. "I have her name."

"Good. I'll have Clark check on the filing. As my personal attorney, when the certificate is not where it should be, he can call McBride's assistant. Everyone present in the front office last night saw McBride email the photo. It makes sense that we'd follow up on the filing." I slapped the surface of my desk. "Fuck, this wasn't an accident."

Leon nodded. "Yeah, that's Noel's thought too, but whoever did it was good. The search warrant should come through any minute. Forensics has already gone over the vehicle and McBride's belongings in the car with no significant findings. Soon, they'll be looking through his house. Right now, it appears he was just an old man who started his car and forgot to open the garage door."

"I don't buy it. Someone wanted the marriage certificate to not be filed." Someone besides Emma. I didn't say the last part, but I felt it.

Leon nodded. "Your plan works. I can call Clark if you want." Before I answered, Leon tilted his head toward the closed bookcase and passage. "Sorry if I interrupted something."

Closing my eyes, I exhaled. "I fucked up." It wasn't an admission I made lightly, and I'd only make it to certain people. Maybe it was because Leon had been honest with me about something personal earlier in the day, I now felt free to do the same. "She's upset."

"But she'll sign again, right?"

I stared at the monitor another few seconds, seeing the empty hallways as the lingering scent of sex and lust clung to my skin. Emma said she regretted marrying me. It hadn't been even twenty-four hours. Her simple answer of *yes* rang in my head, the disappointment in her fucking eyes as well as her damn defiance at every turn.

How fucking hard was it for her to go clean herself?

Emma pushed me at every damn turn.

"Boss?"

I turned my attention back to Leon. "Yes, she'll sign."

"Good. Since I'm here, I have news on Ingalls and Boudreau if you want to hear it."

I lifted my hand. "Let me call Clark and get the ball rolling on the marriage certificate."

Of course Boyd Clark took my call. I filled him in on the information that was known and that which wasn't. Naturally, he was distraught to learn of McBride's death. Overall, the call didn't take long and there was nothing I said that Leon didn't know. As I spoke, he sat back, casually waiting. Once I hung up with my personal attorney, I leaned back. "What is the update on Ingalls and Boudreau?"

Leon sat forward. "Jaxon had an idea."

I shook my head. "Tell me he didn't fuck up. I just installed him as—"

"No, he didn't," Leon interrupted. "He planted a tracker on Ingalls before sending the two men on their bayou adventure. From the information it yielded, it's safe to say the tracker went unnoticed for long enough to give us some good info."

Leaning back, I made the mistake of bringing my hand to my chin. The scent of Emma's essence threatened my concentration. Quickly, I gripped the arms of my chair and moved myself forward, lifting a pen from the desk. "Talk to me."

"Hit the screen, boss. I can show you."

A push of a button descended a large monitor from a hidden compartment in the ceiling. It was another of the office upgrades my forebears wouldn't understand. My trusted men, the ones who had access to this inner office, could then project their information from their phones, be it videos, maps, or statistics, onto the screen, allowing viewing for everyone in the room.

A satellite image of greater New Orleans came on the screen.

"The capos," Leon began, "made sure neither Boudreau nor Ingalls had phones to call for help or use for GPS. They'd already frisked them for weapons. Hell, they didn't even have a fucking blade to cut the ropes."

"How long did it take them to find their way out of the bayou?"

"Not as long as we hoped."

"How?" I asked.

"We ain't certain. Here" —he motioned toward the large monitor— "see the time stamp?"

I did. It said 9:22. That was nearly an hour after Emma signed the certificate.

"That's when Jaxon and his other man were recovered. Boudreau and Ingalls were left afloat. Then before midnight, near the same spot, they were recovered. They should have been taken out with the tide. Either they know the bayou better than we expected or someone who knows the bayou was their guardian angel."

My eyes met Leon's. "Jezebel?"

"Not sure."

"Tell me your gut feeling, Leon."

"If she's calling any of the Louisiana bayou home, the inhabitants know she's there."

While there were well-known communities within the bayou, there was also the less known—the people who have hidden in plain sight for generations upon generations. Centuries of history and survival had given them the means to live within their own culture, impervious to the advancements of the world around them.

"And you think that they're looking out for her and for Boudreau and Ingalls."

Leon nodded. "It is the only way we can come up with for their quick escape."

"Where did the tracker go after the landing?"

"Nowhere." Leon pointed to the screen. "Jaxon went back this morning. The clothes both Ingalls and Boudreau were wearing were left in the boat, pulled up into the muck."

"Fuck. For us to find."

"Seems that way."

"If we're connecting dots here," I said, standing and pacing the width of the office and back. "Boudreau and Ingalls came here to stop the wedding or maybe to confirm Emma's presence. They didn't stop the wedding, but they saw and spoke to Emma. They know she's alive and well in New Orleans. My men took them on what was meant to be a brush with death and in under four hours they were rescued. And..." I emphasized the conjunction. "they left the clothes for us to find, a fuck-you to us." I turned my attention to Leon. "Am I missing something?"

"Based on the time they were rescued, in my opinion, they are both suspects in Judge McBride's death."

I nodded. "If they didn't instigate his death, they could confirm his presence here last night." I turned to Leon. "What are your connections in the bayou?"

"Tara's folks. Generations of Choctaw. Creole in their blood."

"Would they give up information if Jezebel is among them?"

His nostrils flared as he inhaled and exhaled. "They live their own lives and speak their own language. The politics of New Orleans or the damn country means nothing to them. They're separate."

"You're saying they don't give a fuck if a Boudreau or a Ramses runs the greater New Orleans parishes."

"Doesn't affect them."

"Then we need to figure out a way to affect them."

My phone vibrated. Pulling it from my pant pocket, I read the screen. The message was from Ian Knolls.

"MISS EMMA HAS MOVED SOME OF HER THINGS TO THE THIRD-FLOOR SUITE."

I read the message twice before hitting the call button. My gaze met Leon's as I realized he was present. Not that it mattered. He knew I fucked up and now it seemed Ian did too. "Talk to me," I said as the call connected.

"Miss Emma has moved to the third-floor suite, boss."

My head shook. "Why?"

"She didn't give me a reason."

"And you complied?"

"It's not my place to tell her no. You said she was to stay in the house. She's in the house."

Fuck. I had said that.

"There's one more thing, boss. You won't be happy."

I already wasn't happy. "What?"

"Miss Emma insisted that the lock to the hallway be changed."

"What the fuck do you mean, changed?"

"The key is now on the inside."

My free hand went to the bridge of my nose as I squinted my eyes. "Fuck."

I'd break down the damn door if I wanted in. This house was over two hundred years old. I had no intention of letting a door or a lock keep me away from my wife.

Before I could voice that, another call buzzed. A quick look at the screen told me it was Boyd Clark. I spoke to Ian. "I have another call. Tell Mrs. Ramses" — fuck the Miss Emma shit— "to be ready. We may have papers to sign today."

I didn't wait for Ian's response as I clicked to the second call. "Boyd, what's happening?"

EMMA

*B*efore gathering a few things from the suite attached to Rett's, I did as I should have done downstairs and entered the bathroom. My reflection reminded me that Rett had simply zipped his pants and buckled his belt to return himself to a less haggard state. I would need more work to accomplish such a goal.

I ran my hand over my mussed hair, no longer all contained in my braid.

Running a washcloth under warm water and applying bodywash, I found my thoughts somewhere between self-loathing and imagining possible forms of mariticide. That was if we were married. If not, it was simple homicide. As I washed away the remnants of our gratuitous afternoon dealings, my thoughts vied from one end of the spectrum to the other regarding our marital status.

Choosing to save the hot shower, possible bath, and changing clothes for once I was settled on the third floor, I began gathering cosmetics, clothes, and other items. There was the book I was still reading as well as the laptop. One of the few luxuries I lacked was luggage. That meant items were shoved in purses and piled in heaps. As the pile grew, Ian enlisted the help of others.

I recognized a few of the women as those who entered the suite to clean. While in the past they'd stayed silent, it was obvious by their shared expressions that this particular task had their curiosity aroused. Unsure of what to say, I left it to Ian to explain. I heard him say that my suite was about to have a transforming redecoration, and in the meantime, I'd reside upstairs.

"Thank you," I said when we had a moment alone.

Ian nodded.

I reached for his hand. "I mean it, Ian. I'm sorry if this puts you in Mr. Ramses's crosshairs. This is all my doing."

"I've been there before, Mrs. Ramses."

"Emma."

"I hope this can be resolved."

Without replying, I turned to gather more items, unsure if I shared his desire or his optimism. I wasn't certain how things had gone so wrong in such a short period of time, but with each passing second, I felt the weight of my decisions and promises fall heavier and heavier upon my shoulders.

Entering the upstairs suite, I stilled for a moment in the threshold.

I'd forgotten how heavy the draperies were and how dark the rooms were without windows that opened.

Ian stood behind me. "You can change your mind. Your suite doesn't really need redecoration."

"It needs something. Just in case you think this is an emotional reaction, you're right. It is. I also have good reason to be upset, and I am. As you know, Mr. Ramses is a bit..." There were so many words that would fit. "...overwhelming. Right now, I need some time to think, uninterrupted." Dropping my armful of items onto the bed, I went directly to the library and opened the ceiling.

As the people Ian had enlisted came and went from the outer room, I stood for a few minutes, staring up at the late afternoon sky. It wasn't until I returned to the main bedroom that I realized that not only had the ladies Ian called carried the items up from the second floor, they'd also put everything away. The exception was the worn leather bag containing the laptop.

As I took the laptop back to the library, I saw there was an older man with Ian. Despite his small stature, he seemed knowledgeable in completing my request. Nearly a half hour later, Ian called to me to see the finished product.

"Miss Emma?"

I stepped out of the library as Ian met me in the main bedroom. "Is it done?"

He nodded as lines appeared near the corners of his eyes. The other man had disappeared, much as all of Rett's men did. Maybe they were Miss Guidry's spirits instead of living beings.

I extended my hand to Ian. "May I have the keys?"

Ian placed two old-fashioned skeleton keys in the

palm of my hand. I shook my head as I closed my fingers around them. "This isn't enough."

"It's what you asked for, ma'am."

"You're right. I apologize for not being more specific. Let me ask you a question: how many keys exist to open the lock on that door?" I nodded toward the main door to the suite.

It was a bit ironic that after the week I'd spent in this suite contemplating escape, I was now facilitating an ironclad barricade. The difference between then and now was that at this time, I intended to be the one with the power of locking and unlocking the door.

"This is an old house," Ian began.

"It is. Do you have an approximate answer to my question? Say ten keys? Twenty?" My eyes opened wide. "More?"

"May I remind you that I'm here when Mr. Ramses isn't? He has increased the security around and within this house. Truly the use of such locks is more of a risk than a benefit."

"Why is that?"

"You could become trapped."

Holding the old key in my palm, I walked to the window and opened the glass pane, revealing the shutters behind. "These windows don't look down into the courtyard, do they?"

"No, they face the south corner of the house."

I had never been an east-west-north-south type of person. I preferred instructions that included landmarks: turn right at the pharmacy or take the second left. Not only that, I had been beyond the walls of this house only once, and those memories were marred with the terror of my abduction. "If I recall correctly, this house sits on a street corner with a single neighbor to one side. In relation to that...?"

"The windows face the street."

I walked into the library. "These windows are facing a different direction."

"West, toward the back of the grounds." As if to clarify, Ian added, "Above the conservatory."

"I want these shutters removed."

Ian inhaled.

"I'm not going to climb down a drainpipe. You said the concern with my door locking from the inside is the fear I would be trapped. Remove these shutters, and I will have a means of being rescued if needed. Of course, there's always the skylight." I opened my palm and looked at the key before smiling at my ally, the unlikely one who we both knew would report everything to Rett as soon as this was done.

I guess I found comfort in believing that Ian had yet to send that information. "Thank you for having the doorknob turned. I believe in light of the excessive number of keys wandering around and in the possession of God knows who, a dead bolt or latch of some kind on this side of the door is warranted."

"Mrs. Ramses..."

"For the sake of argument, let's say that name is accurate. Nothing that I'm requesting goes against what Mr. Ramses has stipulated. I'm in the house. I'm not leaving. I'm safe from my brother." And from Rett. I didn't say that part. "You're simply complying with my wishes."

Ian pulled out his phone. "I'll have Thomas return."

"Thomas is the man who switched the doorknob?" I asked.

"Yes, ma'am. He's been employed by the Ramses family since before Mr. Ramses's father passed. He will get this taken care of right away."

"Thank you, Ian."

I opened the closet to see the clothes I'd brought from downstairs. Turning back to Ian, I asked, "Are you to stay here? Outside the door?"

"Considering..."

He didn't finish as I grinned.

"I'm going to take some time to relax in a shower. Will you please supervise Thomas for the dead bolt and the shutters?"

"Of course, ma'am. The shutters may take a little longer."

"The dead bolt is the first order of business."

After collecting my robe, I entered the gleaming bathroom. As I did, I had a fleeting thought, wondering why the bathroom was so clean if this suite went mostly unused. Since I'd left this suite weeks earlier, the towels were clean and fresh, and the bath beads I'd brought from downstairs were already in the crystal bowl where they'd been when I first arrived. As I shed the clothes I'd worn downstairs to talk to Rett, I felt a strange sense of familiarity with my surroundings.

With the skirt and blouse upon the floor, I wished for the fireplace of the downstairs suite. I imagined throwing the two pieces of clothing upon the logs and watching as the flames consumed them. My mind told me I was doing everything I shouldn't do in the case of an assault. Then again, Rett said it wasn't an assault.

As I opened the shower doors, I noticed the lack of my wedding rings. They were last seen as Rett put them in his pocket.

Turning the temperature of the shower as high as I could tolerate, I stepped inside the glass enclosure. Loosening my braid, I allowed the hot liquid to fall over me. Much like needles prickling my skin, the sensation was both painful and liberating. Generous amounts of bodywash replaced the scent of Rett with the overpowering aroma of a fresh sea breeze. I grimaced at the tenderness of my scalp as I applied shampoo and later conditioner. It was as I again cleaned my perineum, I noticed the tenderness of my inner thighs. Under the bright lights, a reddish discoloration of my skin could be seen.

Perhaps it was the visual and tactile reminders that I needed to come to terms with my thoughts and emotions.

My knees gave out as I slid down the glass wall and lowered myself to the shower floor. Pulling my knees to my chest, I gave in to the flood of emotions that had been building within me. The falling water masked the sound of my cries as sobs racked my chest. My running nose and tears mixed with the shower's spray, swirling on the tile floor and disappearing down the drain.

There was no sense of time as memories intertwined.

I recalled a warehouse I couldn't see and a cool breeze I could feel—everywhere. My arms and legs were bound. I opened my eyes as I looked down at the faint white lines around each wrist and ankle. In my thoughts, I tried to get away, but even my mouth was gagged. The tones of the men beyond the blindfold taunted me as their words degraded me.

Despite their presence, I was alone.

My eyes opened to the shower stall, seeing the bright lights and shiny fixtures. However, upon closing them again, the space around me shrank. I reached for the doorknob, but it wouldn't budge. I screamed and rattled the handle to no avail. Smoke entered under the locked door as I coughed and gagged.

Again, I opened my eyes, gasping for oxygen.

The heavy, humid air of the shower filled my lungs. Around me was steam, not smoke. Pulling my knees tighter to my chest, I laid my head back against the glass wall.

The scene behind my eyes morphed to Rett's inner office.

I quickly stood, no longer able to combat the memories. I replaced them with thoughts of aspirin or perhaps a sleep aid. Turning off the water, I stepped from the hot stall out onto the soft bathmat and into the cooler air.

Wiping away the steam on the large mirror, I noticed that my reflection was more unnerving than it had been when I entered the bathroom. My hair was wet and clean, but hanging in twisted knots. I reached for a towel and wrapped it around my head. I dried myself with the second towel. As I did, I noticed that the combination of hot water and crying had left my flesh red and patchy.

A quick look at the sunken tub and I determined that I didn't have the energy for a bath. Instead, I chose to check on the progress of the dead bolt. Securing my robe, I opened the door to the bedroom and was met with the tepid air-conditioned air mixed with the warm breeze from the opened ceiling.

As I turned toward the library, standing in the doorframe was the man I planned to keep locked out. His cold, dark stare settled on my eyes as his demand echoed through the suite.

"Talk to me."

EMMA

My head shook once before I tilted it toward the door to the hallway. The exhaustion and frustration racking my body and mind rippled throughout my words. "Leave, Rett."

Reaching into the pocket of his pants, Rett removed my wedding rings. Placing them in the palm of his hand, he extended his hand my direction. "You forgot these."

Instead of reaching for them, I began walking the other way, toward the door—the one that was supposed to be locked—and reached for the knob. Pulling the door inward, I stood silently. For only a moment, my gaze met Ian's. In that same moment, it appeared Ian realized what was happening and with a slight bow, stepped away.

"Emma," Rett said, coming my way.

This was one of those moments. If the door remained open, Rett might leave, but on the other hand, leaving it open meant we had an audience. If I closed the door, Rett's departure was delayed; however, being only the two of us, I had an open floor to speak.

Rett reached over my head for the edge of the door, facilitating the choice.

"Leave," I whispered.

With his lips straight and his expression grim, Rett shook his head as his dark stare stayed fixed on me.

I lowered my voice. "If you close that door, you will hear me out." I was staring directly at him. "If you expect anything else, go."

Holding the edge of the door, Rett replied with pressure to the door.

Fine.

I stepped out of the way, and he closed the barrier to the hallway. For a moment, Rett stared at the addition of the new dead bolt before turning toward me.

Fisting my fingers, I crossed my arms over my breasts. "I don't want you here."

"You're stating the obvious." Rett tugged one of my hands loose, pried open my fingers, and laid the rings in my palm. "These belong to you."

My fingers curled around the set before opening and exposing the two rings—the large heirloom diamond and the diamond band—within my grasp. I lifted them toward him. "Maybe they don't. Maybe our marriage isn't finalized."

"They're yours either way."

When Rett wouldn't take the rings back, I walked to the small table, a place where I ate when in this suite, and laid them on top. Spinning toward Rett, I asked, "What is happening with the marriage certificate?"

"What do you want to happen, Emma?"

"Right now, I want you to go."

"This is my house, *our* house," he corrected.

"You know what I mean."

"I fucked up." His volume rose. "I am sorry."

I clenched my teeth as I studied the man before me.

Was there remorse in his expression or was I projecting what I wanted to see?

In the grand scheme, there was so little I knew about Everett Ramses. I had no way of comprehending how often he apologized or if he ever apologized. In that second, I also had another revelation. It was a new understanding of his response nearly a month earlier when I'd said the same words to him.

"In your words, Rett, apologies are superfluous. You're saying it to make yourself feel better."

He nodded. "I was right then and you are now."

My hands dropped to my sides. "So that's the only reason you apologized, to make yourself feel better. Did it work?" I asked. "Do you feel better?"

"No, and it's not the only reason."

"Did you mean it? The apology?"

"What I said before is accurate. Apologies don't work in this world because usually the result of whatever happened is life or death. This situation is different, and I do mean it."

I wasn't ready to let him off the hook, not now—not yet. In all honesty, I wasn't sure if I ever would be. "It's not good enough." Before he could respond, I went on.

"My feelings are justified. Don't pretend they're not. I'm upset. I'm disappointed and dismayed." I let out a breath and after lifting my arms, I let my hands fall, slapping my robe-covered thighs. "I'm all those things at you and at me. I know that I'm to blame."

Rett took one step closer and stopped. "What you said earlier...I acted like a dick. That isn't your fault."

"You're right. *That* isn't my fault. What happened a few hours ago is completely your doing. My culpability goes back to over a month ago. I'm the one who let you fill me with tales of lore, fate, and deals." A rogue tear fell from my eye, but I didn't bother wiping it away as I steadied my voice. "I fell willingly into this messed-up fairy tale that you fed me. The first night, you told me to admit to myself that it was exhilarating to be pursued by you." I shook my head. "It was. I fell for it all." I shrugged. "I guess that makes me the biggest fool. I am, after all, ultimately the person who's responsible for my being here." My volume rose. "What happened—what you did—earlier today is not my fault. That blame rests solely on you. My mistake was in trusting you."

"Fuck." Rett's Adam's apple bobbed as he nodded. "You can trust me. I never lied. I told you that as my wife, there was an expectation." When I didn't reply he added, "I never hid that I'd have—"

"Wants?" I interrupted, offering him alternatives, each one louder than the last. "Demands? Domination? I'm not Jezebel. I'm not a whore to be used whenever you see fit."

"You don't get it."

"You're right. I don't. And neither do you."

"Jezebel is more than a whore."

His assessment caught me off guard. "What is she?"

Rett sighed as he shrugged. "Some would say a sorceress, others a businesswoman, others still would say she's bent on revenge."

My head tilted as I tried to understand. "Why does she want revenge against you? What does any of that have to do with Kyle?"

"All I care about is how it relates to you. With me you're safe."

Safe.

That wasn't how I felt in his office.

Then again, I didn't feel unsafe or in danger. I felt...

I pushed that thought away—I didn't want to evaluate those feelings further.

Inhaling, I turned and walked into the library. Perhaps it was a change of scenery I desired. I lifted my face to the early evening sun shining through the skylight.

Rett's voice infiltrated the room as the sun's rays warmed my skin. "You said you'd trust me."

I didn't turn toward Rett's voice. Instead, I let his words register, soaking them in like my skin was soaking in the sunlight from above.

"You promised."

I turned to him. "What you did downstairs made me feel like I felt with those men. That evening you saved me. Today you were my assailant."

The tendons in Rett's neck pulled tight as did the muscles on the side of his face. "That's not a fair assessment."

"It's an honest one." The memory of the rings in the other room came back as I turned back to the skylight. "Are we or are we not married?"

"The certificate was signed. The court has record. Due to the unusual circumstances, the court is sending a representative here this evening for us to add another signature to the printed photo. That will then be notarized." He exhaled. "It's unusual, but my attorney has been working on everything and the other alternative is to sign a new certificate. Either way, one more signature and everything is legal."

Taking a deep breath, I peered around the library, seeing that the shutters were still in place.

I'd received a promise from Ian that the shutters would be gone. Did their presence mean he'd lied or that it just hadn't happened yet?

I'd promised to trust. I'd promised to sign. Not doing either at this moment didn't null and void my promise; it was a delay. "I would rather not."

"Fuck, Emma, that isn't an option. Don't you understand that if we're not married, you're vulnerable, not only to Kyle but also to legalities."

"What legalities?"

"I should have told you sooner. It's about Ross Underwood."

"So he is dead, and you knew?"

Rett nodded. "I found out during your first full day here."

My lips came together as I sat on the edge of the long chair and covered my knees with the end of my soft robe. "That would be a month ago or more and you're finally mentioning it?"

"Yes."

"Because you were caught withholding information."

"No, because there was nothing you could have done about it had you known."

I took a deep breath. "You seem to believe you are the almighty imparter of all knowledge, as if you have the right to divulge information to me or keep it from me."

Rett slowly turned, running his large hand down his face. He was still dressed as he'd been in the office, a light blue button-up shirt, the collar open and sleeves rolled up. His dark gray pants fell to his leather loafers, and if I was to guess, my come still adorned his cock hidden beneath. Instead of thinking about that, I concentrated on the fatigue showing in the small lines on his handsome face.

Finally, he spoke. "There was nothing you could have done."

I stood. "That isn't the point. Did you ask me to be your wife, your queen, or your whore?"

"Emma, you're being ridiculous."

I stepped toward the doorway to the bedroom as Rett seized my arm.

"You want honesty?" he asked, his words coming quicker. "I want all three from you."

My breathing stuttered as I stared his direction.

"You wanted honesty."

"I-I guess..."

Taking my hand, Rett dropped to one knee. "My mother was wrong, asking the question isn't easy."

"Why do you want to marry me?"

His nostrils flared as he inhaled. "I want to know that you're always here."

"You don't want consequences for your actions. You want a little woman who is at your disposal."

He nodded as he extended my fingers, ran his finger from the faint white line at my wrist and over my hand. When his gaze returned to mine, my breath caught. I couldn't explain the sensation, but I saw *more*. Maybe it was the glare of the sun through the skylight, but in that second, it was as if I saw deeper into Everett Ramses than I'd ever seen, or maybe for once, I was being allowed to see what he rarely showed.

The timbre of his voice had my attention. "You were conceived to reign over New Orleans. That's why I want you beside me as my queen. It's your fate to rule this city. And as for being my wife, I want that. It fucking kills me to imagine you sleeping up here." His gaze went toward the opening to the bedroom. "And if you think a lock can keep me out, you haven't been paying attention."

I had been paying attention. That was why I also asked for the dead bolt.

Rett inhaled. "As for a whore..." His head shook. "I didn't mean for you to think of me like those men. That possibility never crossed my mind. It also isn't right to say that I have needs that supersede yours but instead that we both have desires. What I want is for us to fulfill them together."

"Rett."

He tugged my hand to his lips and kissed my knuckles. "Emma, you know you can believe me. You said you'd trust me." When I didn't speak, he stood, still holding my hand. "I fucked up this afternoon. However, I've been upfront about what I wanted. I never misled you. I am a man who thrives on power. I crave your submission."

I shook my head as I looked from where he was holding my hand back to his eyes. "I didn't give that today. You took it. It's not the same."

EMMA

*S*ubmission given is sweeter than submission taken.
As I recalled what Rett had told me, I wondered if he meant them—now or then.

"You're right. Don't throw away what we have and what we will have," he said, "because I screwed up." Rett gently framed my cheeks, his palms on each side. "I pushed too far. I'm not offering an excuse. I'm telling you that I know it was a mistake."

I was too emotional for this. I shouldn't want to forgive him and yet I did.

When I didn't reply, he released my cheeks and took a step back. "Signing the certificate is bigger than us. Remember me saying that you may need to speak to someone, to make a statement?"

I nodded.

"It's about Underwood."

Turning, I walked to the tall bookcase and ran my fingers over the spines. When I turned, I said, "You were wrong earlier."

"About?"

"If I'd known about Ross, there were things I could have done. I would have contacted his parents or done something. I can't imagine what they think of me." Another thought occurred to me as I tilted my face to the side. "Wait, Kyle said you killed Ross, but if you *found out...*" The rest of my sentence disappeared.

"Kyle lied." Rett's dark orbs searched mine. "Ross Underwood is the subject that you may need to discuss with authorities. Like I said, I was informed of Underwood's death the day after you arrived here. The cause of death at that time was still undetermined. He'd been found in his hotel room. The thing I also learned was that you were on the NOPD's radar as a possible suspect."

I spun away from the books, pulling the robe tight around me. "Me. Why?"

"At first it was because you were also missing. I later found out that the evidence that put you under suspicion was that the forensics team found your fingerprints in Underwood's hotel room." He inhaled. "Is there something you want to say?"

"No." My mind went back to the day Ross and I arrived in New Orleans. It had been just over a month ago and yet it seemed like another lifetime. I tried to recall. "I was in his room, but Ross was very much alive the last time I saw him. That last time was at the bar. He was at the table and then you hijacked me for dinner. I haven't seen him since." I looked up at Rett. "Ross died that night?"

He nodded. "I never had the impression that the two of you were...romantic."

My nose scrunched and a bad taste came to my mouth. "We weren't."

"Why were your fingerprints in his room?"

"Really, Rett? The first thought you have is that I was there for sex."

"It wasn't my first thought. If it had been, I would have brought this up a long time ago. Tell me why you were in his hotel room."

The response I wanted to voice was that it wasn't any of Rett's business, but then the memories flooded back. Ross's and my flight had been a disaster with layovers and delays and then there were the hotel mix-ups. "I was in his room because my room wasn't ready. There was a mix-up." I walked past Rett to the doorway and turned. "You see, I needed to get ready for a meeting with a mysterious businessman by the name of Everett Ramses."

"Your things were in a different room."

"Yes, Rett. Before Ross and I left the hotel, my room was finally available. He helped me move my things into my room."

"Which would mean his prints were in your room too."

I shrugged. "I would suppose so."

Rett's eyes opened wide. "But they weren't found because when my men took your things from your room, they wiped it all clean."

"Your men?"

Rett nodded. "The police think it was you. They

believe you're a technology wizard, a hacker capable of erasing part of the hotel's surveillance."

"Their surveillance was hacked?"

"There's no visual of anyone entering your room to gather your things."

Which meant Rett or his men were responsible.

I nodded toward the laptop on the desk. "If I was that good at hacking, I'd have figured out your internet. I assume that if questioned, you'd rather I don't inform the authorities of who did retrieve my things?"

"Yes, I'm telling you the truth because I trust you."

I laid my hand on Rett's arm. "Tell me how Ross died."

"Overdose."

"No, Ross didn't do drugs." I went back to the long chair and sat again. "As a matter of fact, Ross had an injury from college that sometimes gave him fits. He was concerned that flying would aggravate it. The pain medicine the doctor prescribed was strong. Ross didn't take it often, but I remember him saying he brought it with him, just in case. When he took it, Ross was extremely cognizant of everything he did, including alcohol." I shook my head, realizing I was still wearing a towel on my head. Leaning forward, I let it fall to my lap and shook out my tangled hair. "No, Ross wouldn't overdose."

When I looked up, Rett was staring at me with an unreadable expression.

"What?"

"What can I say, Emma. I'm standing here looking

at the most fucking perfect woman and I am..." He inhaled.

"You're what?"

"I don't like having you upset."

"Then don't fuck up." I ran my fingers through the length of my messy hair. "Kyle said you had Ross's death declared a suicide."

"It was better than having you as a suspect."

I looked up in surprise. "So it was you? No. It's not better. I didn't do anything to him. Now if someone did, they're out there. I'm innocent. Why should I worry?"

"At first, I believed that Underwood was killed to flush you out. I still believe that's what happened. Did he say anything to you about money?"

"It was all he talked about, getting funding for our computer program. That was what you were supposed to provide."

"I've recently learned more about his financial status." Rett casually leaned against the doorjamb between the library and bedroom. "Apparently, Underwood had the means to fully support your project." Rett shook his head. "I don't know if it would be better for you to go into the police statement blind, but if being my wife doesn't keep you from making a statement, you should know what you're up against."

I stood. "Tell me."

"Ross Underwood had been receiving significant deposits of cryptocurrency for about a year and a half. From what we've ascertained, that money was coming from Kyle and possibly, more directly, from Jezebel."

My eyes narrowed. "Jezebel?"

"My men and I have reason to believe that she's every bit as dangerous as Kyle or Ingalls."

I didn't want to even think about Liam in Rett's presence.

This conversation was becoming more than I was ready to discuss. Now there was information on Jezebel. I'd just found out my birth mother was alive and learned about her past. I wasn't prepared, mentally or emotionally, to delve into her present, especially if it included a nefarious theory. "Rett, please leave. I'm tired."

"Come downstairs to your suite."

I glanced up at the skylight and smiled. "I like it here. It's peaceful."

He looked at his watch. "The clerk from the court will be here in less than an hour."

"You said earlier today that you misled me by allowing me to think I could make deals where you were concerned."

"Maybe I've misled myself."

"I'll be honest with you. I'm torn. I want to sign the certificate and I don't."

Rett exhaled as his dark gaze gleamed my direction. "You want a deal?"

"What do you propose, Mr. Ramses?"

"Sign the certificate." He turned and left the library. When I followed to the doorway, Rett was retrieving the wedding rings. In a stride or two, he was back. "Wear these. Be Mrs. Emma Ramses in the way that will keep you safe from whoever is after you."

"I thought it was Kyle."

"He's part of the equation." Rett lifted my left hand. "May I?" he asked with the diamond band poised.

"I'm not ready to forgive you."

Sun glistened in his dark gaze. "Do you think that one day you may?"

"I hope so." I extended my fingers.

Rett slid the ring onto my finger and then followed with the diamond.

"So sign the certificate and wear the rings and be Emma Ramses..." I said. "Tell me how that's a deal. What concession are you making?"

Rett inhaled as he turned a slow circle. "I will give you time. I'd prefer you took it downstairs, but if it's up here you want, it is yours."

I looked at the rings and back up. "I want something else."

"What is it?"

"By the time the clerk gets here—I don't care where you get it or how you get it—I want you to also wear a wedding ring."

The tips of his lips curled. "Is that all?"

"No. I reserve the right to come up with additional clauses to this agreement as they occur to me."

Rett's lips came to my hair. "You drive a hard bargain, Mrs. Ramses." He started to walk away and stopped. "I'd like you to join me for dinner."

I wasn't sure if we were back to courting, but I couldn't deny that I enjoyed the attention of the courtship-Everett Ramses. "The conservatory."

He nodded. "After we sign the certificate. Our second wedding meal."

"I didn't bring anything appropriate to wear."

He grinned. "It's why you should be downstairs."

I shook my head. "I have connections. I'll be downstairs in less than an hour."

As the door shut, I was uncertain of all the emotions coursing through my thoughts.

The emotion that I thought was gone was the one I found the most welcome.

Hope.

EMMA

*A*fter Rett left, I sent Ian on an errand. I knew the dress I wanted to wear and where he could find it. I'll also give him credit; he too tried to encourage my relocation. "If you were downstairs," he said, "you would have your entire closet."

"But I don't need the entire closet. Remember what you said?"

Small lines formed near Ian's gray eyes as he grinned. "Yes, one dress at a time."

"And, Ian?"

"Yes, ma'am?"

"The shutters?"

"Thomas will work on them while you're at dinner."

It was my turn to smile "Thank you. And please thank Thomas."

As I stepped into the bathroom, there was another knock. Making my way through the bedroom and opening the door, I began speaking, "Did you forget..."

I was met by Miss Guidry's worried expression. "Miss Guidry."

She wrung her hands. "Why are you here?"

"I believe it's where I live?" I said as I opened the door further. "Would you like to come in?"

Her white hair flittered as she nervously shook her head. "This isn't your suite."

"It was and I've decided to reclaim it for the time being."

She reached for my hand, tugging me into the hallway. "Miss Emma, the spirits are worried."

"Tell them it will be all right."

"He needs you. If you're up here, you aren't with him."

I stood taller, still with my damp, tangled hair and wearing my robe. "I'm certain that Mr. Ramses is capable of taking care of himself. I need some time."

"But this is your honeymoon."

Her revelation caught me off guard. I hadn't even considered our honeymoon. "I guess you're right."

She tugged my hand toward the staircase. "Let me help you go back downstairs."

I pulled my hand away. "I'm staying here for the time being."

"Those rings." She tilted her head to my left hand. "Let them remind you of your promise."

"Miss Guidry, I'm not the only person who made promises. You said that Rett didn't marry a woman like Miss Marilyn and that it was a good thing. Right now, I'm not happy with Mr. Ramses. It is all right. It's what people do. We both have growing to do."

"You still want to be married, yes?" she asked as her hazel eyes grew wide.

"Yes." Perhaps it was my first true verbalization of what I wanted, but that didn't lessen its truthfulness.

She exhaled in relief. Her gaze went to the open doorway and back to me. "You don't belong up here. It's not right. Miss Marilyn and Miss Delphine can't help you up here."

Can spirits not climb stairs? Did they climb or float?

I shook my head and asked, "Why do they need to help me?"

Her lips came together in a straight line. "Isn't it better to have help?"

"Why can't they help me up here?"

"You see, the suite downstairs, that's what they know. Mr. Ramses was wrong to bring you up here in the beginning. I appeased the spirits. I told them you would be where you belonged when the time was right. That was then. Now...well, now this isn't where you belong."

I reached out and squeezed Miss Guidry's hand. "I need to get ready for dinner." We both turned as footsteps came up the staircase. Soon, Ian appeared with all I'd asked for: the light blue dress from Rett's and my first dinner, and accessories.

He handed everything my direction. "You didn't ask for the shoes..."

I reached for the dress and shoes as my smile grew. "They're perfect. Thank you, Ian."

After nodding, he turned to Miss Guidry. "Ruth, we should let Mrs. Ramses prepare."

Miss Guidry nodded. "Please don't be misguided, Miss Emma."

I didn't know what she meant. I did, however, know that my time was wasting away. "Thank you." With a nod, I went back into the suite and closed the door. As a cold shiver skirted my skin, I looked at the handle, the skeleton key in the lock, and the dead bolt higher up.

Who would that lock protect me from?

It was a question I wasn't willing to pursue nor interested in pursuing.

Thirty minutes later, looking at my reflection, I smoothed the skirt of the light blue dress. My hair was pulled back on each side and the diamond earrings reflected the lights above the mirror. From the moment that I'd closed the door, I'd spent most of the time in deep conversation with myself.

Apparently, talking to oneself was what happened when one found herself in a situation that neither made logical or even emotional sense. Or maybe it was the influence of Miss Guidry's spirits. Either way, together we—me and I—had gone through the positives and negatives associated with again signing the marriage certificate.

We reasoned that fate had given me another opportunity, one with my eyes wider open than a day before. While there was nothing about Rett's earlier behavior that could or should be justified, there was a glaring reality that he'd so plainly pointed out.

Everett Ramses hadn't lied.

He'd omitted information, such as with Ross Underwood's death.

Yet if I were to believe what Rett finally revealed about Ross, by process of elimination, it was clear that Kyle had been the one who lied. Everett did have a hand in influencing Ross's official cause of death, it being ruled suicide. From what Rett had said, he didn't do that because he was hiding his crime. He did it as a means to protect me.

I admittedly had a difficult time recalling Kyle's appearance last night without recalling Liam's. During our—me and I—conversation as we did our hair and makeup and then dressed, I unsuccessfully avoided a lingering question: was I ready to forgive Rett and move on with this relationship because of the feelings that seeing Liam resurrected?

Or was it the way of New Orleans, the presence of ghosts from the past?

I admitted to myself that my feelings about Liam were complicated at best.

I was a different person when Liam and I had been together—young, trusting, naïve, and undefined. I was what most girls were in their mid-teens—infatuated with an older boy. Since Greyson and others saw me as the little sister, it seemed unbelievable that William, older than Greyson, would notice me.

Our attraction to one another came in stages.

We'd known each other most of our lives. Years passed and over that time, boys became more interesting. Our interests and bodies changed. It was as those changes occurred that Liam and I had a recurring lure.

Shy and unsure, we shared stolen glances. There were tingles when I'd catch him looking my way. My friends thought I was making it up, but then one day, Liam stopped me at school. I was only a freshman and he was a junior, an upperclassman.

Our secret relationship grew.

I'd tell my parents I was with a friend. He'd tell his he had late football practice. Together we'd steal away. Sitting in the front seat of his muscle car, we shared our secrets, hopes, and plans. We shared more than that in that car.

Liam was my first in many things.

And yet we didn't make our relationship public until I was at the University of Pittsburgh, Kyle and Greyson were at Duke, and Liam showed up at my dorm.

Two years ahead of me, Liam was studying engineering at Penn State, only two and a half hours away.

We quickly picked up where we'd left off.

My thoughts, when not concentrating on school, were on him. Weekends were split between my dorm and his apartment. I recalled the big fight the weekend Kyle and Greyson showed up for a football game and found me in Liam's bed. At the time I didn't know which one of us Kyle was the most upset with, me or Liam.

During my senior year at the university, when I received news of the car crash, Liam drove to Pittsburgh to be at my side. He drove me back to North Carolina, helping me as I planned the funeral. He stood beside me as I accepted condolences, and helped as I made legal decisions. And then I returned to school.

Done with his bachelor's degree from Penn State, Liam was living back in North Carolina, working as an intern for the city engineer of Hendersonville, a city south of our hometown.

I couldn't say what happened exactly.

It wasn't gradual.

The end of our relationship was abrupt, as if a switch was suddenly turned off.

While I no longer wanted to be in North Carolina, Liam demanded to stay. There were a few months of emails, calls, texts, and social media. It was too much for me with the loss of my family. Following the advice of my counselor, I turned off my old social media. I moved on and left the people of North Carolina behind, including Liam.

However, it felt as if before I made that final decision, he'd pulled away from me and my pathetic pleas.

As I prepared to sign my wedding certificate again, I admitted that seeing Liam last night brought back feelings I'd buried. I couldn't help but wonder if I was willing to forgive Rett to avoid the feeling of abandonment that seeing Liam evoked.

A new life had found me.

When I'd told Rett that I'd fallen for his talk of lore, fate, and deals, I was as transparent as possible. And now I realized that the promises Liam made were never fulfilled. I'd caught Kyle in so many lies it was hard to keep them straight—the biggest being his death.

Had Rett lied?

Was I blind or was he truthful?

My thoughts went back to the bar near Broussard's. It was in that courtyard that I first saw Everett Ramses. My breathing hitched as I recalled the scene.

My hands were in his grasp, held high above my head. My body was on fire as a man I didn't know caressed and teased me. His question was too personal and inappropriate. "Are you wet, Emma?"

Yet I answered truthfully.

His words came back as if recorded in time, deep in my consciousness. "Listen carefully, sweet Emma. The deal is done. You're now mine. As mine, you will be pampered beyond your wildest imagination. The world is yours. I will lay the heads of your enemies at your feet and indulge your every desire. Your one task is to be mine, ready for me and willing to obey whatever I ask."

Earlier today, Rett called the task due.

I was upset.

I was dismayed.

I was still angry.

And yet, as Rett said, he'd been honest with me from that very first night.

I wanted to trust him.

Another knock came to my door, pulling me from my inner monologue and thoughts.

When I opened it, I was met by Ian.

"Mrs. Ramses, Mr. Ramses is waiting in his front office."

"I'm ready."

RETT

*T*he conversation within the front office stalled as Emma stepped into view. Coming the direction of the stairs, she made her way to the doorway. As I scanned from her golden crown of hair to the toes of her shoes, I made a conscious effort not to audibly gasp at her magnificence. Emma was absolutely stunning. The light blue dress she wore highlighted her vibrant eyes and brought back memories of our first dinner. I had a brief thought about the matching blindfold.

In her hand was a small purse.

For an instant, she stood in the archway and surveyed the front office. By the way the room stilled, this could be one of those moments when the guest of honor arrived, a dignitary or a queen. That was what Emma was—a queen. My marvel wasn't brought on by doubt that she'd keep her word and attend this signing as she promised.

The woman standing in the doorway had never been

untruthful. In many ways she'd been brutally honest about too many things.

My wonder came as a reminder that she was mine.

I lifted my hand as Emma came near. As my fingers encased hers, I introduced her to the two clerks from the Second City Court of New Orleans. It seemed that with what had happened with Judge McBride, the court not only sent two clerks but also a marked police car with two uniformed officers currently waiting upon my driveway. Under normal circumstances, I wouldn't approve of New Orleans's men and women in blue at my doorway, but this wasn't normal.

"Emma, this is Clarence Wilson and Jennifer Snow, both here to witness our re-signing of our marriage certificate."

Emma offered her hand to each as they addressed one another. I couldn't help notice the sensation of pride within me as Emma repeated her name—Emma Ramses.

"Well, Mr. and Mrs. Ramses, we won't keep you," Mr. Wilson said as he held a pen in the air.

I hesitated. Last night, I'd been the first to sign.

Emma reached out, taking the pen. "Where do you want me to sign?"

Ms. Snow pointed to the space above Emma's previous signature. "Once you do, I'll initial."

Emma nodded and signed her name—Emma Leigh Ramses. With a smile, she turned to me, offering the pen. "I believe you're next."

Following Ms. Snow's instructions, I signed above my last signature.

Ms. Snow took the pen and added her initials by each name. Mr. Wilson did the same. By the time they'd both signed, Emma's hand was back in mine. Mr. Wilson removed a notary seal embosser from a small box and crimped the bottom of the photograph.

No longer watching them, Emma's attention had moved to my left hand. She reached for it and turned it from side to side. When she looked up, her blue orbs glistened and her smile grew.

She'd done as I'd asked and signed the certificate.

I'd done as she'd asked, fulfilling one stipulation of her deal.

If I'd had more time, I may have made a different choice. I didn't have more time.

The ring on my left hand had belonged to my father and spent nearly the last eight years secured in the family safe. The ring was larger than I would choose to wear, made of solid gold with a large black onyx stone and diamond-encrusted signets on each side of it representing the family crest.

"Mr. and Mrs. Ramses, we apologize for this inconvenience," Ms. Snow said as she slipped the enlarged photograph into a manila envelope.

"Thank you for taking the time to set everything straight," Emma replied as we all began walking toward the front door.

With my wife at my side, we stood on the front steps as the two officers of the court slipped into the back seat of the marked police car, the iron gate opened, and they drove away. As the iron gates closed, Emma lifted her chin to the evening breeze and sighed.

"I want to change your answer," I said.

She turned my way. "At this moment, I don't regret signing or marrying you. I hope you don't do anything to change that answer."

"I'm pretty certain I'll fuck things up again."

Her lips curled. "A wise man once told me that learning from mistakes was what was important."

"Sometimes he's not as wise as he professes to be." I offered her my arm. "To dinner, Mrs. Ramses."

Before we walked back into the house, she paused. "Tell me that one day we can walk down those steps and out into the world without worry."

I covered her hand, now on my arm. "I can't."

"What?"

"You want honesty, Emma. I'm giving it to you. Today, it's Kyle and Jezebel. Tomorrow, it will be someone else. It's the life you agreed to when you agreed to marry me. But that doesn't mean you're trapped. Security will become second nature to you. I never leave the house alone and neither will you."

Her painted lips pursed as she looked out at the street beyond the iron fence.

"Your safety is my priority."

I watched as her breasts pushed against the bodice of her dress with each breath. Finally, she turned my way. "I'm glad you keep yourself safe too."

The one time in over half a decade that I didn't ensure my safety was for her. Entering that warehouse alone could have been the end to both of us. Thankfully, it was closer to the beginning.

Together we walked into the house as staff closed

the doors behind us. The evening sunshine penetrated the leaded-glass panes, sprinkling the foyer in small rainbows. Emma's eyes grew wide as we walked through the sitting room across from the front office. This was her first sighted journey through these rooms. In her blue orbs I watched the awe for what I took for granted. Our path led through the front sitting room, music room, and another library.

"I love watching you see things for the first time, but I can't stop thinking about the matching blindfold and how I wish you were wearing it."

"Everything is so" —she searched for the right word — "opulent."

It was a good choice.

The fireplace in the front sitting room had an eight-foot-high opening and was made of imported marble. The crystal light fixtures as well as my mother's portrait over the fireplace all added to the atmosphere that had been created.

"My grandmother made a point of redecorating the house once my great-grandmother passed. According to stories, my great-grandmother felt the old house needed to be modernized. I suppose she was right, regarding utilities and such, but my grandmother wasn't a fan of the furnishings. Utilizing old photographs and journals, Grandmother Delphine tried to recreate the feel from the late nineteenth century. When my parents married, all four of them lived here together."

"Sometimes speaking with Miss Guidry, I have a sense of how that felt."

"I'm sure she could give you more detail, but from

what I was told, the search for furnishings was something the two women agreed upon. It was a project that bonded them."

"I heard it was something else."

I shrugged. "Of course, like everything else in New Orleans, I'm not certain of the percentage of fact in many of those old stories."

"Do you remember your grandparents?" Emma asked. "I never have had any of my own."

I patted her hand and nodded. "I do. They passed before I became a teenager."

"So you all lived here together?"

"And Miss Guidry as well as other members of the household staff."

"Sounds cozy."

"This is a big house. Many of the staff still live here or in the building on this property, behind this house."

Emma looked all around. "It's odd I never thought about it."

"You're never alone."

She shivered. "I think that feels a bit" —her head tilted— "creepy."

"No one enters this house who isn't vetted. Anyone with responsibility is fully loyal to Ramses. I wouldn't have it any other way."

When we finally reached the back of the house, the sun was setting, and we came to the conservatory.

RETT

*E*mma's gaze went up to the glass ceiling as her smile grew. "This room is absolutely magnificent."

I tried to see it as she was seeing it, with the wonder that came from lack of familiarity. It wasn't something that came naturally to me. After all, I'd been born into this house. And yet as I followed her line of vision, I saw the colorful evening sky, the shades of purple and pink through the glass. "I suppose it is."

Emma's hand remained on my arm until we reached the dining table I'd had placed in here, complete with the silver vase and single red rose.

Once we were both seated, I sat back and took in the view I found the most magnificent, my stunning wife.

"You're looking at me like that again," Emma said with a blush of pink filling her cheeks.

"What is *like that?*"

"I sometimes feel like you're seeing me, all of me, as

if my dress were gone."

It was my turn to smile. "Oh, Emma, I do love that image, but if I'm again honest with you—"

"It's all I want you to be."

I nodded. "I'm looking at you with wonder at your presence." I grinned. "I guess that word has plural meanings."

She tilted her head.

"You see," I went on, "your presence as in you're here. There was a time earlier today that I wasn't confident we would be here or anywhere this soon."

Her neck straightened. "I had the same concern."

"And also your presence as in there is a presence about you. You're simply regal without trying."

Before we could continue, Miss Guidry entered with a rolling cart and our meal. By the time she finally left, Emma and I both had plates and glasses before us with multiple courses present. Sipping my ice water, I watched as Emma took a bite of her salad and lifted her napkin to her lips.

Conversation came as we ate and drank.

The fear I'd refused to acknowledge—that things would be awkward between us—wasn't realized. It wasn't until our plates were taken away, coffee was served, and we were left alone that I broached the subject I'd been wondering about since I left the third-floor suite. I reached across the table and covered her hand with mine. "There's no doubt that you're far more forgiving than I. And while I am grateful that you are, will you tell me why?"

"I'm not sure you're forgiven."

My eyes opened wider. That wasn't what I expected. I wasn't certain what I expected; however, that wasn't it. "Well, Mrs. Ramses, congratulations for surprising me at every turn."

She looked to the side of the conservatory. "May we sit over there?"

I nodded as we both reached for our coffee and carried it to the table near the loveseat. When she sat, she was facing me. The way she searched me gave me an odd sensation. Maybe it was what she was saying about when I looked at her. My sensation wasn't of being unclothed but unmasked. Most of my life had been spent building up to my coup, to my taking power. Once that power was in my grasp, there was a constant battle to hold it tight. The protection I enlisted wasn't only my men who would risk their lives but included a shield surrounding me.

The shield was metaphoric but present and impenetrable nonetheless.

In Emma's gaze, that defense eroded away, piece by piece and layer by layer. I'd tried to rebuild it earlier today and I supposed I'd succeeded, but I immediately realized the cost was more than I was willing to pay.

"I don't know if you're forgiven," she said again. "I know I want to."

"That's a start."

"But I realized something. After you left the third-floor suite, I had an epiphany."

"Since you're still here, I assume it was a good one?"

She grinned. "Was leaving the house an option I wasn't aware I had?"

"No. I meant here as in having dinner with me."

Pursing her lips, Emma looked down at her hands, twisting the diamond one way and the other before looking up. "I meant what I said about taking versus giving."

She didn't need to elaborate. The contraction in my chest meant I understood.

"I also recalled," Emma went on, "the first night in the restaurant. That night you said what you expected if I were your wife. You didn't sugarcoat it then, and I guess today was the manifestation of that."

Exhaling, I leaned back against the soft cushions and stared up at the darkening sky through the glass ceiling. "This isn't easy for me. I have what I have because I take what I want."

I looked down as Emma reached for my hand.

It had been splayed on my thigh, but now she was holding it between hers. The difference in the size of hers and mine shouldn't come as a surprise, but it did. In so many ways, she would appear inferior, smaller and weaker. And yet today she'd proven the opposite.

Emma Ramses didn't crumple in the face of adversity. She didn't run away or cry. No, this petite, intelligent, sensational sensual woman faced me with more vigor and spitfire than any man in New Orleans. She had a fire burning within her that beckoned such as a lighthouse on a rocky shore. I longed to get closer to the flame, not to extinguish it but to feed it and tend to it.

It was because of her fire that I craved her submission.

I turned her way. "I still want it, Emma."

She nodded.

"Will you ever willingly offer it again?"

I said a prayer to my mother's saints or Miss Guidry's spirits that Emma wouldn't ask me if I'd ever take it again as I had today because she wouldn't like my honest response. While I didn't plan it, I couldn't promise that it wouldn't happen.

Instead of asking or answering, Emma reached for the small purse she'd been carrying. "Miss Guidry reminded me that this is officially our honeymoon. And well, I have something for you."

Our honeymoon.

Emma deserved a real honeymoon. And one day, I'd give that to her.

"Wait." I reached into the pocket of my suit coat and pulled out a small box with a white ribbon. "I have something for you, too. We can call it a wedding gift."

"Not an apology offering?"

"No, you know my thoughts on apologies, and that would mean I'm giving you this to make me feel better. I'm not." I extended my hand with the box. "I'm offering it because you make me feel better."

Her sweet grin grew as she took the box. Before pulling the ribbon free, she shook it and appeared to be contemplating its contents. "I will guess jewelry."

"That would be the most plausible." However, I'd given her jewelry repeatedly over the last month or more. This was something less monetarily valuable. I hoped it would be equally as precious.

Her smile faded. "You've given me so much.

Tonight, I wanted to surprise you with a gift."

"You will. Indulge me, please."

Emma pulled the ribbon free and opened the box. Inside was another box, covered in teal velvet with a hinged top, and satin lining. "I told you—jewelry." Emma tilted back the lid and her blue eyes opened wide. "What is this?"

"It's a key."

She lifted the key between her thumb and finger. "I can see that, Rett. A key to what?"

I would say my heart, but we both knew that didn't exist.

"Your suite."

Her forehead wrinkled as indecision showed in her expression. "The dead bolt Ian had installed doesn't require a key. It only opens and locks from inside."

"No, Emma, to *your* suite. The third floor isn't your suite. You belong by me. That key now operates the new locks on the door from your suite to the hallway, the door to the hallway that connects our suites, and your door to the exercise room. There's no way into your suite that you can't secure."

"And do you have a copy?"

"There is a copy for safety purposes with the staff. No, I don't have one."

Moisture came to Emma's eyes as she wrapped her fingers around the key and hugged it to her chest. "I don't know what to say."

"I guess we can put it on a chain if you want more jewelry."

Leaning toward me, she brushed her lips against

mine. "It's the best gift I'm not sure I'll ever use."

"I guess that decision is up to you."

Opening her hand, she stared down at the key. "Really, all the doors?"

"That's why Thomas was unable to remove the shutters. He's had a busy day as a locksmith."

Again, Emma reached for her purse. "I apologize, I didn't wrap yours."

"I don't need a gift. I have you. And you decided to re-sign the marriage certificate and join me for dinner. I should probably quit while I'm ahead."

Emma reached for my hand and turned it. "Open your hand, palm up, and close your eyes."

A chuckle rumbled deep within my throat. "Are you serious?"

"Yes. Do it, please."

Exhaling, I did as she asked. I felt the sensation of something that weighed next to nothing, but with my eyes closed, I couldn't decide what it was.

"Open your eyes."

"Fuck, Emma." I closed my fingers around the light blue blindfold. "Tell me what that means."

"It means I want to trust you, Rett. I won't give up on you if you won't give up on me."

"You know your way back to the third floor. This house is yours. Do you not want to see it?"

She nodded. "I do and I love learning about the furnishings and hearing stories of your family." Pink filled her cheeks as her lashes veiled her eyes. "I wasn't thinking that we would use it" —she gestured about— "...in public."

EMMA

*T*onight would be my third night on the third floor, and I had to admit my resistance to the attraction of Everett Ramses was waning.

"I don't want you up here any longer," Rett said, standing with me in the suite's library. With the ceiling above us open, under the evening stars, he wrapped his arm around my waist and pulled me closer.

Keeping him at bay during most of our days, I couldn't deny the draw when we were together. In his arms, I was adrift on a cloud of Rett Ramses. The intoxicating scent of his cologne mixed with bodywash filled my senses. The key in my jewelry box gave me hope. And his dark gaze focused only on me was like a ray of sunshine that warmed me from within.

Nevertheless, I knew that I was perched on the precipice of the stand I took—my line in the sand. As my breasts flattened against his wide chest, his upsetting behavior was in the past. In the present, I was once again seeing the fairy tale of honeymoons and happily-ever-afters.

It wasn't that I didn't want those things.

I did, more than I cared to admit.

Despite what he'd done, I was completely under Everett Ramses's spell.

Perhaps my stubbornness in remaining on the third floor stemmed from something deeper, similar to my desire to retain my name, Emma at the least.

This past month and a half had been crazy—to understate it. My world was upended much like a boat capsized during a hurricane. With all that had changed, I needed to hold on to me in some form. If I stayed with the boat analogy, I couldn't sink. I couldn't fall so far into the depths of the ocean that was Everett Ramses that in the process I was lost at sea.

It reminded me of how it had been with his desire for my submission. I wanted to do it on my own terms. I wanted to comply and yet stay true to me—not a version of me created by Rett.

Moving to the third floor had been my stand. I would maintain it for now.

"I'm still..." I wasn't sure how to finish that sentence.

He lifted my chin. "This temper tantrum has gone on long enough. I could insist."

My chest filled as I inhaled. "It isn't a temper tantrum. There is no yelling. This is me making my own decision. I suppose you can insist, but I promise that wouldn't accomplish your goal."

"If my goal is to have you close, it would."

"In proximity" —I laid my hand over the buttons of his shirt— "or here?"

"I've told you there isn't some magical or symbolic organ present in there, Emma." He laid his hand between my breasts. "Not like there is in here. You're too good and too forgiving for your heart to be gone."

"Mine isn't gone, Rett. It was taken and broken, and what remains is guarded very closely. That's why I won't come downstairs yet. I'm not ready. As I said, you could insist, but if you do, you won't like the result."

The tips of his lips curled. "Are you threatening me, Mrs. Ramses?"

"Are you scared?"

"Not in the least. Throwing you over my shoulder and carrying you down the stairs sounds appealing."

I wanted to say that it didn't *not* sound appealing to me, but instead, I moved the conversation forward. "Rett, I'm asking for your patience and calling on our deal, the one we made the other day. I fulfilled my part by signing the marriage certificate again. And you may recall, I added the addendum of additional clauses as they came to me. That is still in effect."

Rett lifted my left hand in the palm of his hand and brought his left hand beside it. "You asked for a ring. I'm wearing it."

I'd looked at the ring off and on since that night but not as closely as I was seeing it now. I reached for his hand and studied the large piece of jewelry. "Is that the Ramses crest?"

"A little smaller than in the courtyard."

"Not much," I said with a smile. "Where did you get it?"

"The safe. It's where most of the jewelry comes from."

"Is that similar to where they keep the Queen of England's crown jewels?"

"Smaller." He inhaled and exhaled as he looked down at the ring and back to me. "You won't come downstairs." It wasn't a question. "I'd like to stay here for a while?"

This new part of our courtship had been growing since my move. The first night after our dinner, Rett had said goodnight to me at the door. Last night, he'd entered the suite for a short time.

A grin came to my lips. "I'm not sure you're used to the word no, so I won't push it." I gestured toward the long chair, wide enough for two. This suite had many things; a place for entertaining wasn't one. "Shall we sit?"

After Rett removed his suit coat and turned off the lights and I slipped out of my high heels, we both situated ourselves on the chaise. With the ceiling open and the night sky overhead, we stared upward. The setting of the sun had lowered the temperature. Still wearing the dress I'd chosen for dinner, I curled into Rett's side.

His arm behind my back pulled me closer. "I like this."

I scoffed. "I'm sure you don't."

His warm breath teased my cheek and hair. "You're wrong. I like having you close."

Again, I reached for his hand. "Will you tell me about the ring?"

For longer than I expected, the library filled with a silent pause, one that lingered as the stars through the ceiling skylight came to life in the black velvet sky. As I was about to comment, Rett began.

"This ring belonged to my father." He turned his hand this way and that. "I quite honestly never intended to wear it."

Part of me wanted to interrupt, to ask questions, but as he spoke, I heard more than Rett's words. His story didn't stop there. There were clues in his pauses and meaning in the tone and timbre of his offering. Instead of speaking, I curled closer, laid my head on his shoulder, and waited for more.

"Most people would assume I hated my father. I am, after all, the reason he's dead."

I couldn't not look up. "You are?"

"I told you once that I sold my soul to become the devil."

"You said that your father and my father decided they couldn't co-rule anymore. You said they both succumbed to their injuries. I assumed the injuries were inflicted by one another."

"Some have assumed as much. After all this is New Orleans and truth seldom overcomes lore. Nevertheless, that wasn't what happened. Those who are important know the truth."

"I don't understand."

Rett sighed and laid his head back on the chair. Though he was looking upward, I had the sense that he was seeing another time. He went on, "I told you that both Abraham Ramses and Isaiah Boudreau underestimated their opponent. I was their opponent. Neither realized what was happening. My father assumed I was present in that warehouse as his son, his second, and the person who had his back. You see, Emma, to rule New Orleans, I couldn't be second. The cost of my position was our fathers' lives. I'd considered every possible scenario where my father would live." He stilled for a moment. "I didn't hate him." His head shook. "There was no alternative. Nothing short of his death would have worked."

I didn't respond. Truly words weren't forming as I let Rett's confession settle into my consciousness.

He reached for my chin, and turned it toward him. "This shouldn't be a shock, Emma. Have I ever led you to believe I'm a good man?"

"Not in words, Rett, but in actions."

"I kill and steal. It's what I do."

I shook my head. "You aren't the monster you profess. The mythical creature with red skin, horns, and a pitched fork wouldn't have saved me when I ran; he wouldn't make me feel special, offer me hope, or give me a key. You may see yourself as the devil, but I don't."

"Even after the other day?"

I kill and steal—it was what he'd just said.

The other day he stole or took.

I inhaled. "You're not perfect." I lifted his hand. "But neither am I." I looked up at the sky and sighed. "Can you explain how that meeting ended in their deaths?"

"I don't care to relive it." Before I could respond, he went on, "I can tell you that it was an unlikely chain of events. There had been problems in the world they ruled. Without details, there are networks that require protection and promises that must be kept. Things were getting out of hand with a supplier of...a product. Rumors flew that pit my father against yours. I wasn't convinced that the time was right to go forward with my plan, but at the same time, the opportunity presented itself and I took it—stole it. Your father was the one who called the meeting."

"Did you do it alone?"

"I didn't. While I'm the one who sits on the throne, taking and keeping that throne requires support. I'd been working toward the coup and had soldiers strategically set."

I wasn't certain what made me think of my next question. There were so many conflicting thoughts in my mind. Yet before I could consider my question's ramifications, I asked, "Did your mother know?"

"That I killed my father?" Rett's head shook. "Did she know that her son, her only child, took the life of the only man she truly loved?"

Instead of answering, I let Rett continue.

"I never told her."

"Did she know?"

"If she did, she made the decision to not confront me. I suppose she understood enough of the world to realize her choice: acknowledge what I'd done and lose her husband and her son or be the grieving widow and hold tight to her son. She chose the second option."

I nodded. I didn't know much about Miss Marilyn, but if I were to believe Miss Guidry, his mother loved Rett. It was true what was said about love blinding people. It didn't have to be the sensual love between two people. A mother's love could also be blinding.

"From everything you and Miss Guidry say, I would have liked to meet her."

It was his first smile. "I wish you could. I suppose in a way I'm responsible for her death too."

I sat up with my hand on his chest, the fabric of his shirt holding his body heat. "You're too quick to assign your own blame."

"No, I'm in charge of everything. I'm ultimately responsible."

"How are you responsible for her death?"

"She never asked what happened, but the loss of my father left her—brokenhearted. Death by a broken heart. I suppose that's why mine is gone, a way to ensure I never suffer the same ailment."

His confessions made me sad. I didn't want to think about the particulars, what exactly happened in that warehouse or how Miss Marilyn suffered without Abraham. Instead, I wanted to help Rett.

"What made you decide to wear the ring?" I asked, moving away from the subject of Miss Marilyn.

"You asked me to, Emma."

I grinned. "I asked for *a* ring. In this magical jewel-filled safe, does there not exist any other masculine rings?"

"I didn't look." He was back to peering upward toward the sky. "I knew which ring I wanted when I set out for the safe. I earned this ring. Not by taking my position. Not by facilitating the death of our fathers, but in the seven years since. Taking power isn't as difficult as maintaining it. I've done that. Having you here beside me has brought that home."

He looked down and turned his hand so ours were palm to palm. Our fingers intertwined as he continued, "My father was a better man than I am. He ruled without question but didn't lose his heart. Even with Boudreau, they had a strange kind of understanding. I never understood it until you."

"Me?"

"Emma, you belong here. I severed a longstanding agreement between our two families that I didn't understand. I've survived over the last almost eight years, but I did so without living. In the last six weeks, I have gotten a taste of what life can be if I'm willing to reinstitute the generations-long agreement. We're now married." He lifted his eyebrows. "Signed, sealed, delivered. The certificate may say a Ramses and an O'Brien, but the reality is we are a Ramses and a Boudreau. Together we will rule the city, the parishes, and wards. New Orleans will continue its path forward, not only maintaining its position in the country and world but increasing its significance in the global arena."

"I'm hardly ruling, Rett. I haven't left this house in those six weeks you've found life."

"There's a lot you need to understand."

"Then teach me."

He was quiet for a bit as I again laid my head on his shoulder. The sound of our breathing lulled me into a sense of contentment. The faint thump of my pulse was a faraway drum. The evening air took on a chill as I huddled closer to Rett's side.

After all that had transpired over the last few days, I was teetering on the brink of slumber when Rett spoke. "Mrs. Ramses, tomorrow evening, I propose a tour of your city and a dinner not in this house."

I sat forward. "What about Kyle?"

"His quest is over. Once you're made public, he won't be able to substantiate his claim. Jezebel North had one child with Isaiah Boudreau, one pregnancy. You are that child."

As Rett began to stir, I bit my tongue. If I didn't, I would have asked him to stay or admitted I wanted to go with him. It wasn't sex that I was after but what we had been doing, were sharing at this moment—his brutal honesty and sincerity.

Everett Ramses was a multidimensional and complicated man. The one with me tonight wasn't the man I met at the restaurant, cocky and confident, domineering and self-assured. That wasn't to insinuate that this Rett was any less the man who had captured my attention. In this shared moment under the blanket of stars, he became more. He exposed a layer he'd kept hidden. I recognized what he'd done as a present. It was as much a gift as the jewelry he'd given and the key he'd tied with a ribbon.

I walked with him to the door.

With my feet now bare, I had the sensation I'd had on our first meeting. My toes stretched as we kissed goodnight. "Thank you for being honest with me."

His long finger skirted over my cheek. "You can and will hate me for things in our future, Emma, but never will I lie to you."

I swallowed and nodded. It was the realization I'd come to, even regarding what had happened in his inner office.

"Goodnight."

After Rett left, I climbed alone into the big bed. As I slipped into sleep, I took a moment to examine the many gifts he'd bestowed, and I realized that each was invaluable in its own way.

What increased their value was the difficulty I believed that it took for him to part with them. Whether it was granting me control of locks or sharing his tragic past, Everett Ramses rarely relinquished anything. The fact he'd given me both was monumental.

RETT

"You've been avoiding my calls," Michelson said, standing as I entered the front office.

"It's nice to see you too, Richard."

"Married." He held up what I could only assume was a copy of my and Emma's marriage certificate. "To a woman you claimed to not know."

"I'm sorry you weren't invited. It was a private ceremony."

"The invitation didn't work out well for Raymond McBride."

I shook my head as I took the opposite chair. "That was unfortunate."

Michelson sat on the edge of the other velvet chair. "It seems a possibility to a few people downtown that perhaps you didn't want witnesses."

"Excuse me? Please be more specific. I've found generalities aren't always interpreted correctly."

He opened the piece of paper. "Ian Knolls and Ruth

Guidry are employed by Devereux Inc." He looked up. "Which is you, am I correct?"

Devereux Incorporated was created by my grandfather in my grandmother's maiden name as a corporation for her to oversee all things related to the house. That included maintenance and salaries paid to household staff. While the entity was in essence part of the Ramses umbrella, the control was transferred to my mother. Currently, it was simply a subsidiary that was devoted to expenses that centered on the house. Instead of explaining that, I simply said, "In a roundabout way."

"So the only nonemployee or nonfamily member who witnessed your wedding is now deceased."

I inhaled. "Are you asking me if I had anything to do with Judge McBride's death?"

"You were aware of it before it was public."

"Boyd Clark followed up on the certificate to be sure it was filed. The rest of the information came from that call." I leaned back. "Why would I eliminate the man who was about to file my marriage certificate?"

"Maybe it wasn't you. Maybe it was your wife. She has a history of association with people immediately prior to their demise."

It wasn't my wife, but I was getting closer to adding Richard Michelson to the growing list of casualties. "I can attest to my wife's whereabouts."

"And she yours. It's rather convenient."

"Who were you with the morning after your wedding, Richard?"

He nodded.

I sat forward. "I have a busy day and the tone of this conversation isn't to my liking. Tell me why you're here."

"Underwood's parents have appealed to the Louisiana attorney general for an investigation into their son's death. They claim that there is no basis for a declaration of suicide. They've gone as far as to make wrongful death complaints. The feds had backed off on the electronic currency trail, but this potential legal maneuver will undoubtedly reel them back in." Standing, Richard paced to the tall window and let out a long breath. "Everett, if the Underwoods can convince the AG to pursue this, their case has merit."

"As you can imagine, Mrs. Ramses was very upset to learn of her friend's suicide. If that isn't what happened, I agree that we need to get to the bottom of it."

Michelson turned my way and exhaled. "You're now behind an investigation that you didn't want to have happen six weeks ago?"

"I know without a doubt that neither my wife nor I were involved. If the Underwoods want justice, I don't blame them."

"And what, Everett? Bring out the fact that my office pushed for the declaration of suicide? That discovery won't help your wife, you, or me. I can't afford to get caught in what could be construed as a cover-up."

"You're right. What do you want from me?"

"I need to speak to your wife. We want her to come to the courthouse and make a formal statement." He came closer. "Hell, unofficially, she was considered a missing person." He shook his head. "I would have put money on the fact that she was dead. And you had her here all along. I trusted you."

Standing, I secured the buttons on my suit coat as I straightened my neck and shoulders. "Did I lie to you?"

"You said you didn't know her or where she was."

"I don't recall saying those words. I do remember you saying that you were worried about her, and that you believed she was a pawn in a bigger game. There's no need to worry. I can assure you that Emma Ramses is safe."

"For how long?"

My jaw clenched. "Forever, Richard."

"Let us get her statement—on the record. The feds were already curious about the cryptocurrency. They'll want to know Mrs. Ramses's connection to Underwood, the last time she saw him, why they traveled here to New Orleans, and her knowledge of his income. If we don't have a statement on record, the feds will want to get their own, and I promise they won't ask as nicely as I'm asking." Michelson exhaled. "Be straight with me, Everett. Did you pay Underwood in cryptocurrency to bring Emma O'Brien to New Orleans?"

"I must admit, I'm shamefully behind the times with the whole premise of cryptocurrency. I have done some recent research and learned there are thousands of different cryptocurrencies traded."

His ruddy complexion grew in intensity.

"Let me be more specific," I said. "No, I didn't pay Underwood cryptocurrency to bring Emma to New Orleans. You yourself said a connection to the digital currency was made to Jezebel North. Perhaps if she is

Emma's birthparent—as you said—she wanted to lure her daughter here."

"And instead, her daughter ended up married to you?"

"Fate has a way of making strange bedfellows."

Michelson shook his head. "I thought you said you didn't kiss and tell."

"She's my wife. My affection isn't a secret."

Michelson looked at his wristwatch. "It's almost noon. We'd like Emma Ramses" —he emphasized her last name— "at the courthouse by three this afternoon. And she'll need to bring her identification."

"She hasn't had time to get an ID with her new last name." Emma also wouldn't show for this command performance, but there was no need to bring that to Michelson's attention yet.

"I'm aware that her identification was used to commission the marriage license and sign the certificate."

Her driver's license was used to first obtain our marriage license, then to show to Judge McBride, and later to the officers of the court who came back here for the second signing.

Richard patted his suit coat. "I have a copy of your marriage license. That and her ID will be sufficient." He lowered his volume. "If your wife is innocent, there is no reason for her not to make a statement."

"She is innocent, yet the NOPD had her under suspicion."

"If she is who I think she is and you didn't lure her to New Orleans, then she would be safer coming forward." Michelson pulled the small notebook from his inner pocket and peeled back a few pages. "Everett, when Mrs. Ramses is asked about meeting you, will her answer coincide with yours."

"I haven't been asked that question."

"You stated that you didn't have dinner with Emma O'Brien at Broussard's six weeks ago."

I nodded. "I had dinner with Emma North."

His eyes opened wide. "Is that how she introduced herself to you?"

Turning, I went back to the chair and sat, leaned back, and lifted one heel to my opposite knee. "If my wife gives a statement, it will be limited to her knowledge of Ross Underwood. It will not be a fishing expedition. I will also be present."

Michelson shook his head. "You may be her husband now, but she's an adult. We'll speak to her alone."

"I don't think that'll be possible." I placed my lifted foot back on the rug and leaned forward. "Don't tell me that this isn't my business, Richard. I think we both know it is." I stood. "I think we're done."

"This will go much smoother with me and an NOPD detective than it will when the feds come calling. If we have Mrs. Ramses's statement on the record, she might be able to avoid speaking to them at all."

"She has the right to representation."

"She isn't being charged with a crime. She's a witness."

"I'll talk to her. The decision is hers."

Michelson smiled. "Of course it is." His gaze went

toward the double doors. "Perhaps I could ask her myself." His gray eyes met mine. "Is she currently home?"

I offered the prosecutor my hand. "Thank you for the visit, Richard. I'll be in touch."

EMMA

The SUV emerged from the tunnel into the evening traffic. Above us, colors filled the sky as the setting sun sent its last rays of the daylight up toward the low-lying clouds, turning the normally cobalt blue to a spectrum of crimsons. My stomach twisted as knots formed on knots, a gaggle of nerves.

I'd imagined that it would be freeing to leave the mansion. Ever since Rett's promise last night of a tour, thoughts of New Orleans swirled throughout my mind. I'd truly only seen a very small bit of the city the day I arrived with Ross. As we were driven north on St. Charles Avenue, I couldn't ward off the uncertainty.

After so long within the protective walls, I had the sensation of a butterfly emerging from the safety of the cocoon. My wings wanted to stretch, yet I was unsure.

What if they wouldn't carry me?

What if I fell?

Rett reached across the seat and gently covered my hand. "You're shaking."

I quickly shook my head. And then for a moment, thoughts of the city streets beyond the vehicle's windows disappeared as I stared into the dark orbs I'd come to know. "I'm...sorry."

"I believe we've had multiple discussions on apologies."

"This isn't life or death. I wish I wasn't apprehensive. This isn't me, Rett. I came down to New Orleans to have a business meeting with someone I didn't know. Now, leaving the house with someone I do has me uneasy."

"No, Emma. After what happened to you, I should have insisted we get out sooner. I'm guilty of wanting to keep you safe."

Tucking my lip behind my teeth, I looked through the windows. "What about now? Is this safe?"

Rett lifted his chin. "We have Leon and Ian here with us and at least ten others stationed around the city and the restaurant."

My legs trembled as the high heels of my shoes burrowed into the carpet. Looking down at my lap, I saw the black skirt of the dress I'd chosen as well as the small clutch with a few important items for a date, such as lipstick and the like.

I turned to Rett. "I'm being silly. I know I'm safe with you and Ian," I nodded toward the driver. He was the same man who told us about Judge McBride. "...and Leon." I turned my hand over so our palms were touching. Rett's fingers encased mine. "I'm anxious, but I'm also excited. When does my tour begin?"

"Now..."

I listened to Rett as the SUV slowed in traffic and he pointed out landmarks. Our home was in the Garden District, the Eleventh Ward. Leon drove us into the business district. The Central Business District wasn't what I thought of when I thought of New Orleans. It was filled with high-rise buildings, boutique hotels, bars overflowing with people, and office space.

In the French Quarter, he took us down to the Mississippi riverfront. The walkway was bustling with people, and artwork, and on the water, large riverboats with paddle wheels were all lit up.

For a moment, I was concerned that we were going to get out of the SUV and walk. And then when we didn't, I wrestled with disappointment. I'd never been an anxious person, and whatever had happened to me, I didn't like it.

Rett kept my hand in his.

"My father," Rett said as we again drove, "was an advocate of history. New Orleans is filled with history, factual as well as fabled. He believed it was important to understand where the city came from and the people who built it, in order to understand where it is today."

"That makes sense."

"You asked about the safety of our underground garage. All New Orleans residents keep flooding in the back of our minds. My grandfather had only recently passed away when Katrina hit in 2005." He shook his head. "The greatest tragedy wasn't the hurricane, a category three when it hit landfall. Though the winds and storm surge did produce damage, the real devastation occurred with the aftereffects. Levees that had been constructed a long time ago and left to deteriorate failed."

I recalled studying Katrina. Suddenly, hearing the information come from a man who was here and who loved this city, what had been only statistics took on new meaning.

"As a point of reference," Rett said, "New Orleans has flooded six times. Before Katrina the most recent was 1969. The average elevation is about six feet and much of the city is below sea level. The levees along the river were strong. It was the ones built to hold back Lake Ponchartrain, Lake Borgne, and the bayous to the east and west that failed. Before the storm hit, our fathers encouraged the mayor to send an evacuation order. It was the first ever. Not all the residents had the ability to evacuate. It was your father's idea to utilize the Superdome. Times of mutual peril can bring about common goals.

"The entire greater New Orleans parishes were affected. Some of the most horrific flooding and loss of life occurred in St. Bernard Parish and the Ninth Ward. Even today in these areas you can see the Katrina crosses left by FEMA."

"What are they?" I asked.

"FEMA went house by house. They painted a big X. In each of the four quadrants they left a code: time FEMA arrived, and then clockwise, what hazards were found, victims, and last, what team entered or didn't enter."

"What happened to your house?"

"No one escaped damage. Mother Nature doesn't care how much money you have. However, for the most part the Garden District and French Quarter are above sea level. It spared us from the aftermath of the flooding."

Rett tilted his head to the side of the street. "We're now in the Third Ward. While I appreciate my father's knowledge as well as knowing the history I just told you or that of that church over there, it doesn't prepare you to understand the current dangers such as the Byrd Gang."

"What is that?"

"They are a who. As my grandfather aged and your grandfather passed, my father and yours established their divide of the city, the wards. Generally speaking, it was the mid-1980s. The city was growing in popularity as not only a tourist destination but a location for long-term business. The Central Business District was booming with construction of tall office buildings. There were numerous avenues for revenue. The two of them were smart and took on all businesses, not only the ones building the skyscrapers."

"What do you mean?"

"While there's much to be gained in construction and establishing fees, the biggest business endeavors that I oversee are the dangerous ones that don't hang a shingle. The Byrd Gang is one of the larger organizations in New Orleans. The New Orleans police gang unit has labeled them one of the most murderous gangs in town."

"And you work with them?" I asked.

"They serve a purpose. We have an understanding. My father began the partnership when the gang originated in a housing development north of the Business District called Magnolia Projects. I've maintained most of my father's contracts. The issues came when your father passed without a successor. For example, in the Ninth Ward, the prominent power is the 39ers Gang. They're a hybrid of sorts. The Upper Ninth Ward's G-Strip and the 3-N-G, a drug clan, joined forces. Your father worked hard to keep their turf from turning into a site of continual mass casualties. He was a significant force in orchestrating their current amalgamation. However, since their allegiance was to Isaiah Boudreau, there was resistance when I took over. We've since come to an agreement, but Kyle has been working to undermine that."

I sat back against the seat. "Why are you telling me all of this?"

"Because your presence with me reinforces my hold. I want you to rule with me. I'm not asking you to barter deals in the Lower Ninth or even be in the presence of dangerous people. Simply an address or a ward number doesn't label the entire population. New Orleans is also comprised of hardworking people who simply want to survive." He gently squeezed my hand. "You, my dear, are not ready for the danger that coexists. However, it's important that you know that organizations such as the 39ers and Byrd gangs are here."

From the architecture, I believed that we'd made a circle and were now back in the French Quarter.

"For you to fully understand how important your presence is, you need to realize the razor's edge that we walk daily to keep this tourism" —he pointed to the filled sidewalks— "as a revenue for our city, as well as the offices full of workers who call the greater New Orleans parishes home. It's a balancing act that I've managed to maintain. In the last year, your brother has been working behind the scenes to undo what I've done."

"And I can help? How?"

"By being you, claiming your lineage and standing with me. You can do more than help; you can solidify our hold on New Orleans."

It was a lot to process. The imagery my husband described was as he'd said, dangerous, gritty, and unnerving.

Gangs and deaths.

Drugs and racketeering.

Legitimate businesses and homeowners.

And yet what I also heard was Rett's desire was to keep all the different worlds balanced. The world that tourists and some residents didn't see as well as the world they did.

Peering out the window, the street looked familiar. "I recognize this place." I pointed to an open gate to a courtyard. "That's where Ross and I went. We're near where you and I met."

Rett nodded. "We are. Tonight, we're dining in the Central Business District across Canal Street at Restaurant August. Along with Broussard's, where we dined" —his dark stare shimmered with lust, twisting my core— "or I dined on an exceptional delicacy, Restaurant August is one of my favorites. I know the owner and was granted a special treat as this is my honeymoon."

I supposed it was mine too.

How long did that last?

Rett and I had spent the last three nights of our marriage apart. I'd accepted his gift of the key and he mine of the blindfold, yet neither had been put to use. It seemed that we had two speeds when it came to intimacy—slow and full-throttle.

They both had their benefits. During the slower times, we talked and shared more. During full-throttle, our attention was focused on the physical.

I appreciated Rett's patience, which I believed exceeded my own when it came to slow. However, this was our honeymoon and I was ready to speed things up again. Before leaving the house, I informed Ian that upon our return, I'd be back in my suite on the second floor. He assured me that when we got back to the house, all my personal items would be back where they belonged.

The SUV came to a stop at the corner of Gravier and Tchoupitoulas Streets.

Rett spoke as I stared out the window. "This is one of the older buildings in the Business District. It's a nineteenth-century French-Creole building. There has been a recent turnover in chefs; nevertheless, they create some of the most unique dishes in New Orleans all focused on Louisiana ingredients."

Ian exited the front seat and opened Rett's door. A

warm evening breeze fluttered my dress as I stepped out onto the sidewalk with my hand in Rett's. Flags flew above the entrance as lights angled up to illuminate the building and streetlights came to life.

My high heels clicked on the sidewalk as we approached the opening doors. The hostess either knew we were coming or recognized Rett. Either way, as she introduced herself to me, Yvonne was lavish with her welcome.

The large dining room we passed was absolutely stunning with large chandeliers, gleaming hardwood floors, stately columns, and mahogany paneling.

My peek was quick as we were whisked upstairs, away from the other diners.

"The chef's private tasting room," Yvonne said as she led us into an equally opulent yet smaller room. "As you asked, Mr. Ramses, we have replaced the normal table with one more intimate." She smiled my direction. "Congratulations on your nuptials, Mrs. Ramses."

"Thank you."

"Thank you, Yvonne," Rett said as we entered the private dining area.

The table they had waiting was not unlike Rett's standard fare, white linen tablecloth, red linen napkins, a silver vase with a single rose, and two glowing candles. Once we were seated, Yvonne relocated an ice bucket on a stand, from the wall to us, revealing a chilled bottle of champagne.

"Compliments of Restaurant August." She smiled. "It isn't every day we learn that New Orleans's most eligible bachelor has married.

Rett reached for my hand across the table as he nodded. "Thank you again. And please convey our thank-you for the privacy."

EMMA

I smiled as I sniffed the aroma of the champagne Rett poured. We were in what I would learn was an unusual state of solitude. Yvonne had left us and our waiters were yet to arrive.

"I'm happy you're amused, Mrs. Ramses."

"I never thought of myself as the one to bag the most eligible bachelor."

"Ah, what Miss Yvonne has yet to realize is that her congratulations were wrongly focused. You see" —he lifted his glass of bubbling wine toward me— "I am the one who should be congratulated."

I lifted my glass. The two met in the middle near the rose and candles with a clink. "Pray tell?"

"Once your identity is fully realized, it will be noted that I'm the one who seized the most eligible bachelorette."

I took a sip of the dry champagne. "Seize is an appropriate word."

"Wooed, courted..."

"Kidnapped, held captive..."

Rett shook his head. "I know you're joking."

Was I joking?

"However, it is worth noting that I have some unpleasant news."

I set my glass on the table. "What?"

"I spoke with a family friend today who happens to be a lead prosecutor, and he wants you to go to the courthouse with NOPD and make a statement regarding Underwood."

The idea made my stomach twist. "When?"

"You had a three o'clock appointment today."

"I what? I was a no-show?"

Rett nodded. "You sent your regrets."

"Wasn't that polite of me."

"Emma, this is serious. I said I wanted to be present, but my attorney cautioned that if I am, it could come back to haunt us. I called him and tomorrow morning he—Boyd Clark—and his associate, Ms. Lynch, will come to the house and discuss what can be said in your statement."

Closing my eyes, I moved my fingers to my temples. "Jeez, Rett, this is like I'm living someone else's life. Shouldn't I just tell the truth?"

"It's very simple. Richard Michelson asked to speak to you regarding Underwood. That's the case they're centered on. What Boyd and Ms. Lynch will talk to you about is staying on topic. This isn't a time for you to offer more than they ask for or for them to go on a fishing expedition regarding you, Kyle, Jezebel, or me."

Before I could answer, the doors opened. Much as it

had been at Broussard's, this room was aflutter with servers. Our first course was delivered along with lengthy explanations of each dish. Royal red shrimp "chop" salad, smoked torchon of foie gras, and cauliflower soup.

Once we made our way through the cold appetizers, our plates were taken away and we were left with charred carrot agnolotti, warm-water lobster spaghetti, and crispy P & J oysters—which I was disappointed but not surprised to learn didn't stand for peanut butter and jelly.

Our champagne was also replaced as glasses of different wines appeared. The waiter guaranteed each was the perfect pairing for that course.

Apparently, Rett hadn't asked for two normal entrees. No, we were presented with small portions of pan-seared red snapper, seared lamb loin, grilled pompano, and roasted duck.

When the waiter returned to ask about dessert, I pleaded defeat.

"I really can't eat another bite or drink another sip."

"I can," Rett replied. And by the gleam in his eyes and twisting in my core, I immediately knew that he wasn't talking about strawberry shortcake or whipped chocolate ganache.

"Mr. Ramses, we would be happy to prepare a plate of all three desserts for the two of you to share."

He lifted his hand. "No, thank you. I must agree with my wife. Dinner was delicious and we're adequately full."

"Coffee?"

Rett looked to me as I sighed. "Maybe at home?"

"Thank you. I believe we're done," Rett said as our waiter nodded and disappeared.

When he reached across the table, I asked a question that had been lingering in the recesses of my mind. "Are we here for us or to broadcast our marriage?"

His Adam's apple bobbed as his lips formed a straight line. "You're very astute. You see, Restaurant August is not only delicious, it's very popular. I had no desire to share you with the diners downstairs, but you're right in that my plan included us being seen together."

I sighed. "Thank you. You were right, I needed to get out of the house, and I'm glad my first excursion wasn't to the police station."

"Then you're not upset that I spoke on your behalf to postpone your statement?"

"I'm not upset, but I would like to be made aware of my options before you decide their outcome."

"I'll admit that I was deterred from talking to you about it."

"Deterred? By whom?" I asked.

"Ian may have conveyed that you were, in his words, nervous and anxious about leaving the mansion."

Lifting my glass of ice water to my lips, I hummed. After my drink, I said, "I can't be mad at him. He's pretty intuitive."

"More so than your husband?" Rett asked.

"A hundred times more."

"That's not true, Emma. I watch and pay attention. I saw the way you scanned this room when we entered.

I know you were thinking about our first dinner and wondering if tonight would end up" —he tilted his chin toward the far wall— "with one of us on our knees."

Warmth crept up my neck, no doubt filling my cheeks with pink.

"Are you going to deny it?" he asked.

I shook my head. "It may sound selfish, but your rendition isn't completely accurate."

He lifted his napkin to the table, pushed back his chair, and came toward me. My breathing caught as he offered me his hand.

"No, Rett, there are people."

He chuckled. "Then, may we go to someplace that is less populated?"

I laid my hand in his. "Home?"

"I like hearing you say that. Could you be more specific about your rendition of your thoughts?"

The warmth returned as I stood. "It wasn't *one of us* on our knees."

Rett's eyebrows lifted.

"It was me."

Memories of exactly that caused my nipples to harden beneath the dress. I reached for my purse and once again, laid my hand in his. As we began walking toward the doors, I said, "There is something else that was supposed to be a secret, but I bet Ian told you."

"Told me what?"

The doors opened as we were ushered toward the stairs. The din of diners, clinks of dishes, and backdrop of music gave me the sense of a movie set. Perhaps it was the antique mirrors and shining light fixtures.

As we descended the stairs, I had the feeling we were back in time, or maybe on the Titanic. As Rett steadied my steps, I worried that analogy had more meaning.

It wasn't until we were back in the SUV with Leon and Ian that Rett whispered his question. "Tell me what secret, Mrs. Ramses."

My gaze went to the rearview mirror, but neither man in the front seat was looking our way. I lowered my voice. "I'm done on the third floor. I want to move back into my suite."

His cheeks rose. "You have forgiven me."

"Maybe."

"Maybe?"

I reached for his hand and continued speaking low. "You weren't right, Rett, but I also agreed to your conditions of this marriage. Work with me, but know I'm ready to do as you said."

He inhaled and his chest inflated. "Yes, I think it's time for you to move back."

"My things are already there."

He leaned closer until our lips met. When we pulled away, his eyes were focused on mine. "I want the world to see you beside me, Emma, because I'm damn proud to have you there. I hope you can say the same."

"New Orleans's most eligible bachelor, it sounds like I'm in an envied position."

"Yes and no."

This time, my eyebrows lifted.

Rett looked at his watch. "With traffic, I would say

that your position in approximately twenty-five minutes would be more enviable."

I shook my head as my mind filled with possibilities.

"And no," he went on, "because there isn't another woman who knows me the way you do. I know I'm not easy."

"No, but you're worth it."

RETT

"*Y*ou're more worried than your wife," Boyd Clark said as he and I stood back against the wall and watched Emma and Boyd's associate Sophie Lynch discuss Ross Underwood.

I kept my voice low. "I understand what's at stake better than she does."

"You need to help her understand, Everett. She can't walk into a deposition unprepared."

"It isn't a deposition. It's a witness statement and preparation is what you and Ms. Lynch are being paid to do." I looked him in the eye. "Paid *very well* to keep me out of legal trouble and now also my wife."

Boyd nodded toward the women. "I thought Mrs. Ramses might work better with Sophie, and it appears I'm right."

Emma and Boyd's associate had been in the front sitting room, talking and going over time lines since nine this morning. It was almost noon. When Emma sent her regrets yesterday, Michelson had rescheduled her appearance at the courthouse for two this afternoon.

This appointment she'd keep.

Boyd was correct in Emma's appearance of calm. Not only was she her absolutely stunning self, she and Ms. Lynch conversed as if they were old friends. I'd told Emma to be honest with our attorneys, and then to only convey to the police and prosecutor what the attorneys deemed appropriate. Most importantly, stay on topic.

"I'll be sitting there with you, Emma," Ms. Lynch said. "If any question seems off subject to me or inappropriate, I'll step in."

My wife nodded as she pointed to some notes they'd made and asked a question.

Leaning against the wall, I fought the urge to keep Emma here in the safety of our home. Hell, I wanted to wrap her in bubble wrap and keep her in protective custody. Yet as much as I sought that, in my gut, I knew my wife was more than capable.

She'd already shown me at every turn that fate had been right. Emma Ramses was meant for me. As my thoughts went back to last night after our dinner at Restaurant August, she turned my way.

Her blue orbs sparkled and her beautiful lips curled into a smile. "Rett, stop worrying."

"I'm not worrying."

"You might want to tell your expression that." She waved me off as she and Ms. Lynch continued working.

Today, my wife was dressed in black slacks and a white blouse. Her long hair was pulled back in a ponytail that hung down her back, her earrings were simple diamond studs, and the heels she wore gave her a few more inches of height.

However, as I looked at her, my mind drifted back to last night's homecoming.

Emma had told me in the car she planned to return to the second floor and by the vise grip I had on her hand as we climbed the concrete steps from the underground garage and then the front staircase, I was holding her to her word.

"I'm not letting you change your mind," I said, standing outside the door to her suite.

Emma's lips brushed mine. "My mind is made up."

The fireplace was lit as we entered, orange flames flickering their warmth and light. Once the door was closed, my patience over the last four days expired. Such as a magnet, I was pulled to her. With my fingers wound in her long golden hair, our lips met.

Unlike the chaste kiss in the hallway, in a matter of seconds we'd both become two people in desperate need for the other. Unapologetically, I took. My kiss bruised her lips as my mouth and tongue ravished everything in their wake. My invasion wasn't met with resistance or a meek acceptance. Hell no, Emma gave as much as I took. Moans filled the room as I backed her toward the wall.

As I removed my suit coat, the scene at Broussard's came back to me, her hands in my grasp and held over her head. Once Emma's shoulders met the wall, I spun her around. The long zipper on the back of her dress had been taunting me since I first saw her up on the third floor. A quick pull and I peeled away the black material, sliding it from her arms, letting it fall to the floor in a black puddle around her high heels. A snap and her bra followed.

With one hand, I gripped her neck. Under my touch, I felt the way she tensed. It should bother me. It didn't. I liked having her on edge, tightly wound, and unsure of my next move. Skirting my touch over her soft skin, I released her and spoke. "Turn around, Emma."

In the fire's light, wearing only her shoes, with her hair freshly mussed, my wife was a fucking goddess. Maybe Leon had been right and sorceress was the correct description. In the back of my mind, I knew I'd pushed her too far the afternoon in the office. My mind reasoned that tonight I should go slow, but my growing desire didn't listen.

A fire burnt within me when it came to Emma, one that exceeded the one ablaze in the fireplace. Beginning as a contained spark, the inferno grew, raging and destroying my resistance and patience. What had been contained was now a powerful, out-of-control forest fire.

Emma's round breasts heaved with shallow breaths as I scanned every inch of what was mine. I stepped closer, my fingers again weaving through her hair as I tugged her head back. A slight whimper filled the room as her neck bent back and her ocean blue eyes stayed fixed on mine.

"You deserve easy after what I did. But being here, seeing you, I don't want to be gentle, Emma. Four fucking days I've waited. I want every minute of my four days with your sexy body."

"Don't be easy, Rett. I'm ready for you, and I want you."

I tugged her hair again. "You don't know what you're saying."

"*I do.*"

Letting go of Emma was the hardest thing I had done, and yet I did. I released her hair and took a step back. I tipped my chin down. "On your knees, beautiful."

Emma complied as she gracefully lowered herself to the floor.

Once she was in place, I asked, "Is this your rendition of the restaurant?"

With her painted lips together and her eyes wide, she nodded.

"Hands behind your back."

I couldn't help but notice the way she fidgeted with her own wanton need as she complied. "Are you wet?"

Her breasts heaved as her answer came between heavy-with-heat breaths. "Yes."

"Spread your knees. Let me see."

One by one, she obeyed. The firelight exposed what she'd just admitted. The evidence of her arousal glistened on her inner thighs. Fuck, I had so many things I wanted to do to her. She was too good for the options running through my dark thoughts.

Emma Ramses was an angel in the hands of a devil.

She deserved better than what I desired of her. She was a queen who deserved the crown and jewels. However, in the dark of night, when we were alone, I needed the whore. I sought to take and dominate. I craved her submission.

How far would I go before she would want to leave?

I crouched down before her and lowered my voice. "One more chance, Emma. Run away. Go back up to the third floor because if you stay I won't apologize for what I do to you or what I want from you."

Her blue gaze stayed fixed on mine and her nipples beaded, growing harder with each phrase I spoke. The tips of her lips curled as she looked at me with more trust than I deserved. "I'm not leaving, Rett. This is where I want to be."

Standing, I unbuckled my belt and worked the button and zipper. In record time, my clothes were lost to the floor somewhere in the shadows with her dress. I fisted my cock as her pink tongue darted to her lips. For a moment, I let her wait as my hand moved faster. The tip of my dick glistened.

"Open."

Emma's lips parted.

She was killing me as she obeyed every command.

Her mouth was heaven, warm and wet. I fisted her hair to keep her close. Emma didn't move away or falter as I fucked her lips, pressing on the tongue, and burying myself until she couldn't take more. As my feet moved apart and balls grew tight, the little noises she made were better than any aphrodisiac.

A pop echoed through the room as I pulled out. Her blue gaze was questioning as my climax hit. My fist pumped my throbbing cock as my come streamed over her lips, down her chin, and across her breasts.

Unfazed, Emma lifted her face as more spewed forth.

"You're mine."

She nodded as she ran her hands over her skin as if she was rubbing in suntan lotion.

"Lick your hands."

Without hesitation, her tongue come forward and did as I said.

Once she was content, I offered her my hand and helped Emma stand.

Though she'd cleaned her hands, the fire's flames glistened in my come on her flesh. As barbaric as it sounded, I loved that she was wearing my mark. That was what Emma did to me, reduced me to a savage with one single focus—acting on my desire.

Taking her toward the fire, I directed her to lean over the sofa and spread her shapely legs.

I'd told Emma that as my wife, her job was to be ready for me, anytime and anyplace. Whether my command was to spread her legs or get on her knees. Four days I'd spent denied and it was time to take what was mine.

As the night progressed, we made up for the time we'd missed. I took her over and over. Unabashed, I brought her to her own climaxes. It was another promise I'd made.

"Be ready, be willing, and you'll be rewarded."

A tangle of arms and legs, we finally fell asleep in her bed, never making it to my suite.

At some point during the night, I woke as her small hand ran up and down my hardening cock. It was the first time I could remember Emma waking me. A grin came to my lips as I realized that not only did my wife willingly take everything I gave, but she was back for more.

I rolled onto my back.

"Ride me."

Slowly, Emma made her way over me. Her expression contorted and her back arched as she, with her knees on either side of me and her hands on my shoulders, impaled herself. With her pussy hugging me tight, I had a fantastic fucking view of her breasts bouncing before me, close enough to lick and bite.

Emma's long hair, now fully untethered, hung around our faces like a curtain as she continued to move. Slowly, she'd lift *and then lower herself. I reached for her hips, allowing her the slow rhythm and concentrating on the way her expression changed.*

Her face was a kaleidoscope of emotions that I could watch for days and never tire.

The suite filled with her noises.

Her pussy quivered as her grip on my shoulders intensified. Panting, she increased her speed and her knees at my side tightened. With my grip of her hips, I helped lift and lower her as her energy waned.

From this angle, watching Emma come apart was better than anything I'd ever seen.

Finally, my wife fell to my chest, her heart pounding against mine.

I cupped her cheeks and brought her satiated gaze to mine. "Fuck, that was amazing."

Emma grinned as she nodded. "I missed you too."

"Four days."

Her eyes opened wide. "Are we caught up?"

"Are you sore yet?"

"Was that your goal?"

"No, it's a beneficial byproduct."

"I am," she admitted. "Sore and satisfied."

"Good. I want you to think of me each time you move tomorrow. Every step. Every turn. Remember, I'm the one who gets to make you feel like that. No one else, ever. You're mine."

"And you're mine." She laid her head on my shoulder as her breathing calmed.

"Mr. Ramses?"

Miss Guidry's voice brought me out of the trance of last night. "Yes."

"Mrs. Bonoit has prepared lunch for the four of you. It is served in the dining room." She added, "Ian said that Ms. Lynch and Mr. Clark would be here for the midday meal."

"Very well." I addressed the room. "Shall we all adjourn to the dining room?"

As we ate, Emma reassured me. "Really, Rett, I'm confident about speaking to Mr. Michelson and the police detective." She grinned at Ms. Lynch. "And Sophie will be there. There's no need for you to keep worrying."

"I'll be at the courthouse, waiting outside the door of your room."

"Everett," Boyd began. "We've discussed—"

"I won't go in to the questioning," I interrupted. "But I've told you what's happening. I have to be sure Emma is safe and no one gets to her."

Her blue eyes came my way. "You said Kyle would stop once we were married."

"He will. Nothing is settled yet." I looked at Boyd. "Except that I'm going."

That was my plan until I received the message of what had just happened in the Lower Ninth Ward.

An hour later, as I stood with Emma in the underground garage, I repeated my plan. "Ian and Noah will be with you." I cupped her cheeks. "Remember me saying that security will become second nature. Don't fight this."

"I'm not fighting. Who will be with you?"

"Leon and others." I exhaled and thought about the message. A shotgun house had exploded. News crews were there. The city was investigating natural gas lines.

None of that was necessary.

The explosion was a message.

The residents within the house were believed to include a woman and two children. The house was the known address for a member of the Tupelo Money Boys. Rumor was that there was a new dispute over drug turf between the Tupelo Money Boys and another gang, the Park Boys.

A few years ago, there'd been another incident between these two gangs.

Dealing with shit like this was what I did. My goal was to curtail the fallout. Brazen acts brought unwanted attention to the crime in New Orleans. That crime made me money. I didn't want it to stop, just exist behind a veil of perceived normalcy.

There wasn't anything normal about an explosion killing a woman and two kids.

"Stay safe, Rett," Emma said. "I'll go and be back before you miss me. Just come home to me."

I kissed the top of Emma's hair. "Nothing will keep me away."

The last thing I said was to Ian. "Protect her with your life."

"Yes, boss."

Since Emma had arrived, I'd watched as a connection formed between her and Ian. It wasn't something I disliked; it was the opposite. The bond they'd fashioned was the reason I could let her go to the courthouse while I went to the Lower Ninth.

My chest clenched as I watched the taillights of the SUV move away down the tunnel. I'd left her over the last six weeks dozens of times. I couldn't recall one time I'd allowed her to leave without me.

Another SUV pulled up to the cement stairs.

Once I was in the back seat, Leon began driving through the tunnel. "Three children, boss. Tupelo Money Boys are after blood."

EMMA

"*C*an you tell us when you met your husband?" Detective Owens asked.

"Detective," Sophie interrupted. "Mrs. Ramses was asked to visit to make a statement regarding Ross Underwood. She has answered every question you and Mr. Michelson have asked regarding the deceased, from their rivalry at University of Pittsburgh, through their partnership with Editorial Inc. If you've exhausted all your questions, we will be going."

Mr. Michelson leaned back against the straight chair, forcing the chair's front legs from the floor. With his arms crossed over his chest, he stared my way. "When did you learn you were the daughter of Jezebel North?"

My gaze snapped to Sophie.

She sighed. "Again, irrelevant."

"Counselor," Michelson said, "We're not in a court of law."

"No, Counselor, we're not. However, this is a sworn

statement that can be used in a court of law. Mrs. Ramses's knowledge regarding anything" —she emphasized the word— "outside of your investigation into Mr. Underwood's death is irrelevant."

Letting the chair drop to all four legs, Mr. Michelson pushed himself away from the basic wood table where we were seated and stood. The room around us was only a little larger than the table; nevertheless, Mr. Michelson paced behind his and the detective's chairs. "This is where we're going to disagree. We have reason to believe that Ms. Jezebel North was involved in luring Mrs. Ramses to New Orleans."

"And that is relevant...how?"

"Were you lured, Mrs. Ramses?"

"New Orleans was a bucket-list destination. When Ross asked me to accompany him in the name of our start-up, I agreed. After all, we were business partners."

His forehead furrowed. "And yet you didn't check on your business partner after the night of your arrival."

"Is that a question?" Sophie asked.

"We have no record of Mrs. Ramses," the detective said, "attempting to contact Mr. Underwood. His phone has been in our custody since the morning he was found."

My stomach twisted with the discussion of finding Ross. During our four years at the University of Pittsburgh, our association was more competitive than friendly. As I'd told Rett, Ross and I were never romantically involved. However, we both recognized that our possibility for success was exponentially increased when we combined our talents. For over nine months we worked on our program. We edited not only our own manuscripts but already-published works. We didn't have our program completely refined, but we were close. We needed financial support. Or that was what Ross said—continually.

I could only imagine the student I knew and the man I'd gotten to know. The descriptions from the detective as well as Mr. Michelson of how Ross was found didn't match how I wanted to remember him.

"Can you tell us again about Mr. Underwood's injury?" the detective asked.

"He hurt his shoulder in a rugby accident at the university."

"The University of Pittsburgh doesn't have a rugby team," the detective countered.

"No, sir. They have a club, the Pitt Rugby Football Club."

"And Mr. Underwood's position was?"

I inhaled. "During his junior year he was a hooker. His senior year, he was moved to scrum."

"Why was he moved?"

I shook my head. "I don't know that."

"But you're aware of the positions he played?" Mr. Michelson asked. "Which did he prefer, forward or back?"

"We never had an in-depth conversation about his preference."

"So he didn't mind being moved to a forward position from hooker to scrum."

My cheeks rose in partial amusement and disgust. "I

know I'm a woman, Detective; however, I happen to know that a hooker is a forward position and a scrum is a back position. It was during Ross's senior year that he was injured. He didn't finish the season. And as I said earlier, his shoulder didn't always bother him, but when it did, it was a distraction. He mentioned bringing his pain medication on our trip. He was concerned that the plane flight would aggravate it."

"A nonstop flight is only two and a half hours."

"But," I said, "as you undoubtedly know, we had a layover in Atlanta. There was a problem with our connection, and we had to find another flight."

"And what was your hurry to get to New Orleans?"

I looked at Sophie who nodded.

"We had a meeting with an investor."

"For your editing program?" Mr. Michelson asked.

"Yes."

"Why would Mr. Everett Ramses invest in a literary-based editing program?"

Sophie answered, "That would be a question for Mr. Ramses. Mrs. Ramses can't speak for her husband as to intent."

"Does he speak for you, Mrs. Ramses?" Michelson asked.

"Not regarding Ross Underwood," I replied. "I have told you all that I know. I didn't contact Ross because I didn't have my phone—and still don't have it. I lost it."

Michelson looked at the detective.

"Did you find it?" I asked.

"No, ma'am," the detective answered. "Cell towers indicated it last pinged off Canal Street at the edge of the French Quarter the night you arrived to New Orleans."

I shrugged. "That would be the last time I saw it."

"And you didn't think to contact your business partner?" Michelson asked.

"I'll admit to being preoccupied."

"With?"

"Not with Ross Underwood," Sophie answered. "And as this questioning is about him, the answer to your question is irrelevant."

Michelson grabbed ahold of the chair where he'd been seated. "What do you know about a woman named Emily Oberyn?"

My eyes opened wide. "What does she have to do with Ross's death?"

"We aren't sure. May I assume, by your response," the detective said, "that you do know Miss Oberyn?"

"I don't know her. I did know her. She dated Ross, back last year before Christmas."

"Can you describe her?" the detective asked.

Sophie spoke up, "I'm sorry. Relevance?"

"Miss Oberyn was spotted with Mr. Underwood after Mr. Underwood left the bar where Mrs. Ramses was last seen."

"Why aren't you questioning her?" Sophie asked.

"We have, Ms. Lynch."

Sophie looked at me and nodded.

My head shook. "I can't say more."

"You can't or you won't?" Michelson asked. "Was there a rivalry? Did you have a problem with the time he spent—?"

"There was no problem. Ross and I weren't like that. It's not that I won't tell you, I can't. Emily dated Ross for a few months. I got to know her a little, casual acquaintances. You know, dinner and drinks now and then. She had red hair and was about my height. She was a real estate broker, or trying to be. She was always about to make that big deal."

"And the last time you saw Ms. Oberyn?" Michelson asked.

"I don't have an exact date. As I said, they broke up before Christmas so sometime last December."

"And the two of you didn't continue any contact? Social media? Text messages?"

"No," I answered. "I had an agreement with Ross. I would be friendly to his girlfriends, but I wasn't any more obligated to continue a relationship than he was. You see, Ross was a lady's man in the sense that he avoided commitment."

"Who broke off their relationship?" Michelson asked.

I tried to recall. "Honestly, I don't remember. Based on track record, I'd say it had been Ross. Or maybe Emily figured out that she wasn't going to change Ross into someone he wasn't and broke it off. I don't think Ross ever explained." I shrugged again. "That was how he was. If he could have installed a revolving door on his apartment, he would have."

"Based on your knowledge of Ross Underwood, would he have been so distraught over seeing Emily Oberyn again that he decided to kill himself?"

"No."

"You don't believe," Michelson asked, "Mr. Underwood would consciously take his own life?"

"Mrs. Ramses," Sophie said, "is no more able to speak to the intent of Mr. Underwood than she is for her husband."

"Based on your friendship, Mrs. Ramses?"

"The Ross I knew," I began, "had one person whom he truly cared about."

"Miss Oberyn?" the detective asked.

"No, sir. Ross cared about Ross. I don't believe he'd hurt the person he cared about."

"What about accidentally?" the detective asked.

"I suppose that's possible," I answered.

"Did you get the financing?" Mr. Michelson asked.

"I believe we're still in negotiations," I replied, suppressing a grin.

"What did Mr. Underwood take for his pain?" the detective asked.

"I don't know exactly. It was a prescription, and he was always conscious of taking it."

"What does that mean?" Mr. Michelson asked.

"It means that when he took it, Ross was conscious about possible interactions."

"What would interact?" the detective asked.

I took a deep breath. "I'm mostly talking about alcohol. When Ross had pain, he avoided alcohol."

"Did Mr. Underwood have a drink the night you were at the bar on Canal Street?"

I nodded. "He did. He had a Hurricane. I think he was on his second."

"So his pain wasn't an issue?" Mr. Michelson asked.

"He didn't mention it."

"Then how did you know about his medicine?"

"Ross and I worked together on our start-up. I knew he had the medicine when needed. On the plane, he mentioned that he might need it. I guess he didn't."

"Are we finished, gentlemen?" Sophie asked. "Mrs. Ramses is a busy woman."

"One more question," Mr. Michelson said. "Why would your husband want Mr. Underwood dead? Did he know you went into Mr. Underwood's hotel room? Was he jealous?"

I sat straight as my eyes opened. "My husband doesn't—"

Sophie stood. "We're done."

"Does he know about you entering Mr. Underwood's hotel room?"

EMMA

My pulse kicked up as I stared at the older man. "It wasn't what you're insinuating."

Sophie spoke. "Mr. Michelson—"

The prosecutor interrupted, asking me, "Does your brother, Kyle O'Brien, know Ross Underwood?"

"You said one more..."

I lifted my hand to Sophie. "Did he?" I corrected. "Yes, Kyle and Ross met multiple times prior to Kyle's death."

"Mrs. Ramses, Kyle O'Brien is very much alive."

"I buried him four years ago. Forgive me if I'm having problems with his resurrection."

The detective and prosecutor exchanged looks before Mr. Michelson spoke again. "Before your brother *died*" —he emphasized the word— "did he and Ross Underwood get along?"

"They didn't *not* get along."

"What about Mr. William Ingalls?" Mr. Michelson asked.

Oh hell no, I wasn't going to discuss Liam.

I turned to my attorney. "I think we're done."

Nodding to the two gentlemen, I worked to compose myself, pushed back my chair, and stood. "I'm very sorry to hear about Ross. As his friend and business partner, I'll mourn his loss. While I don't know what he was thinking, in my heart, I don't believe he would purposely harm himself."

"Ms. Lynch, if you can wait a moment," Mr. Michelson said, "I was recently made aware of Mr. Underwood's wishes." He lifted a manila folder. "Young people today think they're invincible. Someone as young as Ross Underwood doesn't consider death or the separation of his estate. It's my experience that those thoughts aren't entertained until a person has dependents."

"Ross didn't have dependents," I said. "Not that he knew about."

Mr. Michelson nodded. "In most cases, there isn't a last will and testament. It's about filling out the beneficiary line on life insurance and bank accounts."

His gray eyes met mine. "With the current ruling of suicide, most insurance companies and financial institutions, such as the ones Mr. Underwood was affiliated with, refuse to pay death benefits."

"If you're insinuating," I said, "that Ross's parents are only after whatever measly insurance he had, I would argue that they care about their son's memory more than money."

"That's what I found interesting, Mrs. Ramses. You see" —he opened the folder to a page filled with numbers and boxes— "you're correct in that Mr. and Mrs. Underwood are the beneficiaries of Ross Underwood's life insurance policy. It appears they are the ones who took out the policy when he was born. It's only ten thousand."

I shook my head, wondering if the Underwoods needed help. I made a mental note to talk to Rett. After all, it was my husband's choice to not have a prenuptial agreement. That should mean I have some say in where money was allocated.

"That wasn't Mr. Underwood's only asset," Mr. Michelson said.

"He didn't have much. That's why we were looking for investors."

"Mrs. Ramses, Mr. Underwood had a Kraken account."

"Is that supposed to mean something?"

"It's an account for electronic currency. His account received numerous deposits over the last eighteen months."

My pulse kicked up. If I was supposed to look surprised, it wasn't an act. "Again, I don't know what this means."

"It means that Mr. Underwood died a very wealthy man."

I exhaled. "Good, his parents will—"

"Mrs. Ramses, you are listed as the account's sole beneficiary."

"What?"

Sophie reached for my elbow. "As you can tell, Mrs.

Ramses is surprised by this information. She didn't know anything about it."

Michelson's gray gaze narrowed. "Of course not. I'm sure an amount north of roughly three million dollars would have no effect on your statement regarding Mr. Underwood's state of mind."

My rushing pulse rang in my ears as I lifted my hands. "I don't want Ross's money. That doesn't even make sense. He had his parents and a brother. He and I weren't that close."

Mr. Michelson nodded. "Of course you weren't. Again, why were you in his hotel room?"

Sophie reached for my elbow. "We are leaving."

Mr. Michelson feigned a smile. "Thank you for coming in today." He spoke to Sophie. "Should I contact you if we need additional information from your client?'

I wasn't confident in her answer, or anything after that moment.

Did Rett know about the account and that I was the beneficiary?

Why didn't he warn me?

Or didn't he know, and now when he learns, he'll question my earlier answer about my relationship with Ross?

A million questions floated around in my head as we met Ian in the hallway. Together, he and Sophie walked with me to the car.

"Mrs. Ramses, are you all right?" Ian asked.

I nodded. "I want to go home."

He opened the door to the back seat. As I sat, the driver's gaze met me in the rearview mirror. I recognized him as one of Rett's men named Noah. If I knew his last name, at the moment it was escaping me.

"Mrs. Ramses."

"Noah, I doubt there was another option, but I want to get home."

"Yes, ma'am."

Sophie, Mr. Clark, and Ian spoke for a moment outside the car before Ian joined us, sitting in the front passenger seat. Once he did, I closed my eyes and laid my head against the seat.

It had taken us roughly twenty-five minutes to get to the courthouse. I wasn't well enough informed on the comings and goings in New Orleans or its traffic patterns to know if the trip home would be better or worse.

Cars passed in the opposite direction. People walked the sidewalks. My thoughts were back on Ross and that he'd named me as a beneficiary.

Why did he do that?

Laying my head back again, I closed my eyes, shutting out the world I'd been away from for over a month and a half. There were so many people, sounds, and even scents. I imagined I was back in my suite, the second-floor one.

With my eyes still shut, I didn't prepare for the hard jolt preceding a loud crash. My body was thrown forward only to be stopped by the tightening of the seat belt. My eyes popped open. Loud noises rang in my ears as I ducked away from the shattering glass.

Airbags inflated around the interior perimeter of the vehicle as smoke and dust filled the air.

Had we been hit or did we hit something?

"Ian?" I called toward the front seat between coughs.

The door beside me rattled. My first thought was that someone was trying to help.

I reached for the door handle and unlocked it. The hinges creaked as the door was pried open. The eyes staring at me weren't my husband's. Nevertheless, I knew them.

"Liam? What are you...?"

He leaned in and unbuckled the seat belt before pulling me to the street. "You're coming with us."

"I can't." I turned back to the car. I tried to protest through the coughs. "I have to help—"

My knees gave out as a man in a hooded sweatshirt pointed a pistol into the front driver's side window. "No."

Two loud shots reverberated through the air taking away my plea.

Liam held me upright as I wavered. "Oh my God, Ian."

"Get her in the car, now," Liam ordered as a second car came forward.

Another man in a hooded sweatshirt reached for my arm.

"Ian." Tears filled my eyes as I fought the grip. My heels bore down on the pavement. Despite the growing crowd, no one stepped forward. It didn't take long to realize that I was no match for the man pushing me into the back seat of the newly arriving car.

Alarm.

Panic.

Worry.

My body was racked with coughs from inhaling the smoke and powder, and my hands and legs trembled to the point of convulsion. Gasping for breath, I fought to breathe as I unsuccessfully tried to open the door from the inside.

The car was already moving.

"Calm down, Emma. You're going to be all right."

I turned to the voice, a woman's voice.

My chaotic state of mind had blinded me from my surroundings. I hadn't noticed the woman seated only a small distance from me. If I had, I might reason I was peering through a mirror, one with the technology of fast forwarding through time.

As I unsuccessfully fought the terror-induced tears and worked to breathe, I recalled what Rett had mentioned about danger and asked the question to which I already knew the answer, "Jezebel?"

"You can call me Mom."

EMMA

*M*om.

I held tight to my own trembling hands as I twisted back, craning my neck to see what was left of the SUV and of Ian and Noah. My stomach knotted as the scenes outside the windows sped by too quickly. All that I could see of the crash was a plume of smoke rising above a growing crowd. And then we turned and the scene was gone.

My black slacks were covered in the white powder from the air bags.

"Is Ian okay?" I asked.

"He isn't my concern nor yours, Emma." The woman reached over and ignoring the powder all over my slacks, placed her hand on my thigh as she smiled. Rings with large colorful gemstones glistened on each finger.

When I turned, her blue eyes—the same shade as mine—stared back. The shape of her face and even her petite stature were as if I'd been created not by the union of a man and woman but from a copy machine.

My pulse thumped as my mind reeled. Images of the crash infiltrated my thoughts.

"He is my concern," I replied. "He's my...friend."

"He's your bodyguard, Emma. Nothing more. You can get another."

I shook my head as I recalled the last six weeks. "He was both."

"You chose a life with money and power. People are expendable. It's a lesson that is never too early to learn."

I didn't respond, unsure what to say. I knew without a doubt that I didn't believe what she'd said. Ian was my friend. While I didn't know Noah well, Rett approved of both men. They weren't any more expendable than Jezebel or I.

While I'd been trying to come to terms with what was happening, the car we were in had left the city streets.

Beyond the windows, we sped through traffic on the large bridge. The body of water was larger than the Mississippi River. "Where are we going?"

Jezebel tilted her head as she took me in. Her gaze went to my left hand. "I never thought you'd marry him."

I covered my rings with my other hand. "Do you even know him?"

"I don't. I knew his father and mother."

Memories of what Miss Guidry had told me came back. "His mother regrets not knowing you better."

Jezebel shook her head once. "She may now. She didn't then. That's all right. Expendable. I gave up the premise of being a part of that society before you were born."

I looked for my purse, the one I'd carried to the courthouse. It must still be in the SUV. It wasn't like I had a phone or even knew Rett's number to call.

"I wanted to meet you, but maybe this can wait. Where are we going? I want to go home."

"Do you know how long I waited for you to come to New Orleans?"

Jezebel's accent was thicker than Miss Guidry's. The two words of the city's name sounded like one.

"You could have contacted me."

"Before, I did."

"Before what?" The fog from the accident was fading as I concentrated on our conversation. "You did?"

"Before you came here, I did. I visited Pittsburgh."

A cold chill ran over my skin. "I never knew."

"I left you gifts inside your apartment."

The chill continued leaving goose bumps on my arms and legs. "You were in my apartment?"

"I was before that man in the SUV started hanging around."

"Ian was in Pittsburgh?" I recalled something Rett had said about protecting me before I knew it. "What gifts?"

"There was a *gris-gris* containing a necklace. I put it in your jewelry box." She reached into her purse and removed a small cloth pouch. She opened the flap and pulled out a silver chain. The pendant was a piece of jade. "I had it retrieved."

"From my apartment? When?" I reached out and took the necklace. "I don't remember seeing this."

"It was hidden beneath the false base in your jewelry box." She also handed me the cloth pouch. "It's important for you to have it. The pouch is gris-gris, a talisman. The pouch itself is believed to protect its owner from evil and bring luck." She nodded toward the necklace. "Jade is the jewel from heaven. It's a symbol of nobility and wealth. This necklace belonged to your grandmother."

Placing the pouch on my lap, I held the pendant in my hand. "My grandmother? Your mother?"

Jezebel smiled. "No, Emma, your paternal grandmother."

"She gave it to you?"

"Not exactly. Nevertheless, it is yours. It was all right to have it hidden. Much like the gris-gris, the person in possession of the necklace receives its powers, even if that person is unaware of it. Now, Emma, it's past time for you to be aware."

I wrapped my fingers around the necklace. The surroundings beyond the car's windows were changing, becoming more rural. Tall trees framed the road with moss draped from branch to branch. The foliage had grown so thick as to mute the sunshine from earlier. "Are you really my mother?"

"You know I am."

"But what about Kyle? From what I've heard, you were only pregnant once. He's claiming he is the child you bore and that his father was Isaiah Boudreau. Are you saying he isn't your child, and that I am?"

"No, that's not what I'm saying. I understand this is going to come as a shock. I promise that I've done all I could do to protect you and Kyle. He goes by Isaiah now. That was his decision, not mine."

"You were pregnant twice? Both times you gave birth to Isaiah Boudreau's child?"

"No. I had one pregnancy. It was difficult. I won't lie to you. I nearly died."

The car was moving slower along a less traveled lane.

She went on, "That was what he wanted, for me to die, my children too. I was a reminder he didn't want. He was wrong. You see...even evil intentions can produce good."

I had the memory of Rett telling me that I was good, that evil doesn't always produce evil; it can produce good. My stomach twisted as I spoke. "He raped you." I didn't ask the question. I knew the answer.

Jezebel smiled as she lifted her chin. "Good for you."

"I don't understand."

"No, you do. You understand because you're a woman. It took your brother a long time to come to the realization that the two of you were not conceived in some make-believe rendition of a fairy tale. The Brothers Grimm understood what fairy tales were, not what Disney has transformed them to be. The tales they wrote were dark and unnerving because that's what life is. As women, Emma, we must know that truth deep in our souls. The charms I left you were to protect you because I wasn't there; the O'Briens were gone. I couldn't leave you alone, so I offered you to the spirits to protect as I had done since before you were born."

I wasn't noticing the increased darkness or the dense foliage beyond the car's windows. My attention was focused on the woman speaking.

"Women like your husband's mother, they chose to ignore or maybe they refused to see the darkness. Either way, those women aren't better for it. They spend their lives with blinders on that limit their opportunities." Her smile grew as her blue eyes opened wide and she stared into my gaze. "I should have known it would be my daughter who would fulfill the prophecy."

I was still trying to comprehend what Jezebel was saying about being conceived; the spirits' protection, fairy tales, and dark realities were beyond my current understanding. "I'm your daughter."

Jezebel nodded.

"Kyle isn't your child."

"The two of you shared my womb."

She was saying we were twins.

The car bounced as the tires left pavement and drove over uneven packed earth.

"No," I said in response, shaking my head. "Kyle's older. Eight months. Our mother never explained it. Once I learned I was adopted, I assumed he was the biological child of the O'Briens."

Jezebel sighed and waved her beringed fingers. "I'll share more. We're almost home, and I need to rest."

The trees opened enough for sunlight to enter. An old large plantation-style home came into view. I held my breath as I took it in. The architecture reminded me of the Old South as if it would be depicted in a movie. Trees filled the landscape, momentarily blocking the view. As we got closer, I felt the chill from earlier as a sense of foreboding settled into my bones.

"You see," Jezebel said, "I rarely go out among so many souls. It's so loud hearing their pleas. However, I'd come to the conclusion that if I wanted something done right, I needed to be present myself." As the car came to a stop, her eyes closed and opened, and she took a deep breath. "This is right, Emma. It's what the spirits wanted all along. It has taken twenty-six years and four months, but now, I feel the relief that has been missing from my soul." She waited until the driver came around and opened her door.

He hadn't said a word, and his silence continued as he offered his hand for her to step out.

Jezebel's fingers curled, gesturing for me to follow.

I pushed the gift she'd given me into the pocket of my slacks.

As Jezebel stood upon the ground, golden bracelets that must have been up in her sleeve in the car jingled from her wrists. Her colorful long dress unfurled in the humid air and combs with colored jewels glistened in her long gold hair. Her appearance reminded me of a priestess in the French Quarter.

Once we were both standing on the packed-dirt driveway, Jezebel reached for my hand.

Before she could speak, my focus went to where our hands were connected. Her multiple rings glistened. That wasn't what had my attention. It was that despite the oppressive heat around us, Jezebel's hand was ice cold.

When I tried to pull away, her grip tightened. "This is where you belong," she said.

"I don't..."

Jezebel shook her head. "Close your eyes, Emma."

It took me a second to comply.

Before I did, as insects buzzed, I scanned the area around us.

For as far as I could see, there were tall trees with low-hanging branches and veils of moss. Dark shadows lurked in the distance beneath the canopy of foliage. The hard-packed ground we stood on was an island of sorts, surrounded by pools of water and mud.

I knew enough about this ecosystem to be cognizant of the dangers that could lurk under the murky water as well as in the air. Mosquitoes and horseflies multiplied exponentially as their larvae matured in the stagnant water. There was a circle of life —the fish and frogs ate the insects while larger reptiles ate the fish and frogs. The area wasn't without animals —mammals.

In a place like this, the mammals, even those with the advantage of opposable thumbs, weren't always the highest on the food chain.

I looked up through the trees.

With the lush foliage, I wasn't even sure if the large house was visible from the sky. In that second, I realized my only hope of leaving—of escaping—was to convince Jezebel North that I would listen and cooperate.

Running away as I'd done from Rett's wasn't an option.

Exhaling, with my hand still in Jezebel's, I did as she asked and closed my eyes.

"Listen," she said, "and they will talk to you. You are a child of the spirits. They protected you and me as you grew within me. They strengthened both of you when I wasn't able. Let them speak."

Opening my eyes, I pulled my hand away. "Jezebel—"

"I very much appreciate the hard work of Marcella O'Brien," she said, interrupting. "She accepted the task of raising you and Kyle. She agreed to my stipulations and conceded to accept what the spirits had decreed, knowing by doing so she was saving your lives." Jezebel's chin rose as she looked from me to the house and back. "However, I've waited nearly twenty-six and a half years to hear you call me Mother."

I concluded that she meant from the time she knew she was pregnant, as I'd only recently had my twenty-sixth birthday before coming to New Orleans.

She continued, "I must insist that you use some form of that word." Her volume lowered. "After all, Jezebel isn't my name, not the one my mother used."

I sucked in a deep breath and forced the moniker from my lips. "Mother, I'm married. I married Everett Ramses, and I need to contact him. He'll be worried." I pushed away my concerns of Ian and Noah.

The sound of a slamming screen door brought our attention to the house.

A woman appeared on the front porch, small in

stature with skin that was as dark as Leon's if not darker. The gray in her hair and the wrinkles in her face were reliable indicators of her age. Her eyes shone brightly, like beacons in the shade of the trees near the house. The woman smiled as she fanned herself with an old-fashioned wooden collapsible fan. "Lawd, praise be, Miss Betsy. She's here. You did it. Our girl is home."

EMMA

M iss Betsy?

"Edmée," Jezebel said as she reached for my arm. "Please show Emma to where she'll be staying. I'm afraid I've overdone."

Edmée hurried down the stairs and over the packed dirt. She reached for Jezebel, wrapping her arm around Jezebel's waist. Her dark orbs turned to me. "Help me, girl."

I did the same, supporting Jezebel as we helped her up the stairs.

"Over there," Jezebel said, nodding toward a row of rocking chairs.

"No, miss," Edmée said, "You best lay down. The spirits have been too hard on you."

"The chair is fine."

Once Jezebel was seated, the sound of heavy footsteps from inside the house caused me to turn toward the screen door. Before I could see through the mesh, the door creaked and slammed against the house as Kyle burst onto the porch. In that instant, he was the brother I remembered, wearing blue jeans, Chuck Taylors, and a tight-fitting dry-fit short-sleeved shirt. His skin was tanner than I recalled and his blond hair was longer, mussed, and slightly curled.

While Kyle looked at me, he didn't verbally acknowledge my presence; instead, he hurried to Jezebel. Holding the arm of the chair and crouching down in front of her, he asked, "Are you all right, Mom? Can I get you something?"

Turning at the sound of tires on loose dirt, I watched as the car we'd arrived in disappeared to somewhere behind the house. Holding the porch post, I stared out again to the land beyond this island of sorts that held the house, pondering if there was a route to escape. While I couldn't recall driving over a bridge, from where I stood, it was the only possibility.

Gripping the post tighter, I knew I was again captive.

There might as well have been shutters covering windows.

The difference between where I was now and one of Rett's suites was size.

Instead of being trapped in a nine-hundred-square-foot suite of rooms with a guard outside my door, I was captive in the middle of an untamed wilderness, my escape guarded not by a man but by insects and alligators.

The sweltering heat added to the uneasy feeling the landscape instilled. Large trees reached up to the sky, their roots—some visible—disappeared into the muck.

High above, the leaves created a green ceiling successfully obscuring this settlement from the sky. At the waterline, the roots created cages and mazes where insects, reptiles, and animals could live, hide, and eat.

I turned to my left as bubbles surfaced in nearby wetland. As the others on the porch tended to Jezebel, I waited and watched. The bubbles grew larger and then stopped. Nothing surfaced and the water was too dark and dirty to see the source.

The realization came slowly.

We were in the interior of the bayou that Rett had mentioned.

I turned my attention back to Kyle and Edmée. They seemed to work in unison to placate Jezebel. Leaning back in the rocking chair, Jezebel fanned herself with Edmée's fan. Her hand trembled and I noticed how her complexion had paled since I first saw her within the car.

"May I get her something to drink?" I asked, trying to help.

Three sets of eyes came my direction.

Jezebel was speaking, but from my distance, I couldn't make out what she was saying.

Kyle nodded and stood.

Somehow, as he approached, my assessment of moments earlier shifted. Kyle had changed, grown, and matured. He seemed more muscular and taller than I remembered. I hadn't noticed those features while in the grandeur of Rett's home, but here on this porch, he was different.

Did men continue to grow after the age of twenty-three?

Even Kyle's voice seemed deeper, more in command. "Come with me, Em."

I shook my head and held on to the porch post. "Kyle, I need to call my husband."

Kyle tilted his head to the inside as he opened the screen door.

"What about Ian and Noah?" I asked.

His expression hardened as he moved his head from side to side.

I'd seen this expression years before when he wanted his way. When we were ten and eleven it meant he didn't want to hear my thoughts. Sixteen years later, I believed the meaning was the same.

With a deep breath and one last look at the bayou, I let go of the post and followed, careful of my heels not catching between the slats of wood on the porch floor.

Once we entered the house, the floor improved. The temperature seemed to rise not lower.

Perspiration beaded on my forehead and dripped down my back and between my breasts with each step. With the uncomfortable heat, I barely noticed my surroundings. Yet what I saw was unquestionably beautiful—polished hardwood floors, crystal lighting fixtures, and expensive furnishings. It reminded me of Rett's home on a slightly less ostentatious scale.

Kyle continued to move deeper into the house, not saying a word.

Scanning my surroundings for a plan as we walked, I peered right and left. Within this hallway, we passed a wooden staircase with ornate banister posts, that led upstairs. There were also multiple doors and archways.

From what I could see, the rooms were filled with natural light, the windows all opened. And yet the draperies hung motionless as no breeze infiltrated the stagnant air.

By the time we made it to the kitchen in the back of the house, my white blouse was sticking to my skin. I lifted my ponytail from my neck, wishing I had a clip or some way to keep it off of me.

The sound of our footsteps announced our arrival.

A couple—a man and a woman—turned our way. It appeared they'd been doing something with vegetables along a far countertop. When they saw us, or maybe when they saw Kyle, they both nodded, stopped what they were doing, and departed through the rear screen door.

Kyle walked around the counters and cupboards to a small hallway on the right. I followed a few steps behind. He stopped at a big wood door and pushed back a dead bolt, not unlike the one I'd had installed in the third-floor suite. Turning the knob, he opened the door.

"The heat takes some time to get used to," he said. "You'll be more comfortable down there. It isn't really a basement, not like what we had in North Carolina. Edmée calls it a cellar."

My neck straightened. "What? You expect me to go down in there?"

"It's what Mother wants."

"Oh hell no."

"It's not that bad, Em." His deep, authoritative tone mellowed, sounding more like the brother in my memories. "We've all done our time. Now it's your turn."

My head shook. He'd been right about the heat. It was suffocating. "I don't care what you did, Kyle." I looked around the kitchen, pulling at the collar of my blouse. "Is there water?"

"In the faucet."

"I was thinking bottled."

"The water is like the cellar," he said. "It takes time, but your body gets used to it. Now I have a suite upstairs." He grinned. "Look at you; you're sweating like crazy. You'd never be able to sleep up there."

I didn't care about his suite. My thirst was growing by the second. "You drink the water?"

"You will too. Once the fever passes, you'll be better than new. Mother knows what's best."

As I tried to generate saliva, I had the sensation of a bad movie, *Children of the Corn* or something. Finally, I spoke, "I'm worried about Ian and Noah. Do you know what happened to them?"

"I wasn't there. You'll have to ask Liam when he returns."

"Returns?" I asked, looking around and seeing a refrigerator. "If there's electric, why isn't there air conditioning?"

"Mother doesn't like it too cold."

I recalled Kyle's comment about Liam. "You said return. Liam doesn't live here too, does he?"

Kyle nodded. "For now. It's safest. Greyson was here too" —he paused as a dark shadow covered his expression— "before your husband had him killed."

According to Rett, Greyson was trying to kill me. Instead of going down that rabbit hole, I said, "What about the refrigerator? Is there something to drink in there?"

Kyle went to a cupboard and reached for a glass. With a huff, he lifted the faucet and filled it with a cloudy liquid."

He turned, handing it my way.

"I'm not drinking that."

He smiled and set it on the countertop. "You will."

I spun around the kitchen that was both old-fashioned and modernized. There were no hard-surface counters or spectacular lighting fixtures. The counters were metal and the lights plain. Yet everything that was mandatory seemed present. "Where are we?" I turned to Kyle. "Tell me what's happening."

"Are you asking about the details on the monster you married?"

Closing my eyes, I imagined the man I married. When I did, I didn't see a monster or a devil. I saw a man who I desperately wanted to contact, not because he'd be upset or worried, but because I didn't want to be the cause of his distress. I'd tell him I was safe. This place was weird and a bit creepy, yet for some reason, I didn't feel that I was in danger.

I'd admit that my new biggest worry was for him.

It was more than worry.

I cared.

No matter how hard I'd tried to protect my heart, as I stood in what could rightfully be described as hell's kitchen, my concern wasn't for me but for him. I told

Rett he couldn't have my heart, but now with the passing of time, I could admit, if only to myself, that when it came to Everett Ramses, I cared—deeply.

"No," I replied, "I'm not asking you about Rett. I want to know what the hell is happening here, where we are, and when I will be able to contact Rett."

"I would tell you, but Mother wants to explain." Kyle tilted his head toward the cellar. "You should rest. Our mother keeps odd hours. When she calls, you need to come."

"How is she *our* mother?" I stared up at the person I'd always considered my brother. For a while, I wondered if it was biological. Now, I'm confused by what Jezebel said. "What she said doesn't make sense."

"I'm not supposed to say." Kyle flashed me his six-hundred-watt grin, the one that let him get away with too much when he was in high school. "But like when we were kids, Em. I can't tell you, but if you guessed..." He shrugged.

"We can't be siblings. Jezebel only had one child."

"That's what she wanted our father to think."

"She said we shared a womb." The answer hit me—another movie plot. "Shit, am I Princess Leia?"

Kyle nodded. "Yeah, you got it. That makes me Luke."

I recalled the conversation in the car. "Jezebel said—"

"Don't call her that. She's our mother. She deserves the title."

"Why? She gave birth. She didn't raise us."

His expression darkened. "Stop, Emma. Don't let the spirits hear you talk like that."

God, he sounded like Miss Guidry.

I shook my head and peered around the kitchen. Nothing made sense.

I decided to focus on the one question and avoid the usage of proper nouns. "*She* said we shared her womb. But we can't be twins, Kyle. We have different birthdates. I don't mean one day and the next. You're eight months older than me."

Kyle shook his head. "Let her tell you. She's waited a long time to tell us both what happened and is happening. It's been planned out...fuck...for longer than we've been alive." He was back to holding the edge of the door.

"Kyle, I'm not going in that cellar." I looked pleadingly at him. "You remember how I am about locks."

"Fuck, the smoke."

"It was fire, Kyle, not just smoke. I was trapped."

"The fire was outside. You only thought you were trapped."

A group of us kids had been playing a game—truth or dare type. Greyson and Kyle dared me and my friend to go into the hall closet and see how long we could stay. At first it was easy, until we realized the door was locked. Even so, neither of us panicked until the smoke. Our first thought was that the house was going to burn down with us trapped in a closet.

Ironically, it was Liam who opened the door.

Even today, thinking about the chain of events made my skin crawl.

I wasn't going to debate this incident with him again fifteen years after it occurred. "I won't go down into that cellar if the door is going to be locked." When Kyle didn't reply, I added, "Mom and Dad understood."

His lips formed a straight line. "The O'Briens always gave into you, Em. It's time to grow up."

"Grow up? I'm not the one living with my mother."

Kyle's jaw clenched and his nostrils flared as he took a deep breath. "Go down in the cellar. It's furnished and not bad." When I didn't move, he added, "If you want, I'll go down with you. But you have to stay, and I'll tell everyone the door can't be locked."

My eyes closed as a tear slipped down my cheek. I wasn't sad. Frustrated combined with a lingering uneasiness would be a better description of the cause. "I need to call Rett."

"Even if I handed you a phone, there's no reception, not with regular phones. There's something about the ground out here, it defies reason."

"Is there internet?"

"Do you know his phone number?" Kyle asked, his tone turning mocking.

"No, but..."

"His email?"

My heart was pounding faster. "You do, don't you?"

"And you're married to the man, sis. He doesn't love you. You're his captive. Face the facts. Mother has plans, and Everett Ramses knows his time is about to end. You were nothing more to him than a means to an end. Well, I have news; it's not going to end well for him."

I felt the twist in my chest. Rett and I had agreed to leave love off the table, but I cared. Damn it, I cared.

Part of me feared that it was an epiphany I'd made too late.

I pushed that thought away.

"Kyle, Rett's been honest with me. I know what I am to him and what he is to me. He's my husband. Please, Kyle."

Kyle lifted his chin. "My name's now Isaiah, use it. There's a toilet and sink down there. Go. Unless you want to drink the water."

Avoiding the doorway seemed impossible. "You said you'd take me down?"

"Fine, follow me."

Before we could venture through the door and down the steps, voices came from the front of the house, loud voices. My breath caught at the loudest one. It was a man's voice, and he was saying something about Eugene from the Park Boys.

"What is a park boy?"

"Wait here," Kyle said as he walked past me toward the front of the house.

EMMA

As Kyle walked away, my mind went back to my brief lesson on New Orleans. I couldn't recall Rett mentioning a park boy. Did it mean someone who was at a park?

Low voices turned my attention away from the front of the house to the back, through the kitchen windows. The two people who had been in here when we entered were now out on a back porch. For a moment, I wavered between asking them for help and following Kyle to learn what had happened and maybe learn about Ian. If I were becoming truthful with myself, I cared about him too.

Getting home was my first desire.

Standing taller, I looked one way and the other.

I made my decision.

After all, when would I have another opportunity to speak to anyone?

With a quick look over my shoulder, I confirmed that Kyle was now on the front porch with Liam. Their conversation had quieted so that I was unable to hear individual words. From their body language, I would gather they were somewhere between sharing information and a celebratory atmosphere.

Not exactly my current state of mind.

"I'm in a *Twilight Zone* episode," I murmured as I tried to think straight.

The back door creaked as I pushed it open. For only a moment, I lifted my chin, enjoying the fresh yet still air. "Excuse me?"

The man and woman both turned my direction.

They were both slight in stature. Their skin was leathery as if they spent a lot of time working in the sun. She had on a dress and he was wearing overalls. If I didn't know better, I'd think I'd been brought to a bad movie set with stereotypical costumes. However, this was real life and there was no director to call cut.

When the two moved, I saw piles of red beans and a large pot. Their fingers were dyed by the red, almost looking like blood. I moved my gaze to their faces.

"Hello." I waited, but neither one spoke. "My name is Emma."

They nodded.

Okay, well, they understood me.

"Can you help me? I need to make a phone call."

I didn't know Rett's number, but I had come up with a plan. The only number I could recall was Ross's and during the questioning, the NOPD said they were in possession of his phone. I could call it; they could call Rett. It might be farfetched, but my choices were limited.

The woman looked to the man. I thought for a moment I had a chance, but the man shook his head and spoke, not to me but to the woman. His voice was deep. The language he spoke was unfamiliar, yet I recognized the tone and speed of his speech.

In the last month and a half, I'd had a crash course in the meaning of different tones. I'd learned enough to recognize that there was something in this man's tenor that indicated he wasn't pleased.

I waited.

The woman's reaction confirmed my suspicion. Without turning to me, she went back to the beans. His pale eyes came to me and he shook his head.

This conversation was over.

I peered out from the back of the house determined to find another way to get home. The landscape wasn't significantly different than from the front other than the presence of two other buildings surrounded by tall trees. Their structure was less grand than this house. The wood siding was weathered, and the wood shingled roofs were covered in moss. I reasoned that at least one of the structures was a garage. After all, the car had come this way.

Maybe if I could get into the buildings...

"Emma."

Through the screen, I heard and saw Kyle returning to the kitchen. I had the sensation of getting caught doing something that I shouldn't. A quick look at the couple and the way the woman's hands now shook let me know that if I didn't do something, I could be a cause for their trouble. Biting my lip, I reached for the door handle.

"Are you going to tell me where we are?" I asked.

"This is our mother's home."

I spoke quieter and asked, "What language do they speak?"

"Most call it Creole. It's heavy on French with a lot of made-up words. They don't think they're made up, but it takes time to understand. Honestly, there are so many dialects that in all these years, I'm still floundering."

"Language never was your forte."

"Well, your writing isn't what we need either." He tilted his head toward the front of the house. "Mother is going to rest. She said she won't be able to unless she knows you're being taken care of."

"A cellar isn't taking care of me. Let me call Rett." My attention went to the glass of water waiting upon the countertop. My thirst had subsided, but seeing the milky liquid caused it to return.

"Again, Em, if I handed you a fucking phone, you couldn't make the call."

I looked to him as his gaze went to my left hand, my wedding rings, and back to my face.

"How is that marriage thing working for you?"

Any patience I'd tried to summon up was wearing thin. "Shut up."

"We're not kids anymore. You can't talk to me like that."

"I want answers."

"When Mother is ready."

I sucked in a breath, ready with a retort, as Liam came around the corner, stopping at the doorway.

In my conversation with Kyle, I hadn't heeded the second or two warning when I'd heard footsteps on the hardwood. I was admittedly unprepared as Liam and I came eye to eye.

Instinctively, I scanned the man I'd loved a long time ago, from his dark hair to the toes of his shoes. I hadn't noticed when he appeared outside the car earlier today, but he was dressed in a suit, not unlike the ones Rett wore. His shoes were leather loafers, not tennis shoes like Kyle's. Despite the heat, much like Kyle, he appeared unaffected.

Liam's chest filled with air, testing the buttons on his suit coat as he stared my direction.

Gripping the countertop, I stood straighter, not looking away.

Besides the few minutes in Rett's foyer, the last time I'd seen Liam he was driving away from my apartment in Pittsburgh. The memorial service was history, and he'd made it clear that so were we.

This moment might be easier if I could look back on that particular time in my life with pride—if I could say I kept my chin high and didn't reduce myself to a heartsick ex-girlfriend. While I eventually came to that outcome, first I'd mourned—my family and the loss of my hopes and dreams for Liam's and my relationship.

I'd missed classes and sat up nights crying. I'd left messages on his cell phone and personal messages on social media. They'd been pathetic, sad messages—and every one of them went unreturned. I even did what I said I'd never do and stalked him via social media.

Finally, I stopped.

At that point, I cut off everyone from my childhood and hometown.

I took the path I should have taken when Liam said goodbye.

In my defense, at twenty-two years of age and after the loss of my family, I wanted someone to lean on. I believed that William Ingalls would fill the huge void my family had left. I had faith that our forever wouldn't end. I'd been wrong.

As Liam's green eyes met mine in this strange kitchen in the middle of a Louisiana bayou, I had an awakening. It was more than an epiphany. If this were a novel, I had the epilogue.

First was my awareness that today I was a stronger woman and a stronger person than I would have been if my relationship with him had continued. It wasn't that Liam deserved credit for my growth. I deserved that credit.

He deserved nothing.

The other realization was that he knew. When he walked away from me, left me alone in Pittsburgh mourning... he knew Kyle was still alive. He left me alone, and he knew.

That jolt gave me the strength to look him square in the eye. "You motherfucker."

The green in his eyes glistened as his smile grew.

I waved my hand. "No, you don't deserve the time or energy that it would take to say what I want to say." I took a breath. "But I want to know something. You were there. Today"— I clarified— "at the accident. Tell me about Ian and Noah."

Liam's smile grew wider as small lines formed near his eyes. There was a coldness I never saw before. It was enough to bring a chill even in this heat.

"Oh, you're talking about your drivers? Or were they your bodyguards?"

"They're people I care about."

His smile transformed to a straight line. "I suggest you find new people to care about." He walked to the refrigerator and pulled out a beer. After twisting off the lid, he handed it to Kyle.

I wasn't a beer drinker, but compared to the water, seeing the condensation form on the glass bottle was mouthwatering.

Liam retrieved another, twisted the lid, and took a sip before adding, "I know who you could care about. How about my brother? Oh no. That's right. Your fucking *husband* killed him. Hey, but if you're desperate, there's always me, Em." He winked. "We were good together."

"Fuck you, Liam."

Kyle laughed.

Liam and I both turned toward Kyle.

He spoke to Liam. "I told you to leave my sister alone." Taking a sip of beer, Kyle leaned against the counter and crossed his arms over his chest. "Maybe I was wrong. She's feisty around you. I'll get the popcorn and watch how this turns out."

"It's not turning out," I said. "I'm married."

Liam's expression turned to disgust. "In name only."

It was my turn to laugh. "Is that what you think? Do you think that there's no man who can come after William Ingalls?" I didn't let him answer. "Compared to Rett, you're a kid."

Liam leaned my direction, lowering his voice. "But he did *come* after me."

My pulse raced as I bit my tongue.

"I suppose if he wants leftovers."

Straightening my neck, I lifted my chin. I wasn't going to let Liam degrade me for moving on. My thought was petty—but true. I shouldn't say it, yet I couldn't stop myself. "Honestly, compared to Rett, I'm not even sure I'd know you were there."

"Fucking—"

I smiled at his reaction.

Before Liam could reach me, Kyle stepped forward, standing between us. "I was wrong," Kyle said. "This is boring. Liam, you heard Mother. Get her the information she wants." He turned to me. "Go downstairs."

I spoke to Kyle. "I don't know why you think you're the commander and chief around here."

"Because I am, Em. Learn to listen."

I stood taller. "Whatever you think your plans are for me, you're wrong. I'm not staying here. Rett will find me."

Liam straightened his lips. "Oh, so you cared about him, like your bodyguard?" He shook his head. "That list of yours is getting shorter by the minute."

My circulation stilled as blood rushed to my feet.

My body was overtaken by a sense of queasiness his words instilled. "What do you mean?"

"I mean your husband—your *late* husband..."

Liam continued talking, yet the word late had my head in a spin.

Slowly, Liam's voice emerged through the fog. "...Lower Ninth early this afternoon. You see, there have been some problems between two rival gangs." Liam shrugged. "Crossfire is a bitch." He shook his head. "I don't think he'll be coming to get you. But the good news is we couldn't any record of a prenup. That doesn't mean there isn't one with Ramses's attorneys, but damn, Emma. Between Underwood's money and Ramses's, you will make your momma real proud with the finances you can bring to this organization."

Organization?

I refused to consider that what Liam said about Rett was true.

"What organization and how do you know about Ross's money?"

"Later," Kyle said.

Frustration and lack of control caused my voice to rise. "I don't want Rett's money or Ross's. I want to leave here and never come back."

"Rest."

We all turned as Jezebel appeared in the doorway. Her complexion appeared healthier than it had earlier on the porch. There was something about her—maybe the way the combs now looked like a crown or the presence she radiated. It was a majestic look that held my attention yet was hard to describe.

"Listen to you three," she said. "I told the spirits I had adults ready to take their rightful places. You sound like children." She turned to Liam and her cadence slowed. "William, the past is over. Emma is my daughter and will receive the respect she deserves. I can't speak for the O'Briens, but I've known you and Greyson for the last four years. You've both been like sons to me." Her expression hardened. "But don't let that fool you. Isaiah and Emma are my blood. Don't overstep, William. The spirits won't approve."

It was as if her speech sucked the air out of the room.

That was a figure of speech.

In reality, it was as if the heavy humid air grew thicker. The tendons in Liam's neck protruded as his jaw clenched.

Finally, he turned to me. "It's good to see you again, Emma. I'm at your service."

I wanted to tell him to go to hell or fuck off—there were multiple phrases echoing in my head. Instead, I nodded. It wasn't until I saw Jezebel looking at me that I added, "Thank you."

Jezebel grasped my hand and turned it over. While her touch was cool, it was no longer freezing.

Reaching into her pocket, she pulled out two small blue tablets and dropped them in my palm. "These will help you rest, my dear. The spirits reminded me that this is new to you. There is much for you to process. Take the tablets, rest, and things will become clearer."

My blue eyes met hers. "Rett isn't dead. If he were, I'd know." My mind briefly went back to the underground parking garage the first night I was there. I'd barely gotten to know him, yet when his car drove away, I felt the loss. I looked at her gaze. "I can't explain it, but I would know."

She nodded toward the tablets. "Take those and go to sleep. I'll wake you after I rest." She turned to Kyle and Liam. "Get Emma some water."

My pulse sped up as Kyle stepped to the counter and retrieved the glass from earlier. His smile mimicked Liam's, cold and calculating. Taking a step toward me, he handed me the glass. "Drink up, sis."

EMMA

$\mathscr{A}$s I reached for the water Kyle offered with the tablets in my other hand, the milky liquid quivered within the confines of the glass. I stared down, recalling Kyle's words—*after the fever*...

I spoke to Jezebel. "I'd rather have a beer."

"You don't drink beer," Kyle replied.

"And you're dead. Time changes things. I want a beer."

Jezebel shook her head. "Give her a beer."

Once the glass was taken and a cool bottle was in my hand, I nodded toward the cellar. The one place I didn't want to go was now my escape—at least temporarily. I took a step, but Jezebel stopped me.

"Emma, you need to rest. Take the tablets."

With my hands trembling and three sets of eyes upon me, I lifted my hand with the tablets to my open lips and followed them with a sip of the beer. Swallowing, I turned back to the stairs. Before I made it through the doorway, Kyle reached for my hand and pried open my fingers. His blue eyes met mine. I saw his determination, wanting to catch me in deception.

Once my fingers were straight, all that was left was a smudge of blue on my palm left by the tablets from when they'd been captured in my overly warm hand.

I gave him my best fuck-you smile.

"Rest," Jezebel said.

Nodding, I left the beer on the nearby counter, hurried through the doorway, and rushed down the wooden stairs. My high heels luckily didn't falter. I barely noticed my surroundings as I ran for a partially open door and pushed it open. Turning on a light and closing the door, I spit the contents of my mouth into the toilet. Quickly, I ran the faucet. More of the milky water spewed into the sink. Ignoring the color and odor, I cupped some fluid in my hands and brought it to my lips.

Resisting the urge to gag, I sucked up the liquid, rinsed and spat again.

I repeated the procedure a few more times until I was sure there were no remnants of the tablets left in my mouth. When I looked up, my reflection staring back at me appeared weary, but unlike Jezebel, my complexion was the opposite of pale. My long hair had taken on the curl of the humidity. While most was still secured back into the ponytail, I had small frizzy spirals surrounding my face.

Removing my hair tie, I lowered my head, gathered my long tresses together and piled them onto my head and away from my neck. A few twists of the hair tie and I now had a messy loose bun.

After I splashed more water on my face, I took a deep breath. Unbuttoning my blouse, I saw the bruise from the seat belt across my chest, interrupted only by my lace bra. Gently, I smoothed more water onto my neck and chest. Each application lowered my temperature and washed away a bit of the perspiration. A fine white dusting from the airbags disappeared from my skin with every douse. The powder was ingrained in my black slacks. It would take more than dirty water to clean them. When I looked again at myself, my eyes seemed clearer and bluer and my cheeks had lost a bit of their rosiness.

In that second, I had the realization of what Kyle had told me. The temperature in this cellar was at least fifteen to twenty degrees cooler than upstairs. I hated to admit that he'd been right. Slowly, opening the bathroom door, I looked around the room I'd only sprinted through.

The walls were cement blocks. Stepping inside I splayed my fingers on the rough surface. I felt the coolness they must transmit from the earth underground. Looking up, I saw that the ceiling was wood. It wasn't a ceiling at all but the underside of the floor above.

As a matter of fact, the boards creaked above me as people stepped. If I strained, I was able to hear voices, but I couldn't make out their words. The floor beneath my high heels was smooth and made of concrete.

Along the wall next to the steps was a twin bed complete with a pillow and bedding.

Compared to the beds I was used to sleeping in, this

one looked small, as if it were meant not for an adult but for a child. Turning, I saw an old upholstered chair and a lamp. The current illumination was coming from two light bulbs in white sockets attached to the ceiling/upstairs floor.

I walked around, running my fingers over the furnishings. Everything was spotlessly clean and interestingly old. The similarities to Rett's third-floor suite seemed ironic. In one corner, sat a small round table with a Formica top and two chairs. It looked as though it belonged in an old-fashioned ice cream shop, not a cellar.

"Furnished," I said under my breath.

My freshman dorm at University of Pittsburgh had better furnishings.

If I were to compare this cellar to the third-floor suite, there were a few obvious omissions. The ever-filling refrigerator complete with bottled water was one, and as I turned a complete circle taking in everything around, above, and below me, there was no magical ceiling with a skylight.

It was then that I noticed the bottom landing of the stairs. Where in my haste, I'd turned left into the open room, to the right was a door—a closed door. Walking quietly to the landing, I peered up the stairs. From where I stood, I could tell the door was closed. Its status as locked or unlocked was unknown.

If I were to believe Kyle's word, it was unlocked. However, in my rush to spit out the tablets and small sip of beer, I hadn't taken the time to listen for the sound of a dead bolt moving.

I reached for the handle of the door to the right of the landing.

The handle didn't turn.

I had an idea. When we were younger, each room's lock opened with the insertion of a long pin-like key. We often kept them on top of the doorframe. Biting my lip, I looked up the stairs. With the coast clear, I ran my fingers over the top of the frame. As my fingertips made contact, a straight piece of skinny metal fell to the landing.

Surely, there was better security.

Then again, who would find this house?

With another quick look up the stairs, I inserted the metal piece in the small hole in the middle of the handle. Just as it did in our childhood home, the lock clicked and the handle turned. Slowly, I pushed the door inward.

From the light coming from the room I had been in, I saw the desks and screens. It was a computer setup. As I stepped in, I decided it was more elaborate than I'd expected, not that I'd expected anything—maybe a canning room.

I ran my fingertips over a keyboard and a screen came to life.

It was as far as I would get.

The screens were blank, not even a clock in the corner and each keyboard was password protected. Even if they weren't, Kyle had been right. I couldn't email my husband. I didn't know his email.

Dejectedly, I pressed the button in the middle of the knob and shut the door. An unsuccessful twist of the doorknob let me know the door was again locked. Putting the key back on the frame, I resolved that this attempt at rescue was thwarted. Having the door locked would keep that attempt hidden. No one needed to know.

The more I paced, the less I saw similarities in this room resembling Rett's third-floor suite.

The entire space was as small as the library, and like the exercise room, there were no windows. I'd never considered myself claustrophobic, but with each passing minute, I was beginning to reevaluate that particular neurosis.

I pulled back the covers on the narrow bed.

Everything was clean and fresh.

The same thoughts and questions I'd had when I'd arrived at Rett's returned.

Why was everything clean and fresh?

Had Jezebel expected me to be here?

It seemed she'd made her trip into the city for the purpose of acquiring me; nevertheless, was she so confident that she had this room prepared?

Removing my shoes, I lay back on the pillow and stared up at what was my ceiling.

No matter what other thoughts came to mind, one dominated.

That seemed appropriate.

Even in my thoughts, Everett Ramses was a dominating presence.

Lifting my left hand, I stared at my wedding rings. "You're safe, Rett. I know you are." I was speaking aloud, but there wasn't anyone to hear. "I feel you.

Maybe that's what Jezebel meant by listening to the spirits. Maybe it's Miss Marilyn talking to me, reassuring me." Tears prickled the backs of my eyes. "I am safe, too. Please, Miss Marilyn, if you can hear me, let Rett know I'm safe. I don't know how or when, but I'll get back to him. It's what I want with all my heart."

The words were off my tongue and out of my lips before I could retract them.

No one else had heard my declaration, but I had.

I believed that it was seeing Liam that confirmed what I was afraid to admit.

Sometime during the last six weeks, not only had my broken heart found its way back together, but it had slipped through my fingers and been given to another. I swallowed the tears, refusing to give them notice. For so long I'd thought I was incapable of feeling love again. To protect myself from reliving the pain of a lost love, I'd taken what remained of my heart and hidden it away in a place where even I couldn't find it.

And while I was busy, I'd forgotten to guard it, to keep it under lock and key. My mind and energy had been focused on a man I barely knew yet knew intimately. I wasn't only talking about sexually. Yes, I knew Rett that way and I had no regrets. When we were together it was as if it had been God's—or the spirits'—plan all along.

Two pieces of a puzzle.

The yin and yang.

But that wasn't the extent of our connection.

Rett brought out a part of me I never knew existed. He brought out a part of me that I'd been afraid to face.

After what happened with Liam, I never thought I could trust anyone—man or woman—the way Rett asked me to trust him.

A smile came to my face as I recalled the stupid blindfolds.

I hated those things, and now, thoughts of each one brought me joy.

Rett had taken away something as simple as my sight in benign situations to teach me something I didn't know I needed to learn. The simplistic act of walking to dinner night after night became easier each time we did it. My agitation at the strip of cloth morphed to acceptance and even anticipation. He didn't rush me or force me. Each evening, I willingly handed him my independence and as he promised, he never allowed me to fall.

And when I did fall, when I ran, he came after me.

He saved me.

Rett didn't let that misguided attempt to flee stain the progress we made. No, he continued with the blindfolds until I was so comfortable that I offered him one in return.

As I lay looking up at slats of wood, I accepted that I'd failed miserably in keeping my heart from Rett Ramses. That realization fueled a new goal; I wouldn't allow him or me to die without him knowing the truth.

I loved Rett Ramses.

As I lay there, I had no way to judge how much time had passed.

No clock, computer screen, or even a view of daylight.

Jezebel had said she'd wake me, but as I'd lain upon the small bed, with each passing minute, my thirst had grown and my hunger was beginning to rear its ugly head. If I were to survive this place and these people, I needed sustenance.

With my high heels left behind, I walked slowly and quietly up the stairs in my bare feet.

Taking a deep breath, I reached for the doorknob and twisted.

The handle turned.

Remembering the dead bolt, I knew that it wouldn't stop the doorknob from turning, only block the door from opening. Gripping tighter, I turned the handle and pulled.

RETT

"Where is Boudreau?" I growled.

The man's lips moved, but no words came as his head moved slowly from side to side. His light brown hair was matted with dried blood. The flesh around his wrists was raw from the coarse ropes and more blood ran down his arms.

My grip fisted his filthy shirt and pulled him forward. "I asked you a fucking question."

"I-I don't know where he goes. He just shows up and then he leaves." Blood dripped from his swollen lip and the skin around his left eye was red, changing to purple and black by the minute. That eye was only a slit.

The man was looking at me with his other eye.

I didn't give two shits about this man. He was one of the disposable, fucking a dime a dozen. New Orleans was crawling with scum willing to do dirty deeds for next to nothing or maybe in search of their next fix.

"When was the last time you saw him?"

"I-I..." He coughed and more blood splattered on his shirt. "Ingalls, I saw him today. I ain't seen Boudreau in over a week. Ingalls been the one making the rounds."

My blood boiled as it surged through my circulation. And my teeth were in dire danger of splintering with the amount of force I was applying. I stepped back and scanned this man. The rope securing his wrists was laced over a large hook suspended from the ceiling of the warehouse with a thick linked chain. It was similar to the way sides of beef or hogs hung in meat coolers. With his shoes gone and ankles also bound, his toes barely reached the concrete floor.

I would guess that this guy was at least eight inches shorter than me and probably fifty pounds lighter because even in his current position, I towered over him.

He'd been worked over before I arrived. The beating he took made his face less recognizable. When Leon and I arrived at the warehouse, I was informed of this man's crimes against Ramses, not of his name, and I didn't fucking care.

This piece of shit didn't deserve an identity.

A long time ago, my father once told me that every soul deserved a name, and then with a laugh, he pulled the trigger of his gun, shooting the man who had wronged him between the eyes. The loud explosion echoed, blood oozed from the bullet hole, and chunks of brain matter sprayed over the floor and wall. The dead man wet himself as his body convulsed, still hog-tied on the floor of a cargo car in the train yard. My dad looked at me and with a grin, he patted my shoulder and said, "We'll call this one Johnny."

Fuck, after we left the train yard, my father took me for ice cream before heading home.

At the time, I was no older than thirteen, and my only instruction was to not tell my mother.

I don't know why that memory was significant. Nevertheless, it's something I'd never forgotten. In the schoolhouse of life, that afternoon was one lesson that stuck with me.

In my years before and since I'd taken control of this city, I'd left a trail of dead Johnnys in every ward and beyond the greater parishes of New Orleans.

"You sure it's Ingalls?" I asked.

Johnny nodded as spit and blood dripped from his chin.

There was every reason to believe this guy was telling the truth, at least about that. From the traffic cameras near the accident, Ingalls had been identified as the man who opened Emma's door, who pulled her from my SUV, and who handed her over to this guy—this Johnny. Johnny then shoved her into a Cadillac sedan.

My men didn't find Ingalls, but unluckily for Johnny, they found him. They also found the kid in the hoodie, the one who took the shots through the windows of my SUV. Maybe Johnny here was lucky—he was still alive. The kid wasn't.

My fist made contact with his torso. "You fucking touched my wife."

The air expelled from his lungs and more blood

dripped from his lips. Johnny's knees lifted, pulling his toes from the floor, and the chain groaned as Johnny swung with the force of the punch.

His face hung forward as if by the minute his head was growing heavier.

"Fucking look at me." I demanded.

Slowly, Jonny lifted his chin, bringing his one good eye toward me. "I-I didn't know who she was."

I shook my head.

"Do you know who I am?" I asked.

"Mr. Ramses, sir." He nodded. "I didn't mean nothing against you. Ingalls paid me cash. I got a sick kid."

I pulled a pistol from the holder on my side. "I don't give a shit about a kid. I care about my wife."

I moved the barrel next to his temple. The man's eye closed as he turned his face away. "You're going to die today," I said. "You know that, right?"

Snot dripped from Johnny's nose as he nodded.

We were getting too close to the begging stage.

I fucking detested that stage.

"I'm going to give you one more chance," I lied.

His non-swollen eye came my way.

"Give me something, anything, to find my wife, and I'll see that your kid gets medical treatment."

"I-I don't—"

I pressed the end of the barrel harder against his temple making the chain creak. Then I pulled it away and pressed it beneath his chin. "Do you know why this isn't a good way to commit suicide?" I didn't wait for an answer as I moved the gun again. "Open your fucking mouth."

Johnny's lips came together as he shook his head.

"Open your goddamned mouth or I'll knock out your teeth." I tilted my chin over my shoulder. "Or one of my men over there will take them out one at a time. Marcus, the one with the black jacket" —I knew Johnny didn't truly care which one was Marcus— "has a collection of teeth. He's always itching for some more."

His one eye came my way as he slowly opened his lips. I shoved the barrel of the pistol between his teeth until he gagged and coughed. "This is another bad way."

When I pulled the pistol out of his mouth, Johnny nodded until I brought the barrel back to the soft flesh beneath his chin and pointed the barrel toward his sinuses.

"Most of the time, the barrel isn't aimed correctly." I moved the barrel around.

The man's whimpers morphed to sobs.

"And then what happens," I went on, "is when you pull the trigger, instead of dying, you end up surviving. Do you know what would be worse than me killing you?" I wasn't pausing for answers. "Letting you live without a frontal lobe of your brain. More than likely the nerves to your eyes—they call them optic nerves— yeah, well, the bullet shreds those motherfuckers. And your tongue is half-gone. Hmm, you won't be talking. Hell, you might not even be able to eat again. Not like takin' a big old bite out of a juicy Po' boy." I shook my head. "Won't matter that your teeth will mostly be gone, part of your jawbone too. None of those things are what makes this a bad idea. It's the damage to the brain that's real important. See, you could live without eyes, a jaw, and teeth."

I tapped his forehead with the barrel of my gun. "The frontal lobes of your brain are what you use to talk, if your tongue still worked. It also controls voluntary movement. Shit you want to do, like walking, sitting, and fucking your woman. None of that shit will happen. You might think about them, but the neurons won't connect. And the worst part, you'll still be able to think. You'll know that you're nothing more than a fucking vegetable. That sick kid of yours, if he lives, he'll watch his old man shit and piss himself as he changes your feeding tube, the one stuck through your neck and your diaper. That is why this" —I shoved the barrel into the soft skin under his chin— "is a bad idea."

"I-I got something," Johnny managed to say.

I pulled back the pistol. "Talk."

"Ingalls, he said things about..." Johnny's eyes closed and nostrils flared.

"About what?" I pressed the barrel back under his chin.

With his chin held as high as possible between his stretched arms, he said, "My kid. He needs medicine. My wife lost her job and our insurance, we can't afford..."

"What did Ingalls say?"

The man shook his head.

I lowered the gun. "Talk."

"Mr. Ramses, you got to know, none of us knew who she was...that blonde. Ingalls showed us pictures and she's right pretty." The large links of the chain creaked as Johnny's trembling increased. "We didn't know that she was your wife. He said things..." A tear ran down his face from the swollen eye.

"He?"

"Ingalls."

The barrel was back under his chin. "I'm going to give you to the count of three," I said. "One. Two—"

EMMA

The door moved, coming inward toward the stairs. The temperature rose as I moved upward as if the air became thicker as well as warmer. I took the next step, and the last, until I was at the kitchen floor. The shadows had grown while I'd been in the cellar, indicating that the sun was setting. It was still present, but getting lower in the horizon.

"Emma."

I sucked in a breath as I stepped around the corner of the hallway.

Jezebel was seated at the table beyond the kitchen counters and appliances. No longer dressed in a colorful dress, she was wearing blue jeans, a plain shirt, and a sweater that hung below the chair. Her long hair was braided, not unlike the way I wore mine from time to time.

She didn't look my way. Her attention was toward the back windows. "You didn't take the tablets."

"I'm hungry," I said honestly.

Jezebel motioned me toward her. "Edmée made you a plate. I told her you'd be up soon." Her gaze met mine. "Come sit with me."

I eyed the refrigerator, wondering what other wonders of drink it held within its chilled depths.

"Come," she beckoned.

My bare feet padded over the wood floor until I reached the table. Holding onto the top of one of the chairs, I had the strange sensation of childhood, of being caught in a lie. Looking down, I confessed, "I didn't take the tablets. You know that because I didn't sleep."

"No, child, I know because I know. Those tablets wouldn't have made you sleep. They were sugar pills."

I pulled out the chair and sat. "It was a test."

Jezebel nodded.

"I'm sorry, Mother." I made myself say the proper noun.

Jezebel took a deep breath and stood. "Let me get you some dinner."

Rett's concern that Jezebel was also responsible for the danger he warned about fueled my questions as she walked past me to the working area of the kitchen, only to return with a plate. There was no silver dome as there would be if Ian brought me food.

I swallowed, not ready to think about him.

The plate she brought was filled with red beans and a dark green leafy salad. It had pecans, sliced oranges, and red berries all mixed with a raspberry vinaigrette dressing.

"The beans are fresh, just shucked today," Jezebel

said as she went back and returned with a bottle of water.

My eyes opened wide. "Kyle said—"

"Kyle took the tablets."

I opened the cap, hearing the click, and hurriedly drank nearly half the contents of the bottle. When I finished, I inhaled, enjoying the common sensation of the cool moisture on my lips and tongue. "I may need a second bottle."

After retrieving a second bottle, Jezebel took the seat where she'd been sitting, placed her hands in the pockets of her sweater, and leaned back, all the time keeping her eyes on me. "Tell me about yourself, Emma."

Lifting the fork, I moved the food around the plate, mentally weighing if I believed it was safe to eat.

As if Jezebel could read my mind, she offered, "I'll taste the food for you if that will help you eat."

I set the fork down. "Kyle took the sugar pills?"

She grinned. "And slept for fourteen hours straight."

"I thought you said they were placebos."

"They are. The mind is the most powerful drug. And some minds are easier to manipulate than others. Tell me, is your husband easy to manipulate?"

I stared for a moment, appreciating Jezebel's directness.

My lower lip disappeared behind my front teeth as I considered her question. "Mother, you're speaking of Rett in the present tense. That means he's all right." I shook my head. "I should know that doesn't matter; Miss Guidry speaks of everyone in the present tense."

"That's because Ruth speaks to everyone in the present. As for your husband, you know he's alive."

There was no way to describe the relief that came with that simple sentence of verification. I blinked away the tears and picked up the fork. Jezebel's question came back as I took a bite of the red beans. While I'd expected them to be tasteless, they weren't. "These are sweet."

"Yes, they're grown on the property. I suppose they'd be called a hybrid."

I ate some more. "They're very good."

"Your husband," she prompted.

I shook my head as I took another drink of water. "I'd say no; he's not easily manipulated."

"Your brother?"

I nodded with a scoff. "I mean, he was. I haven't seen him, and I suppose people change."

"William?"

Thoughts and memories came to my mind. "I didn't think so. Again, it's been years. Now, I don't know. I'd say Liam is less so than Kyle."

"And on that scale, where does Mr. Ramses fall?"

"The least of them all." I finished the beans and moved on to the salad. After a few bites, I turned to Jezebel. "I don't understand. If the blue tablets were a test and Kyle took them but I didn't, who passed the test?"

Jezebel took a deep breath. "Do you love him?"

As I contemplated her question, I had no desire to be anything less than transparent. "I didn't want to."

She leaned forward, placing her lower arms on the table.

I pushed the ingredients of the salad around and looked back up. "I let my heart be broken a while ago. I didn't want to do it again, but Rett is" —I grinned— "a force of nature."

Her forehead furrowed. "Emma, has he hurt you?"

"No," I answered quickly. "Rett accepted my counterproposal. The first night we met he said we'd marry. I know that seems...presumptuous and odd, but even though we'd just met, I believed him. I never argued that outcome, but I told him he'd never have my heart."

"He's a man. He only cares about your body." She nodded. "And you gave that or did he take it?"

"I gave it...willingly," I added. "I don't regret that. But my heart, I thought I had it shielded, and now I realized I didn't. He didn't take it, Mother. In less than two months, it slipped from my grasp to him. I don't even know if he knows. I want to tell him."

"Will he reciprocate?"

"Will he say he loves me?" I asked, repeating what I thought she meant. With my lips together, I stared out the back windows. The world beyond the kitchen was growing darker. I turned back. "It doesn't matter."

Jezebel tilted her head. "What?"

I shook mine. "It doesn't matter what he says. I want him to know my feelings."

"And you'll be all right if he doesn't offer you the same?"

I shrugged. "It's been less than two months. I didn't

go into our relationship looking for love. Neither did Rett. If he can't say the words, then I don't need to hear them. I feel it." A smile returned to my lips. "It's in the things he doesn't say. It's in his eyes when he stares at me and the sweet gestures that I know are outside of his natural character. I guess if I could ask for one thing, I really want him to know."

"Why doesn't he know?"

This time I laughed. "Because he's a man."

Jezebel grinned.

"Not all men are intuitive." I thought of Ian. "Some are. I think it has to do with their responsibilities. Rett has many. His attention is rightfully divided. I couldn't bear if Rett never knew the way I feel."

"You passed," Jezebel said. "Twice and counting. You've shown me that you can think for yourself. And with what you just said, you have self-confidence that I admire. Kyle is...not the same. He requires continual confirmation. He also tries hard to please. It was how he was before he learned the truth about your conception. Since he learned that I was hurt, his desire to please has become obsessive. He will say or do anything he believes will please me or bring me my goal."

"What is your goal?" I asked.

"I want what the spirits promised."

"Control of New Orleans."

Jezebel nodded.

"And you arranged for it to look like Kyle died to help you claim that control?"

"I did. I made a choice. I now see that it was also a mistake."

My food was gone and so were both bottles of water. If there had been anything in it to hurt me, I wasn't feeling the effects. I pushed my plate away from the edge of the table and leaned back in the straight chair. "Thank you for dinner. What was your mistake?"

"Believing the lies of misogyny I'd been fed all of my life."

"Misogyny? You mean choosing your son over your daughter."

"I didn't do that. I wanted both of you here as you are now. And yes, I made assumptions based on gender." She smiled. "Incorrect assumptions of the city's acceptance of fate. I'm very proud of you, Emma."

I didn't understand all she was saying, but I wanted to. "Tell me how Kyle and I are twins."

"That's the whole story, Emma. You were conceived at the same time, born nearly twelve hours apart. Twins are no mystery. They have been born throughout the ages."

I shook my head. "But our birthdates—"

Jezebel lifted her hand.

It was the same thing Rett did to silence people.

She took another breath. "The spirits keep reminding me that of everyone here, you know the least."

"Miss Guidry has told me some."

Jezebel grinned. "Ruth means well, but her allegiance is divided."

"What do you mean?"

Jezebel shook her head. "One thing at a time. Nearly thirty—no, more specifically, twenty-eight years ago, I went to Isaiah Boudreau for his help and blessing to begin a business because to succeed in New Orleans, I needed either his or Abraham Ramses's support. That choice too was a mistake."

"He raped you."

"Not right away. He led me to believe he would help me. He set me up for a fall, for public failure that he believed would rid him and New Orleans of the likes of me forever. That was his plan. This all occurred when I was younger than you are now. In hindsight, I should have gone to Mr. Ramses."

"Rett's father."

Jezebel nodded. "When I did, it was too late. They had an agreement. You see, I had received a bank loan, and I had a business plan."

"Event planning," I said.

She smiled. "Ruth has told you. Now it's my turn. Let me tell you my story."

I nodded.

"I'd worked hard to create an upstanding business. New Orleans was booming. I didn't have the education, but I did research. I talked with successful entrepreneurs. I read anything and everything I could find from books in the library to business journals. I scoured city records. Everything is public if you know where to look. I analyzed the value of land and the cost of construction. It made sense to have a small investment in brick and mortar and a bigger investment in people.

"My plan was to provide all aspects of event planning. For catering, I'd have that building, a kitchen, and cooks. New Orleans has some of the most talented cooks who never prepare anything other than dinner for their own families. I'd hire servers and waiters. There were numerous people I knew who, if given the opportunity, would make their way out of the small niche where life had placed them. These were men and women who were hard workers and willing to learn.

"Instead of investing in space for the events, I'd work with the businesses already growing, the hotels and convention center. Events didn't need to be limited to spaces under roofs. The riverfront was developing. We have beautiful parks. I knew the cost for renting every space in the greater New Orleans parishes.

"What I lacked were people with the money to make it happen. The bank loan was a start, but I'd worked the spreadsheets and I knew, to be successful, to hit the ground running, I needed more cash flow. Mr. Boudreau arranged a meeting." She took a deep breath. "It was supposed to be with other investors, people who had the capital to invest. He had connections to some of the biggest and most influential people in Louisiana." Her chin rose. "Some of those people were present."

"For the meeting?" I asked.

"The gathering wasn't what I'd expected. I arrived prepared for questions. I had folders of research and data to substantiate my business plan." She inhaled. "That wasn't why they'd been invited."

The recently consumed dinner churned in my stomach.

She continued, "Isaiah believed my humiliation would be greater if the act was witnessed."

My eyes blinked but words were difficult to form. "No one helped you?"

Jezebel shook her head. And yet watching and listening, there was no emotion in her expression or voice, as if she was telling a story about another person, not the horrific details of her own assault.

Silence fell over the kitchen as a breeze came out of nowhere, rustling the curtains beside the windows.

"The spirits are here. They want you to understand."

RETT

*J*ohnny coughed.

"Tell me what he said," I growled.

"Ingalls said she's a good lay, and he said he wanted her back to teach her a lesson."

My jaw clenched as my grip on the handle of the pistol tightened. "He said that?"

"Yeah, like they was real close, and he talked about shit, but we didn't know she was married. God, you gotta believe me. We didn't know she was your wife."

The scene around me was covered in a hue of red. My blood had reached its boiling point. I made myself breathe. "How do I know what you're saying is true?"

"'Cause my kid."

"You can do better than that."

The man shook his head until his good eye opened. "I'm sorry, Mr. Ramses. You asked..."

"Go on."

"Ingalls, he said he never fucked her ass. Said she was real good at blowing and he might pass her around, but he wanted her ass. He said if her ass was as tight as her pussy—"

My fist connected to his torso again. As Johnny coughed and spit, I asked, "Did Ingalls pay you?"

"Half. He paid half."

My jaw clenched. "When and where do you collect the second half?"

"Desire, tonight. That old Baptist church. It's boarded up. The one near Pleasure and Metropolitan Streets. There's a board loose near the back. Inside, he's got a place he meets with people."

I knew exactly the place Johnny was describing. Desire, in the Upper Ninth, had a reputation worse than the Lower Ninth. It was a neighborhood that needed cleaning up, and I was ready to light a match to the whole damn thing.

"What time?" I asked.

"He said two. Two in the morning."

"Why two?"

"Bars still open. Good folks gone home."

"How much does Ingalls owe you?" I asked.

"Half a G."

Taking a step back, I spun the pistol in my grip and landed the butt of the handle on his temple. Johnny's head fell forward and at the point of contact, his flesh sliced and more blood oozed down his cheek. His body went limp and the chain creaked. I spun on my heels, my gaze avoiding my other men, I looked at Leon.

"Five hundred," Leon said.

I knew what half a G was. My mind was on my wife.

"Ingalls offered a measly fucking thousand to get Emma."

"I'll off this one for you," Leon offered.

"No, he's got a paycheck to collect." I took one more look at Johnny's limp body and turned back to Marcus and the other Ramses soldiers. "Get him cleaned up. If he does what we say and brings Ingalls to our trap, I'll make good on my promise for his kid. Either way, it's good night, Johnny. He can decide his kid's fate."

As more of my men entered the room, I cleaned the blood from my gun and hands and wiped the splatter from the top of my Italian loafers using disinfectant wipes. The soldiers did their job without saying a fucking word.

Walking to the SUV, Leon said, "Boss, Ingalls didn't leave with Mrs. Ramses."

My jaw clenched tighter. "He fucking touches her and I'm going to enjoy watching him die."

Once I was back in the SUV, I pulled up the information from earlier on my phone.

The hackers on my payroll had a network that was invisible to the rest of the world. Logging into it, I took another look at the traffic cam footage from earlier in the day. I started it a few seconds before the collision.

The car carrying more of my men that I had following Emma from the courthouse was cut off at an intersection one block before the point where her SUV was hit. By the time the car with the backup made it to the scene, she was gone.

Even watching the footage for the tenth or more time, curses flew from my lips.

If I wasn't so fucking furious, I'd be impressed.

The entire maneuver was exceptionally well timed.

Starting with intercepting the backup car, to the SUV's collision, and the intervention of a black Cadillac sedan, the whole chain of events took less than ninety seconds. It was enough time for my SUV to collide in the perfect way that caused the airbags to deploy.

The black Cadillac swept in and was gone with Emma inside of it in less than forty-five seconds from the time she was removed from the SUV.

That bit of footage, I'd watched more times than I cared to admit.

As fucking upset as I was and as much blood as I wanted to shed, watching Emma forced into the Cadillac without Ingalls gave me something else. It gave me hope. My wife was alive and uninjured in the collision. It was the piece of this puzzle I held onto.

She was alive.

I couldn't dwell on the thoughts of what Ingalls told others. I had to think straight.

Slowing the footage, I watched as Emma was pulled from the SUV, walked and then screamed as shots were fired. Even as Emma was pushed into the Cadillac and the car took off, I concentrated on the fact she was unhurt and alive.

She *is*.

Nothing else mattered until I got her back.

My hackers followed the Cadillac on traffic cameras as it sped away across the Lake Pontchartrain Causeway.

The fucking cameras at the Chinchuba exchange weren't working. And at that point, her trail went cold.

Of course, the Cadillac in question was part of a rental fleet that had been stolen four months ago from a lot in Shreveport. Four of the same models had been taken. One was found parked outside a nightclub in Baton Rouge three days after they were reported stolen. The other three had been MIA until now.

There was no way to link the Cadillac to a person. The license plates were also stolen. Nevertheless, I didn't have any doubt that Isaiah Boudreau was connected. He and Ingalls had recently been recruiting men in a warehouse in Baton Rouge. A man we had on the inside reported back to Leon the night before last. He said Boudreau seemed more agitated than normal. And then at the last called meeting, he wasn't there, only Ingalls.

That matched what Johnny said.

While our informant never mentioned Jezebel when Leon questioned him, the mole relayed news that things had been tenser as of late and there was chatter among the ranks that someone else was pulling Boudreau's strings. They were mumbling about a puppet master.

I'd taken that news well.

Talk was it was Ingalls planning a coup of his own.

My trusted men believed it was Jezebel.

Either way, there was no better way to bring down Boudreau than from the inside. Get his own men to question his authority and watch as the empire he'd tried to build crumbled from within.

"Johnny's dying tonight," I said as Leon's eyes met mine in the rearview mirror. "No pass."

"Boss, just 'cause Ingalls tells people that stuff about Mrs. Ramses don't mean it's true."

Clenching my teeth, I turned toward the window. As I did, I didn't see my city outside the windows. It wasn't the blue evening sky over the skyline. No, I was seeing Emma's stunning blue gaze and the way her orbs swirled with emotions. I fucking wanted them all. I wanted her passion and excitement, but I'd take her anger and even her fucking disappointment. I'd willingly put up with more displays of the power I'd let her think she had. Hell, she could spend a fucking month on the third floor if she wanted. I'd put up with anything she wanted to give me to have her back, safe and sound.

"Men talk," Leon said.

I grunted.

He was right. They did.

I didn't know the extent to the truth in Ingalls's loud mouth or in Johnny's rendition, but I knew that what Johnny said had basis. That wasn't solely because I knew how tight Emma was and how good it felt to be inside her or how she could wrap her lips around me and do this thing with her tongue.

I knew there was some validity, not because she told me, but because during my research, I learned that Emma and William Ingalls had been involved. When I asked her the first day she woke in my house if she'd been in contact with any of her or Kyle's friends, the day she identified Greyson in the photo, I knew about William.

She didn't say.

I didn't push her for answers. My reasoning was that I wasn't going to spend the rest of my life obsessed with her past. Emma's future was my concern. Even so, I knew.

And if that fucking past wanted to broadcast shit no one needed to hear, if he wanted to put himself on my radar, I had no trouble removing him for good.

If those motherfuckers want a war, they got it.

"Boss, the doctor's calling you about Knolls."

Leon's voice penetrated my thoughts. Looking up, I saw the caller's name upon the dash of the SUV. I hadn't even heard the phone ring.

Snapping out of my haze, I lifted my phone. "Ramses here."

EMMA

I stared at the curtains, suddenly curious of the breeze, the first I'd felt here. "I want to understand." I did. This wasn't me pacifying Jezebel for my escape. The woman who gave me life was sharing with me, and I wanted to know how she'd gotten to this place in her life.

"Know that I'm not ashamed of my past, Emma. I'm telling you to show you that you come from strong genes. The man who fathered you wasn't a good man, but he was powerful. He was a man who used people for his benefit. I learned from him. I want you to learn too."

I nodded. "When did Isaiah Boudreau learn you were pregnant?"

"When it was too late for him to do anything about it. That doesn't mean he didn't try. He wasn't alone. You see, his wife never conceived. She saw my pregnancy as a personal affront to her. Of course, Isaiah denied that he could be the father." She placed her hands on the table and splayed her fingers. The multiple gems on her fingers glistened under the light hanging over the kitchen table. She moved her gaze back to me. "It was difficult to deny something witnessed by so many. Up until that point, I'd worked hard to become more than my mother. She was a good woman, Emma. Don't think less of her because of her profession. Truly, it took me realizing that every woman sells her body. It doesn't matter if she is born with blue blood or red, the color of her skin, the language she speaks, or the money she has. Some women complete that transaction once with vows" —she nodded toward my wedding rings— "others nightly. Your maternal grandmother accepted her fate. I didn't. However, you should know, I considered options to terminate my pregnancy before I told anyone."

I swallowed. "Okay."

"That isn't a reflection on you. It was a dark time. Not only had my body been abused, my dreams were shattered and scattered on Canal Street for everyone to see. The latter was the most painful. Through it all, I was all alone."

"What about your mother?"

"She was no longer in this world." Jezebel stared toward the window as a smile crept to her lips. "I decided to leave New Orleans." She inhaled. "Even though doing so would have given the Boudreaux what they wanted, I believed I was without options. Then one night, Edmée came to me, telling me she was sent by the spirits." Jezebel scoffed. "I'd lived my whole life in New Orleans, but I'd never believed as others did." Her blue eyes met mine. "That night, I believed.

"That night Edmée explained to me what was happening and my role in the future of New Orleans. Not only my role, that of my children. She knew I had two babies inside me long before anyone else knew I was pregnant. She took care of me through the sicknesses, she taught me to listen and heed the spirits, and in doing so, she resurrected my determination.

"Because of her, I knew I'd survive, we all would. And then the warning came."

"The warning?" I asked.

"The spirits warned her that Isaiah was a danger to my children and the fulfillment of the future she'd seen." Jezebel reached for my hand on the table.

As hers covered mine, I realized that this time hers was the warm one. Her story had stilled my circulation. And even in the humid air, I was cold.

"I wanted to raise you, both of you," she said, "but the spirits knew what was best. You needed to be safe. And the best way to keep you safe was to hide both of you and not let anyone know that I had two children. You and Kyle were born on the summer solstice." A peaceful expression settled over her. "As you know, it's the longest day of the year. The spirits believe in the power of the sun. Centuries ago, they worshiped the sun. It has long been the symbol of goodness, life, and positivity. You, Emma, were born first. You came into this world strong and vocal. I named you for the woman who delivered you."

"Edmée?"

She nodded. "Yes, and your brother finally arrived just before midnight."

I narrowed my gaze. "Kyle's birthday is in February. I was born eight months later, in October. I realize the math never worked, but as children, we didn't question it."

"We believed that because boys grow faster than girls, it made sense to pretend he was older. I had the help of a young attorney. He forged birth certificates in exchange for other things. It stands to reason that even if Isaiah and Lilith didn't know the date you were born, they'd be looking for a child adopted out of Louisiana with a June birth date."

"Lilith?"

"Your father's wife."

I patted the gris-gris in the pocket of my slacks. "Was the necklace hers?"

"No. It belonged to your father's mother. When I was young, she wore it with pride."

I thought back to her story. "What did you exchange?" As soon as the question left my lips, I knew the answer.

"That is a story for another night, Emma. You see, every woman sells herself. After what happened to me, I decided that my commodity would help me prepare for now."

"When did you change your name?"

The sound of footsteps quieted our conversation. We both turned as Liam and Kyle came down the hall toward the kitchen. My shock was visible as I took in the woman with them.

"Emily?" I questioned, scanning the pretty woman with long red hair. She was wearing a short skirt and tight blouse. What had my attention was the way she was clinging to Kyle's arm.

Her smile seemed forced. "Emma."

Letting go of Jezebel's hand, I pushed back my chair and stood. My eyebrows knit together as I asked, "Why are you here?"

"We thought you'd still be sleeping," Kyle said. "I guess there's no time like the present. Emily, you've met my sister, Emma. Emma, you've met Emily." He smiled her direction. "What you might not know is that Emily is my fiancée."

His fiancée?

"You were with Ross," I said, "the night he died."

Her face tilted and her lips came together. "Oh yeah, I heard he died. That's too bad." She shrugged. "Taking pain meds after an earlier hit of Oxy..." She shook her head. "I thought he was smarter than that."

"Oh my God." I stepped closer. "It was you. You knew he had pain medication. You killed him."

"Interesting theory," Emily said. "Of course, I wasn't the one to benefit from his death. That would be you."

Kyle let go of Emily and walked past me, his shoulder bumping mine. "Your husband is the guilty party. I guess he married you for the same reason you married him." He rubbed two fingers with his thumb. "Bet he knew you would inherit Underwood's fortune."

Ignoring Kyle, I looked at Emily. My thoughts went back to right before last Christmas when she and Ross were dating. "How long have you and Kyle been engaged?"

She smiled. "Over a year." She waved her hand, the

one with the large diamond. "Don't try to figure it all out. I was doing my part for Mother, like we all do."

"Mother?"

Jezebel's gaze met mine. "They are to be married."

"When?" I asked.

"Once everything is settled," Emily said, "we're going to have a big New Orleans wedding."

"Settled?"

"You know, once Kyle and Liam are in control of the city." She shrugged. "Kyle said we can have your house."

"Kyle said what?"

Liam spoke. "Ramses destroyed your father's home. It was nicer than yours, but they don't mind redecorating."

I thought about Rett's house and his story about his mother and grandmother, how they worked together to decorate. "What are you saying?"

Kyle responded, "This is war, Em. Once it's over, the spoils belong to the victors. We will be the victors."

"Spoils?" I repeated. "You're certifiably crazy. Rett's house isn't available to take. It has been in his family for generations."

Liam had remained quiet, but as I turned his way, his gaze narrowed. I couldn't describe the way he was looking at me. A chill scurried over my skin as the tips of his lips curled upward. "Kyle and Emily can have the house. I've been promised something else."

"You aren't getting anything of his."

I turned to Kyle, hoping for some sanity.

My brother was no longer a part of this conversation. He was sitting in the chair where I'd been sitting, his hands on the table, whispering to Jezebel. He turned to me with disgust. "You didn't take the pills?"

"No, I didn't."

He turned back to Jezebel. "Mom, we were wrong to wait to get Emma. She isn't one of us. Ramses's fucked with her" —he hesitated— "head. Leave the plans to me and Liam." He stood. "She is...dangerous. Forget her. The spirits' prophecy doesn't need her to make it happen." His volume rose. "We don't need her. Our numbers are growing. Ramses doesn't know how many of his men have turned. Soon we'll have your city, Mother. I'll lay it at your feet."

"What is it with men and laying shit at our feet?" I asked.

Jezebel smiled as she stood. "You are both my children. The prophecy is that you will rule this city; you were conceived for that purpose." She turned to the three of them. "You listen too much to folklore and fables." She reached for my elbow. "Come, Emma. There is much for you to learn."

"What did I misunderstand?" Liam asked.

We'd begun to walk, but she stopped. "Emma, show them your necklace."

I reached into my pocket and pulled out the gris-gris, opened the flap and removed the silver necklace with the jade pendant.

"So?" Kyle said.

"Emma, tell them who it belonged to."

Looking up from the necklace, I turned to Kyle and Emily, both near the table, and then to Liam standing near a counter. "Jeza—Mother said it was my grandmother's, my paternal grandmother." I looked at Jezebel.

"Is this supposed to mean something?" Liam asked.

Jezebel smiled. "Yes. Start listening to the spirits instead of rumors and let me know when you have it figured out." She turned to me. "Come, we'll sit on the porch."

EMMA

I walked beside Jezebel down the long hallway and toward the screen door to the porch. Before we made it to the door, she led me into a sitting room. In a basket were blankets. Jezebel lifted one and handed it my direction.

"It has to be eighty-five degrees," I said as I took the wool blanket.

"It's not for the temperature. Sitting outside, there will be mosquitoes. Wrap up and they won't get you."

The scratchy blanket was in my grasp. "Do you have any bug repellent?"

Jezebel shook her head. "I don't believe in chemicals."

"You gave me tablets to sleep."

Her blue eyes met mine as a smile came to her lips. "There was nothing in them."

We both wrapped the blankets around our shoulders and settled into two big rocking chairs. The hum of flying bugs began the chorus of night noises. Crickets and toads added their sounds until the dark world beyond the porch was vibrantly alive in my mind. Not all the creatures I imagined were capable of being kept away with a wool blanket.

"If the bugs are too annoying," Jezebel said, "Edmée has a recipe for a lotion that will help in the future."

I sighed, looking out into the darkness. "I don't want to stay here long enough to need that."

Jezebel nodded. "Your brother was right about one thing." She didn't let me try to guess what that was. "We should have brought you here sooner."

Standing, I readjusted myself, sheltering my feet from the mosquitoes. Sitting again, I pulled my bare feet up onto the chair and tucked the blanket around me. There were probably already a few nibbles to my exposed flesh. Once I settled, I said, "I don't have an answer for that."

"It's true. You've been influenced by your husband."

My head shook as I swatted away something flying close to my head. "I suppose I have."

"My earlier question about manipulation...has he manipulated you?"

Sighing, I gave that some thought. "I don't think I can give that an unbiased answer. I'd like to think I'm not manipulated." I turned to her. "No, he hasn't manipulated me. He's informed me. He was the person who explained who I really am and my role in New Orleans."

"What did he say?"

"That I was to marry him and rule with him."

"With him?"

"Beside him, Mother."

"And you feel he was honest about that? He wants your input?"

My mind filled with instances where my input had been welcomed and other times when it wasn't met as fondly. "I think he'll listen. When we're together and alone, he will listen."

"And you think you have a voice, or is it part of the manipulation, him only letting you think you do?"

I rose to my feet and stood at the railing on the edge of the porch. The pitch darkness seemed to go on forever. Without turning, I asked, "Are you trying to say you don't think I have a voice?"

"Emma, my experience is very limited with what goes on between a husband and wife. I've never married. You said you willingly married him and that now you think you love him."

I spun toward her. "I do love him. I don't *think* I do. I know I do." A day ago or maybe even hours ago, I might have been surprised by the conviction I heard in my own voice, not now. I knew I meant every word. "And I have a voice. Rett listens even when he doesn't want to." A smile came to my lips as I recalled our dinner in the conservatory and opening his gift of a key.

Wrapping the blanket around me, I sat again in the chair.

Jezebel reached over to my hand and covered it. "You are..." She didn't finish her sentence.

"I can't imagine what you think of me. I'm not Kyle and I'm not you. I honestly don't know what you expected to find."

Taking her hand back, Jezebel laid her head against the back of the chair and rocked, the runners of the chair clicking on the wood floor of the porch. "Emma, I've thought a lot about you since before you were born. Life has taught me not to make assumptions or snap decisions. As I said, I've also watched you and tried to protect you."

"When did you go to Pittsburgh?"

Jezebel exhaled and continued rocking her chair back and forth. "After I gave you to Mr. Michelson, I made myself stay away from you and Kyle until I couldn't. The first time I traveled to North Carolina, I believe you were five. Since then, I've gone where you and he were whenever it was right."

My mind wasn't computing her entire sentence. "Mr. Michelson?"

"Yes, he was the young attorney who helped me with your birth certificates and placement. He found the O'Briens and made sure they would raise you both with the stipulation you were two different ages."

"The same man who is now a prosecutor for Louisiana?"

She turned my way. "I'm surprised you know that. Yes, that's him."

"He questioned me today" —I looked out at the darkness— "or yesterday." Before Jezebel could answer, I added, "When Kyle and I were very young, we lived in Tennessee. I don't remember any of that. When I was four..." I realized I'd need to do that math again. "...anyway, before we started school, we moved to North Carolina. Because of college, I moved to

Pittsburgh. After everyone died, I decided to stay there."

"The O'Briens understood the threat of danger to both of you. It was difficult for them to pretend you were eight months apart when you were babies. That's why they had to move later." She sighed. "They were good people. They gave up their family and friends to keep you safe."

"Wait? We had family?"

"Yes, you have me."

My head shook. "No, I'm talking about the O'Briens. I had this memory of grandparents, but I thought it was something that I concocted in my young mind. Because once I really had memories of my childhood in our home in North Carolina, we didn't have any extended family."

"Marcella's parents are still alive. I believe Oliver has a brother."

I laid my head against the wooden chair. "I didn't contact them. They don't know what happened to their family." I turned to Jezebel. "How do you know this?"

"I listen to the spirits and pay attention."

"Did you...?" I thought for a moment, wondering how to phrase my question. "Were you involved...? Are they really gone?"

Jezebel smiled. "That's the most indecisive I've heard you be, Emma. Come, that won't do. Show me your strength."

"I guess I'm afraid of what I'll learn."

"Tell me why?"

"If the O'Briens aren't dead, that means they agreed

to let me think they were, just like Kyle. And that would be...hurtful. And if they are dead, and I learn you were involved in their death after even you admitted what good people they were...it would affect the way I see you."

"How?"

"How could it not?" I responded.

"What is it that you find upsetting or repulsive?"

"I didn't say repulsive." My mind pondered her question. "In the car you said Ian and Noah were disposable. I don't see life that way."

"I didn't use the word disposable. I said they were expendable. There's a difference." She inhaled, wrapping her blanket tighter around her. "Is it the act of killing you find hurtful?"

"It is...wrong."

"Even if it serves a greater function?"

I shook my head, conflicted.

Jezebel nodded. "What do you think your husband does to maintain his power?"

I knew the answer. There were rebuttals on the tip of my tongue, excuses even. However, as I sat there in the darkness with the chorus of insects buzzing and toads croaking, I was beginning to see Jezebel's point.

How was it right to excuse him and not her?

"You were involved in their deaths." I didn't phrase it as a question because it wasn't.

"Yes, Emma, I was involved but not as you assume. The accident was supposed to be survivable for all three. I don't know what happened, but while Kyle survived, the O'Briens didn't. It was an unfortunate byproduct. They had done all that was asked." She sighed. "Sometimes we must simply accept outcomes even if they aren't exactly what we intend. If you're to fulfill the prophecy, you'll need to face decisions of life and death. No city can be run by a leader who isn't willing to deliver the necessary consequences. There will be times that personal feelings may want to interfere. It's easier not to have those types of emotions, but eliminating them takes time."

My mind filled with memories of the O'Briens. No longer did I concentrate on their deception, how they never told me I was adopted. I now saw their choices through a clearer lens. They'd been charged with protecting me and Kyle. When we moved to North Carolina before starting school, they sacrificed their own family for us, for *our* family unit. They created the illusion that was necessary for our safety.

"They were good parents," I said. It wasn't meant to hurt Jezebel. I hoped it would help her, to let her know that we'd been well taken care of.

She sighed. "The world isn't black and white. It's full of all the different shades of gray. It's difficult for people to always see that. The spirits have a clearer view. Learn to listen to them. They've been with you since your conception."

Closing my eyes, I let my mind speak to Miss Guidry and Miss Marilyn. My message was the same as it was earlier in the night: tell Rett I'm safe.

"However you learn to see the contrast," she went on, "in order to succeed, you must see it. Either people are for you or they're against you. There's no middle ground."

The echo of the back screen door reverberated through the house as determined footsteps came our way. The small hairs on the back of my neck stood to attention, waiting for whoever would emerge from the interior. I couldn't explain the sensations I was now feeling around Kyle and Liam. The only way I could describe them, even to myself, was uneasy and different.

EMMA

The screen door opened and Kyle appeared.

He'd changed his clothes from earlier, now wearing a blue suit, crisp striped shirt, and a silver tie. "We're going out."

Jezebel lifted her chin. "Stay safe. I assume this has to do with business."

"Yes, we've received word about something." His gaze came to me.

"Something to do with Rett?" I asked.

Kyle shook his head. "Not exactly." He looked back at Jezebel. "I also promised Emily some fun. Killing two birds."

The shake of our mother's head was almost imperceptible, but I saw it. "The time is near, Kyle. Don't let down your guard."

His blue stare came to me before turning to Jezebel. His fingers balled to fists at his side. "I don't understand how you two are just sitting here."

Our mother looked up. "What is troubling you?"

"Her." He pointed at me. "She didn't take the sleeping pills. She married him. She doesn't understand any of what's happening and you're...fucking socializing."

"Emma is my daughter, the same as you're my son. When you arrived here, we talked."

His head shook. "She's not with us." He narrowed his gaze my direction. "I see it. Liam sees it. She chose her side and that decision is as obvious as the fucking rings on her finger."

Despite Kyle's outburst, Jezebel remained perfectly calm. "When you first arrived, you had questions."

He inhaled.

Jezebel explained, "Emma is in a different position than you were when you woke here, in *my* home."

"Yours? I thought it was ours?" Kyle ran his hand over his hair, stirring the waves he'd combed back, before turning his heated blue stare my way. "It feels like Emma's the damn prodigal son. I've been here, doing every goddamned thing you ask, taking care of you, making my name known and...fuck."

"Do you love Emily?" Jezebel asked.

My eyes opened wide. Even though I wasn't directly part of this conversation, I felt the shift in the atmosphere. Kyle was also obviously taken aback.

"Yeah, we're engaged."

I couldn't help but think of what Miss Marilyn had told Rett. Asking for a hand in marriage was the easy part; being married was when it became difficult.

"Have you told her?" Jezebel asked.

"Of course."

Jezebel nodded. "And she's told you in return?"

"Yes, what does this have to do—?"

"Could you love her," Jezebel asked, "if you weren't absolutely certain of her feelings?"

I sucked in a breath, realizing how this question related to me and Rett.

Kyle walked to the railing and back. "Yeah. Maybe. Hell, I'm not sure."

"If you were to have children, could you love them and her?"

"Yes."

"Because love isn't an emotion in limited supply," Jezebel said. "It's infinite." Before Kyle could respond, she asked, "Now that Emma is here, are you doubting my love for you?"

"No, but fuck, I'm your son. I'm the rightful heir to Isaiah Boudreau. I need to be seen, Mother. *Me*. Isaiah."

Jezebel's grip of the rocking chair's arms tightened each time Kyle used that name. Besides her discussion of love, this was the first display of emotion I'd witnessed from her. While mostly covert, it was still there. In the mosaic she'd painted, one that lacked emotion, the blanching of her fingers as her grip tightened was a neon sign.

When I looked up, Kyle was looking back into the house, unaware of what Jezebel had done.

"Why change your name?" I asked.

I supposed the question could go to both of the people with me, but I was directing it at my brother.

His attention snapped to me. "Kyle died."

"Okay. Why choose the name you did?"

"Study our father, Em. Learn about his power and control."

"Do you emulate him?" A man who would forcibly rape a woman in the company of others to prove his point and his power. Even though I didn't add the last part, I couldn't understand how Kyle was unable to connect the dots.

Kyle looked at Jezebel and back to me. "He made mistakes, but his mistake made us. I can't really be upset about that, now can I?"

"And you think that if you change your name to his, you'll suddenly have the power and influence he had?"

By the way Kyle shuffled his expensive shoes on the porch and the tendons in his neck pulled taut, I knew my questions were not welcomed.

"I'm taking his power and control," my brother said. "It is my birthright. You have the same blood, Em. When I rule, I won't forget that."

"When *you* rule? Why shouldn't that be us or me?" It wasn't a question I'd ever posed before, not even to myself.

Kyle's laugh disappeared out into the dark bayou. "You're funny, Em. You think you can ride into New Orleans, the people will slaughter the fatted calf, create hashtags, and like the magic they practice, you'll suddenly have control?"

"That's not what I said." And I was having difficulty connecting all of his metaphors.

His blue eyes narrowed. "What the fuck do you know about ruling New Orleans?"

"More than you think."

"Right," he said with a scoff. "This is bullshit. I've spent the last four years learning and infiltrating this city. I've been in every fucking parish, every ward." His volume rose. "I have a reputation. You've been here for a few weeks and want a spotlight. Your husband may think he's in control, but let me tell you, he's not. No wonder he's using you for attention. It won't work."

"Using me?"

Kyle went on, "There are people, a lot of people, loyal to our father who even seven years later aren't willing to stay in step with a Ramses."

"And when you take over," I asked, "those faithful to Ramses will bow at your feet."

"It'll take time, but it will happen. This city needs to come together."

I stood, taking the blanket with me. "Interesting."

Kyle shook his head. "Don't act like you understand."

Pursing my lips, I nodded. "The truth is getting clearer by the moment. I understand that you're missing the fucking point. Here's a hint, Kyle. I'm the point. And I'm standing right in front of you."

He shrugged. "So?" He paused, turned his attention to Jezebel and back to me. "Jeez, Em, you're talking in riddles like Mom and Edmée. This city doesn't need riddles. It needs a leader who will unite the city."

Unite the city.

A Boudreau and a Ramses.

I wasn't sure how many times Rett had given me a similar speech. Of course, his was delivered differently. And yet for me, this was the moment it all came together. It was as if the nighttime sky parted and rays of sunlight shone down. Maybe that was the metaphoric spotlight Kyle meant.

Kyle was wrong.

I hadn't sought that.

As I stared up at the darkness, I lifted my chin to the sky, feeling the invisible warmth shining from above.

No, I hadn't sought the spotlight for the uniting of the two families.

It found me.

Inhaling, I nodded, sat, and looked at Jezebel.

She lifted her chin to Kyle. "Your position is unchanged, Kyle. You know the risk of going out, especially now."

"I'll have Liam with me and we have soldiers stationed around. No one would dare get near us."

Someone would dare.

I knew that in my heart.

I knew that someone intimately, and currently, my only concern was for his safety. As far as for Kyle and Liam, my concern was waning by the minute.

As Kyle said goodnight to Jezebel, I wondered about subtle distinctions.

What is the difference between confidence and cockiness?

My husband radiated confidence.

I saw that quality the first night our gazes met across the bar. I was drawn to it. Others saw it, too. I recalled the way the sea of people parted when he walked through the crowd. Rett's position made him the king of New Orleans, and he wore that title proudly. He didn't need to say a word; his assuredness was on display like a royal mantle. His crown was invisible, but it was there, seen by all those who served him and those who didn't.

Kyle saw it, whether he wanted to or not.

Staring at my brother, I saw a boy trying to play a man's game.

It wasn't the difference in their ages. It was the differences in their maturity, experience, and understanding. Kyle said I didn't understand.

I believed I did.

It was he who didn't.

According to our mother, the prophecy was that she was carrying a child to rule New Orleans. The city had been co-ruled for generations. As crazy as Rett sounded when we first met, I now saw that he was right; he'd been right all along.

And so had the prophecy.

It was Kyle who was wrong.

Jezebel and I sat un-talking after Kyle went back inside the house. The resounding silence faded as the insects and toads resumed their chorus. It was as if Kyle's visit had prompted an intermission and the overture they sang meant it was time for the second act.

Two cars came from around the side of the house. Their tires rolling on the hard-packed earth and the hum of their engines momentarily replaced the natural melody. And then, like the glow of their red taillights, they were gone and the sounds of nature were back.

As the night noises created their own lullaby, my eyes grew heavy. The day had been long, and the more we sat, the less uncomfortable I was wrapped in the scratchy blanket.

I may have nodded off.

I saw images and scenes, disconnected, such as discarded clips of a movie. They came the way one sees things in dreams. As they progressed, I was less present, more a voyeur.

Rett's dark stare glistened in the candlelight as we dined and his deep voice relayed stories about his family. And then he faded away. However, I knew I was still in his home. It was their voices I heard first. We were in the sitting room with the large fireplace in Rett's home. Of the women present, I'd only met one—Miss Guidry. Yet I recognized the other two from their portraits, Delphine and Marilyn. Though the three ladies were conversing and I couldn't hear what they were saying, I felt their emotions of worry, concern, and maybe even fear. A smile came to my lips as they held each other's hands. The house faded away. The streets of New Orleans were filled with people, chants, and candles. Liam was there, watching. His emotions didn't fit the others. He was apart from them. His anger seemed palpable. The others were sad and worried. I wanted to ask what had happened.

Had someone died?

I woke with a start, unsure of the scenes that had slipped somewhere between my conscious and subconscious.

I also wasn't certain how much time had passed when Jezebel spoke.

"You hear them, don't you?"

I turned to her. "Hear who?"

"The spirits. They're unusually loud."

Was I hearing them?

Were they the ones who made things clearer?

"I don't know if I do," I answered honestly. "How can you tell if you're hearing them or maybe your own thoughts?"

"You listen." She closed her eyes and continued rocking.

The night sounds combined with the rocking of chairs filled the air.

Before I could reply, a shrill scream came from inside the house.

Jezebel and I both sprang from our chairs, leaving the blankets behind as we hurried inside.

RETT

*N*ighttime enveloped the neighborhood, settling over the darkened streets of Desire. My pulse thumped as it raced through my veins, not from nerves, but the unmet desire to bring Emma's kidnappers to justice and my wife home. The tips of my fingers tapped an undetectable rhythm on the armrest in the back seat of the SUV as Leon and I stared through the windows from our place in the shadows.

Twenty years ago, it would have been easier to remain less conspicuous or hidden in Desire. There was more here at that time—more people, more buildings, and more places to fade into. The population of this neighborhood had dropped exponentially over recent years.

Katrina was partially to blame.

It was too easy to blame all of New Orleans's woes on that one hurricane. As I'd told Emma, she—Katrina —had a bum rap.

While she'd been a category five out in the gulf, by

the time she made it close to us, she'd weakened down to a category three. Forecasters said New Orleans had dodged the bullet when she'd hit landfall forty-five miles away, keeping her powerful winds farther away.

But she was a deceiving bitch.

Her power wasn't in her winds.

New Orleans had handled 125-mph winds before and since.

No, her power came in the over ten inches of rain and over eleven feet of storm surge she brought.

A plan had been developed to rid the sea-level city of water, but the structures hadn't been maintained. The levee system failed. And even now, nearly two decades later, people speak about the devastation of Katrina when what they should talk about was the abject failure of those sworn to protect the city, its structures, and its people.

My city.

My people.

Emma's and my father both had tried, but evacuating a city that had never before received such an order was a feat in and of itself. Even I had to admit that using the Superdome was a good idea. Then again, it brought forces within the city to a level playing field —literally. That caused its own problems.

Now, as I peered out the windows, I saw lot after lot in Desire where houses once stood, now empty. While most of the damaged structures from 2005 had been removed, many hadn't been replaced. Instead, they left grass and mud as well as cracked-asphalt remains to fill the spaces.

The church Johnny had mentioned was a block away.

In this area, overgrown brush and abandoned buildings were more abundant than homes with full-time residents. Leon had our SUV parked behind an old gas station, hidden in the shadows of what was at one time a carwash.

From where we sat, we could see the back of the church.

At a little after midnight, the men started to arrive. One or two at a time, all on foot, they'd made their way along the rutted dark streets and slipped behind the loose piece of plywood. It was now a quarter to two and the head count within was seven, including Johnny. And from our vantage point, there was no sign of life.

I had a car with my men watching the other side.

No one had left.

This abandoned old church made for a well-hidden hideout.

Initially, I'd wanted to wire Johnny for sound.

The reason he wasn't fitted with a bug was because of the work that had been done to him—swollen eye, fat lips, and bruises on his body. I knew from good sources that Johnny's presence would be questioned. He'd obviously been caught by my men. There was too great of a chance that he'd be searched and wires would be discovered.

That didn't mean he wouldn't double-cross us.

He could.

My insurance policy—Johnny's wife and kid—was currently at a motel in the Fifteenth Ward with two guards watching their door. The research my men did today confirmed that Johnny's wife had been recently let go from a big-box store in the Lower Ninth. She'd missed too many days of work; supposedly, her absences coincided with their kid's doctor's appointments and days their kid missed school.

I didn't want to know any more.

That information was enough to confirm Johnny's story.

He was now in that church to get his money. It was his only job.

Johnny also knew if my plan went south, he and his wife wouldn't need to worry about medical appointments. I'd take the three of them out.

Johnny, Mrs. Johnny, and little Johnny.

Damn, my list of Johnnys was growing.

Then again, if he came through, things could look up for the Johnnys.

Leon spoke quietly, "Boss, no reason why Ingalls would need to pay his own bill. He could easily send someone."

Meaning Ingalls might not show.

"I've thought of that, but what are our other options. If Ingalls or Boudreau appear, I want them fucking tailed from every side."

That wasn't all that I wanted.

While I'd considered torching the church at the onset of their meeting, I decided against that for one reason: killing either Ingalls or Boudreau tonight wouldn't bring my wife back to me. It stood to reason that if Ingalls helped abduct Emma, he was in contact with who wanted her, who had her—most likely Boudreau and then there was the added possibility of the elusive Jezebel North.

A text message came through, and I hit the icon.

"Fuck."

Leon's dark gaze met mine in the rearview mirror.

I lifted the phone. "Boudreau's showing his face at some high-class establishments. And he has an interesting piece of arm candy."

Leon's head snapped sideways until our eyes met. "Not Mrs. Ramses?"

"Fuck no. Remember the name Emily Oberyn?"

His brow furrowed. "The ginger who was spotted with Underwood."

Leon wasn't asking.

"It now seems she's with Boudreau." I read the text. "Right now, they're at Restaurant R'evolution. I'm just fucking learning that earlier they were seen at Galatoire's 33."

"Making the rounds," Leon said as his head tilted to the side. "Seems like a ruse. They want your people watching them."

"My people are. My people are also here and around the entire fucking city."

"Word's getting around. Thought you should know."

My focus went back to Leon. "Word? What word?"

"Mrs. Ramses. The shit Ingalls started is getting out but not the way he thinks."

"Go on."

"People saw you and her at August. Some reporters

took her picture headed into the courthouse. They're slapping it all over social media."

"Fuck." That wasn't what I wanted. "That's why I've been getting calls from Michelson and a few detectives at NOPD. I'm not ready to have them nosing around."

"Probably how they know," Leon said with a nod. "But, boss, it ain't like you're thinking. They're rallying around her."

"Rallying? They? Who?"

"Talk is that Mrs. Ramses, she's married to you and is Ms. North's daughter. Hell, they have pictures of the two women up on Twitter. Jezebel's are from some time ago, 'cause she ain't been seen for a while." He shook his head with a smile as he stared down at his phone. Leon looked up. "There ain't no denying Mrs. Ramses looks like her momma."

"Wait?" I was trying to wrap my head around what he was saying. "You're saying Emma's picture is on social media?"

Fuck. This is why I wanted to keep her home. She didn't ask for this.

"Boss, the people, they're worried, even though she ain't been reported missing—"

"Because like I said, the last fucking thing I need," I interrupted, "is NOPD sticking their nose where they don't belong."

"You said Michelson called? You not trusting him now?"

Exhaling, I met Leon's gaze. "I did. Right now, I'm not trusting anyone outside my ranks."

"That's the thing, boss, the people, they care.

They're worried. I got word earlier tonight; there was a prayer vigil for Mrs. Ramses at St. Charles and another one at Franklin Baptist."

A prayer vigil?

"Why?"

"You know New Orleans. There's a saint or a spirit for every need."

"Emma isn't dead."

"Not saying that. They're worried she's missing. Hell, we ain't the only ones who saw the video from the cameras. Those cameras belong to the city. One person gets a copy and posts. The one of her being pushed into the Caddy has over a million views."

I wasn't sure how I felt about this.

It was good, right?

"Saint Anthony," Leon said.

"Excuse me."

"He's the saint of missing people, things too."

I shook my head. "Miss Guidry was going on earlier about the spirits. Saying my mother talked to Emma, and she's safe. Of course, my dead mother didn't relay Emma's location." I was growing tired of Miss Guidry's tales. "What the fuck good are spirits?"

"Boss, don't you see? You've been busy with Mrs. Ramses, Knolls, and Herbert, too. Your mind's been occupied. The spirits talk but that don't mean all people listen."

I had another thought. "Franklin Baptist, that church is in the Lower Ninth."

"Yes, boss, it is. And they are praying straight to the Lord. All over the city. Different denominations and different people. Like I said, they're rallying behind Mrs. Ramses."

Exhaling, I leaned back against the seat. "Well, fuck. The Lower Ninth is Boudreau turf."

"For seven years, that's been Ramses territory. They know something else. They know she's a Boudreau."

Leon was right. That ward had become Ramses territory, but we both knew there were still those people who had been true to Boudreau for generations and were slow on making the transition. Those were the areas Kyle, a.k.a. Isaiah, had worked the hardest. Pockets of old-timers with young bucks that don't want change.

I looked out the windows. We were parked in one such area.

"Earlier today," I said, "I had the idea to cleanse Desire, fucking torch it." I met Leon's gaze. "You're better at knowing what's happening on the street. What can I do to help Desire or the Lower Ninth? The gangs here listen, they don't like it, but they do. Except, fuck, the house that exploded yesterday had three kids. That shit can't go on."

"You ain't going to turn New Orleans into a park. Your daddy and Mrs. Ramses's daddy knew that. They knew what you know. It's about men on the ground. And you know who controls those men?"

"Me? Boudreau? Their local leaders?"

Leon scoffed. "You're getting closer. I ain't saying it is one hundred percent, but you know who was filling those churches this evening, walking the streets with candles, posting on social media, and saying prayers to gods and spirits in Mrs. Ramses's name?"

I couldn't help but smile. "It wasn't those men. If history means anything, it was the women."

"Ninety percent. Now, don't get me wrong. I ain't saying they're soft. Hell, there're tough women out there, ones who'd shoot you as easy as look at you. There's a salon or two that cleans more cash in this city every month than the gambling boats combined." He scoffed. "I've watched members of gangs get pulled inside their house by their ear. Ain't no one standing in the way of a momma.

"The women, they know how this city runs as well as their husbands or daddies. They also talk to their husbands and sons. No man worth his weight doesn't listen. He may not like listening, but if the women be like Tara" —he whistled— "they talk...a lot."

"And right now," I said, "you're telling me that the women of New Orleans in Ramses and Boudreau wards are worried about Emma?"

"That's what I'm saying."

A new thought came to me. "Leon, if she wasn't my wife, would I be threatened?"

"You ain't talking about you, are you?"

"We need to get to her. I've been saying Kyle wants her dead. If he hears about this, that piece of shit will take her out like I've been saying because she's his competition. I'm starting to hope that our theory is right and Jezebel is somewhere in this mix."

Leon nodded toward the front windshield. "Ingalls just arrived."

Two men got out of a black Cadillac.

"Looks like Boudreau and the ginger aren't here," Leon said. "Told you, they're a distraction."

"Are you fucking me?" I asked, seeing the car. "Ingalls is driving the same fucking car that took Emma."

"Then that means that car took her somewhere, left her, and now is back in the city."

"Get our men moving," I ordered. "Get his car wired and if Boudreau has a car parked near R'evolution, it better be wired too." We'll wait until this meeting is over and we're following Ingalls back to wherever he goes.

I wanted to watch him die after what he said, but tonight wouldn't be the night.

He needed to lead us to Emma first.

EMMA

*J*ezebel and I hurried into the house, the screen door slamming as we both came to a halt at the bottom of the staircase. Lying on the last steps and onto the wood floor was Edmée. I scanned her, searching for injuries. Her arms and legs appeared intact, bent at the correct angles. There was no blood or sign of trauma. She was simply splayed on the final steps.

"Do you think she fell?" I asked, my hands trembling from the scream and scene.

Jezebel shook her head. "We need to help her."

Together, we wrapped our arms under hers, not unlike the way Edmée and I had helped Jezebel upon my arrival. Her head wobbled on her neck as we lifted. Edmée couldn't weigh more than a hundred pounds, yet in her current unconscious state, she wasn't easy to maneuver.

"It's the spirits," Jezebel said. "Sometimes, they're too much. Tonight, they're louder than I've ever heard."

"So she fainted?" I asked, trying to make sense of...well...anything.

Jezebel nodded.

Finally, we were able to get Edmée to the sofa in the front sitting room, the same room where we'd found the blankets.

Jezebel crouched in front of her and laid her palms on each side of Edmée's face, framing the other woman's cheeks as she spoke. The language wasn't English, not what she and I had been using. It reminded me of the couple on the back porch. As I listened, I recognized the French influence, but the meanings of the words were lost on me.

Edmée's eyelids fluttered as she woke and concentrated on Jezebel.

There was a moment of silence between the two of them as if they spoke to one another without words. Maybe they were speaking or maybe it was the spirits talking to them. I took a step back, my arms around my midsection and watched. Tears filled Edmée's eyes as she nodded.

And then Jezebel released her friend's face and they both turned their focus my direction.

It was as if I were watching them from another realm, unable to understand what was happening between them. Yet they saw me, all of me. It wasn't the way Rett looked at me. No, Jezebel and Edmée were looking at me in a way I could feel more than see. I closed my eyes as if to hide, but that didn't help. When my eyes opened, they were both still focused on me.

Jezebel shook her head and lowered her chin.

In that second, she appeared defeated, and yet I couldn't imagine what had happened.

Finally, she inhaled and stood.

There was no question that Jezebel had a natural beauty about her, poise and stature. Isaiah Boudreau may have tried to defeat, demean, and humiliate her, but she'd overcome. With her chin high, she turned to me.

"I didn't fully respect the city." She smiled. "I thought I could keep you" —she swallowed as tears came to her eyes— "for at least a little while. They love you."

"What?" I shook my head. "Who is they?"

Edmée sat up, pulling herself higher. "Child, you have everyone talking, live and dead."

A chill settled over my arms as I rubbed my hands over each one. It was impossible to be in this house in the middle of the bayou and not be affected by the talk of those who had passed on before us.

Edmée spoke to Jezebel as her expression turned somber. "Do you hear what they're saying?"

Jezebel nodded, her expression also darkening.

"Miss Betsy, it's time."

My mother's mask of indifference shattered before me as tears leaked from her blue eyes. "I want more, Edmée. I deserve more."

"You did your part." Edmée stood and walked to Jezebel. "And, baby, you did it right."

Hearing Edmée call my mother baby was odd, and

yet the years showed on Edmée, in her wrinkled skin and white hair. Even her hands showed the signs that come with time. And while Jezebel had given birth to me and Kyle, she'd said that when she did, she was younger than I was now. Without a change in my birthdate, I was twenty-six on my last birthday.

Jezebel was probably near fifty.

Suddenly, she appeared younger and sad.

"Mother." The term I hadn't wanted to use less than twenty-four hours ago now came much easier.

Edmée continued to speak, holding Jezebel's hands. "We can't control time. Ain't nobody who can. Even the spirits. They teach us to respect it, to use it for good. You did that, Betsy."

Jezebel clung to Edmée's hands as her face fell forward and her shoulders quaked. "I made mistakes."

"You stop."

Jezebel looked up at Edmée.

"Miss Betsy, you are a proud woman; that isn't going to end. We all make mistakes. It's what happens when we try. If you don't try, if you did nothing, moved away and lived a different life, things would be different, but there'd still be mistakes."

Jezebel's nostrils flared as her lips tucked between her teeth. It was something I knew I did from time to time. Seeing the woman who bore me have the same mannerism gave me a sense of peace.

"I'm not ready," Jezebel said.

Edmée's head shook from side to side. "Ain't your call, baby. The spirits are woke. The city's bustling. You know what we have to do."

"Together, we believed."

Edmée nodded. "The city's spoke. If we don't move fast..." She shook her head. "I ain't heard this kind of warning since before your babies come into this world. The danger is real."

Jezebel turned to me. The whites of her eyes were littered with red lines. "I'm sorry, Emma. I'm so sorry."

My hands dropped to my side. "I don't know what's happening."

Jezebel turned to Edmée. "I don't know if I can go back. The spirits are loud here. In the city..."

"You going to send Emma out there alone?"

Jezebel shook her head. "No. Get Daniel." She inhaled. "I need messages sent."

Edmée nodded.

As Edmée walked back toward the kitchen, Jezebel sat on the edge of the sofa and sighed.

I couldn't stop the pull I had as I went closer, crouched, and laid my hand on her knee. "What is happening?"

She covered my hand. "I wanted so much."

"I don't understand."

"The prophecy told me that I carried within me a leader for New Orleans. It warned of destruction that would come and lives lost. It said to protect my offspring and help him understand."

"Him? You mean Kyle?"

"No, child. The spirits are blind to gender, unlike most of us. A leader isn't based on the chromosomes within their genetic makeup. I wanted to believe that the spirits were also blind to sibling rivalry. That both of my children would take their rightful place." She exhaled. "If I hadn't done what I did, that might have happened."

"What did you do?"

RETT

"They're fucking with us," I said after the trackers on Ingalls's and Boudreau's cars had taken my men on a wild goose chase. "They know we've tracked them."

"I thought," Leon said, watching the same screen I was watching, "they'd take us into the bayou. Ingalls's car crossed the river just like the Cadillac with Mrs. Ramses had earlier. It seemed like he was heading in, but now he's on I-12. And Boudreau, he went near where our boys dropped him and Ingalls off for their bayou adventure, but he passed all the roads too. Headed west on 10."

"Where is the warehouse our mole within Boudreau's organization talked about?"

"Northeast of Baton Rouge, near the train yard."

Leon and I were back in my inner office. We'd gotten what we wanted from the meeting in the Upper Ninth. The jury was still out on the Johnny family. That verdict wasn't as important as Emma. Even though the sun was about to rise, I wasn't tired. No, I was the opposite, ready to jump out of my skin if we came up with one more dead end.

My phone vibrated with a text message. Looking at the screen, I saw the message PRIVATE NUMBER.

"Fuck."

I hit the text. Words appeared as a circle in a whited-out picture spun.

"COME GET HER."

I gripped the phone tighter as the picture populated. "Fucking Christ," I mumbled.

"What is it, boss?"

The picture was of Emma. I knew every inch of what I saw. I also recognized where she was. This picture was taken over a month ago, before we'd rescued her. She was tied to the chair. Her face was covered with a black cloth bag, but every other inch was exposed.

I knew my wife.

While it should be reassuring that the picture wasn't recent, it wasn't. I killed the two sons of bitches with her. Either they snapped this picture and sent it to someone else or we missed someone else in our presence.

"Get the car, Leon. We're going to Baton Rouge. That's where Emma is. I feel it."

He stood and stretched his neck. "I'll go, boss. But something don't feel right to me."

"I can't sit here."

Images of Emma tied to the chair in the warehouse in the Eighth Ward came back as my fingers balled to fists. I looked at my watch. It was nearing four in the morning. "We're going."

Within minutes, we were out of the office, down in the underground garage, and driving on the streets of New Orleans. This was the time of day that the city rested.

New Orleans never truly slept, but this was later than the bars and patrons and earlier than the early risers. I watched with fascination as the two parts of New Orleans conducted their daily meeting.

As Leon drove us out of the city limits, my cell phone rang. My jaw clenched as I read the name: *Richard Michelson.*

I'd been avoiding his calls as well as others from the NOPD. Now, before daybreak with over an hour's drive to our destination, I finally hit the green icon. "Richard. I would assume you know my aversion to phone discussions."

"This is my private number, Everett. Fuck, answer a damn call."

A fucking drum line was keeping time in my temples. I closed my eyes. "Later, come by the house."

"I can come by now."

"It's the middle of the night. I'm asleep," I lied.

"You sound awake to me. And if you really care

about the woman you married, I'd put money on the fact you haven't slept a wink."

"The woman I married," I replied, "would be safe in our bed if she didn't go to answer your fucking questions. I heard from Sophie Lynch. You didn't stay on topic."

"What did she tell you?"

My nostrils flared as I exhaled. "Eleven o'clock in my front office."

"Everett, I saw the footage like everyone else. The city needs someone to come forward and make a statement. I've talked to Mr. Clark, but he said you were busy. The people of New Orleans are following this, but there hasn't even been a missing person report filed yet."

"We're working on this. If you don't think I am..." I took a breath, lowering my voice. Fuck, my nerves were stretched.

Of course the warehouse where she'd been held before had been searched. I had people checking out every shipping container at the docks as well as those at the train yard. As strange as it sounded, I was finding a bit of comfort in Miss Guidry's repeated statements of optimism. The woman was bat-shit crazy, but currently, I needed to hear her brand of crazy.

"Everett," Richard said, "the son of Isaiah Boudreau was making a splash at the high-end bars last night. Your people in NOPD were watching. He's getting out of hand. There are some officers here who want to bring him in and end the shit he's stirring up."

"Are you asking my permission?"

"No, I'm warning you. As loud and boisterous as Boudreau is, William Ingalls is your biggest threat."

I shook my head. "He has no claim to this city."

"You're right. He's working behind Boudreau's back, and I've seen this ploy before in other cities. Chicago went through something similar a few years back. They beat it, you need to too. This city is so entrenched in its history, Ingalls thinks he can wipe it all away and start fresh."

"Maybe you should warn Boudreau."

"I have."

It was like a fucking punch to the gut.

There were words I wanted to say, but I had to remember this was a cell phone and while my line was secure, I couldn't say the same about Richard's.

"Nice. I guess you've chosen your side."

"It's not like that, Everett."

"You said you believe that Emma is Jezebel's daughter. By process of elimination, that removes Kyle or Isaiah from contention."

"Fuck, I swore I'd never say this."

"What?" I asked.

"Things aren't as they appear. Ms. North, she did what she needed to do. Give it some thought, Everett. You'll know the answer and once you do, you'll realize how maybe the younger Isaiah isn't the enemy."

I shook my head. "What the fuck, Richard. He's after my city. He's claiming something that isn't his to claim. He's working to undercut my men. I'm not fucking blind and they're not stupid. He's not as powerful as he thinks."

"In a way you're right. You're also wrong. Watch Ingalls. He has one chance at a claim to this city."

"He has no fucking chance." I was ready to end this phone call. "Good night—"

"Your wife," Michelson interrupted. "He's the one who took her. And my gut says he wants everything that's yours, Everett. Everything. Listen, I'm laying my family and my career on the line because Abraham did the impossible. The scum who was after my daughter...if I'd have been the one to...I'd still be rotting in prison and you know what? To protect her, I'd do that. You know what happens to prosecutors in prison? You should know that's not something I want to think about. Abraham, he did my daughter even one better. I'm being as fucking honest as I can be."

"Tell me about your questioning of Emma."

I turned my attention out the windows as we headed west. The pink morning sunrise was in our rearview mirror as we got closer to Baton Rouge.

"It was taped. I'm walking a fucking thin line here."

"When did you learn who was named as Underwood's beneficiary?" I asked. I'd just learned last evening from Clark and Lynch.

"I couldn't tell you. Mrs. Ramses's reaction had to be genuine."

I'd give Richard Michelson a genuine reaction as soon as I had my wife back.

"Tell me something," I said. "Since we spoke, I've been looking into this electronic currency. The deposits to Underwood's Kraken account seem to be attached to a number sequence that could point to Jezebel North as you suggested weeks ago."

"That's what our investigator here at NOPD figured."

"Did she also explain the beneficiary process?"

"What do you mean?" he asked.

"The information you blindsided Emma with yesterday isn't completely as it seems. You see, in the case of this particular transaction, the sender of the currency stipulates the recipient and the secondary recipient, or as you called her, the beneficiary. My people have determined that it wasn't Underwood who put Emma's name on those transactions. It was the sender."

"Jezebel?" Richard asked.

"That is the untraceable part."

"Fuck." Richard took a deep breath. "I'll be at your front office at eleven."

I didn't wait to say goodbye. Instead, I hit the red icon and tossed my phone onto the seat. Leon's dark stare in the rearview mirror said what my inner voice was saying. I'd given Michelson more than I should have. I let him know I had people investigating.

The morning sky continued to lighten as we came closer to the eastern edge of Baton Rouge. There were three other cars of men on their way. I wasn't walking into a trap by myself. I'd gone in alone last time, and my gut told me that if either Boudreau or Ingalls were responsible for Emma's abduction, they were counting on me to enter alone again.

I checked my phone. A program that my men had

set up allowed me to see all my cars as dots on a map. Some had come this way before I decided to join the party. Others were called and were a little bit behind us. Given the time of day or should I say night, we made what was usually an hour-and-twenty-minute drive in record time.

As I stared down at the other dots, I wished one of them was Noah Herbert and that Ian Knolls was back at the mansion watching over Emma.

This wasn't the time for wishes. It was time to get my wife and if in the process, we settled this ridiculous attempt at a coup, so be it.

RETT

*S*itting straighter in the back seat, I realized where we were, not simply east of Baton Rouge but the exact location. Time had made its mark. Nothing was exactly the same as it had been, but that didn't change the fact we were here. I was here again. "This isn't the fucking warehouse," I said as the lightening sky brought the buildings into view.

"Yes, it is," Leon answered. "I told you, it don't feel right."

"I had the damn place leveled."

"Building's different. Place is the same."

"Fuck." I should have bought the land and made sure it wasn't rebuilt.

The realization of where we were was as if a dam had broken. Memories I had kept at bay gushed into my thoughts.

Over seven years ago, I'd accompanied my father to this same location. Being outside of New Orleans city limits was agreed upon by both my father and Isaiah

Boudreau. My father hadn't been the one to call the meeting, but he knew once it was called, he needed to attend. The factions of discontent in the different wards were growing. The issue at hand had been a supplier of Molly to the city. Molly was the street name for ecstasy. People came to New Orleans to have a good time. Ecstasy was a popular drug especially with the younger tourists who were willing to pay more than necessary for it. The main supply had been arriving via cargo ship to our busy ports on a regular basis. Unfortunately, the drug lord who was our biggest supplier had been arrested on a litany of rigged charges while in the US.

No one dared interrupt that chain while Félix was in control, but with his arrest, there were upheavals in his ranks. Those events opened a window for new suppliers. A few of the bigger gangs saw that as an opportunity to avoid the middleman and work directly with the new suppliers, leaving my father and Boudreau out of the mix.

Out of the mix meant out of the money.

A few of the smaller gangs in the Tenth and Eleventh Wards decided they wanted in on the rebellion, so they organized under an umbrella of sorts, calling themselves the 110ers gang. The whole way of independent thinkers was getting out of hand. Ramseses and Boudreaux ruled for a reason. They kept each individual subset in check. The recently established 110ers had to be an example to other gangs on why our families were essential within the chain of command.

Abraham and Isaiah chose to not extend their protective cloak to the 110ers. They wanted independence, they got it. That joint decision opened the 110ers to more than they expected.

In reality, Abraham and Isaiah's decision killed two birds.

It gave the city a perceived win on their fight on crime, the mayor's NOLA FOR LIFE project, and it cut the 110ers off at the pass, reinforcing to others why it was important to keep the status quo with our families.

With our protection gone, the multi-agency gang unit from the Orleans Parish district attorney's office received a sweeping fifty-one count racketeering indictment against fifteen members of the 110ers. The indictment wasn't limited to their drug activity. It also connected members to over ten murders that they may or may not have been responsible for and money-laundering charges.

Rumors began to fly.

While the other gang leaders fell in line, there were rumblings and questions.

Some of the non-indicted members of the 110ers went back to their smaller gangs where there were questions about money. Many assumed it was the multi-agency taskforce that confiscated the cash; the staggering amounts rumored to have been under their control were never listed on any reports. Accusations and fighting ensued between the surviving members, pitting small gangs against one another.

I hadn't had a hand in the disappearance of funds, yet I'd been involved in starting the rumblings. Never had I expected for things to happen as rapidly as they did, but when Boudreau called the meeting here, I knew it was my time to act. The city was ripe and ready for a coup. The people were riled up and itching for something new.

I was that something new.

The last time I was on the property where our SUV was now parked, I walked away as the new king of New Orleans. Taking a deep breath, I fought the sense of déjà vu.

"Ingalls and Boudreau are already here," I said. The evidence was the trackers.

"This feels like a trap," Leon said.

"I can't walk away if Emma is in there."

"Wait for the rest of our men." Leon looked at his phone. "Ten minutes and we'll outnumber them."

"Unless they have more men on the inside," I said.

Leon was right. This was not how I normally did business.

Since I'd found Emma, nothing was normal.

Leon and I with two others of my men entered from the rear near the loading docks. There were four other Ramses men entering from the front. The door moved silently as if it were well maintained, yet I'd learned during research while in the parking lot that the warehouse had been rebuilt only three years ago and had remained without a tenant.

The area we entered would serve as storage for shipping if it were in use. Thankfully, the sun had risen. Windows near the ceiling allowed the early morning light to enter. Rays of sunshine shone down, creating pillars of light containing particles of dust floating through the air.

Our shoes on the concrete floor echoed in the nearly seven hundred thousand square feet of emptiness. There wasn't a corner that was hidden as we scanned the perimeter.

"Are we sure they're here?"

"No, boss, just their cars."

I took a deep breath.

The meeting that occurred with my father and Boudreau hadn't happened in the large storage facility but in the attached offices. I tilted my chin toward doors on the far side. My men who entered through the front should already be in the offices.

As we continued with our guns drawn, the sound of gunfire reverberated through the large building. Leon, my men, and I rushed to the edge of the room and continued along the wall. Loud voices came from within the office structure.

Leon's hand was on the doorknob when another shot was fired.

Pushing our way through, we all stopped.

On the floor, lying in a puddle of blood, was William Ingalls.

My breath caught at what I could see in the attached room.

Isaiah II had his gun aimed. Not at me but at the back of my wife who was sitting in a chair. Facing the other direction, her long golden hair cascaded over her shoulders. Her head was tilted to the side as if she were unconscious. And her hands were tied behind her.

"No," I screamed, my gun aimed at Isaiah as I entered the office.

He didn't turn or even acknowledge that I was there.

"Drop your weapon," a deep voice ordered from the shadows to my right. When I hesitated, the barrel of the gun came closer.

I didn't recognize the man giving the order.

"Don't hurt her," I said as I lowered my gun to the floor.

Out of the corner of my eye, I saw my men who had entered the front. They were close enough to see, but they hadn't been discovered.

Isaiah spun my direction. "You did this."

"Fuck you."

"You set her up, seeing if I'd save her." He pointed at Ingalls's body. "Him too. We both got your texts."

"I didn't fucking send you a text message. I received one."

Isaiah's brow furrowed beneath a crown of hair the same color as Emma's.

Slowly, I took a step toward Emma. "What did you do to her?"

He shook his head. "This is how we found her."

"Let her go," I said, lifting my hands. The words came out before I could give them too much deliberation. They didn't make sense, went against every sin I'd committed, but I said them anyway. "The city is yours. Let Emma go back to her life. Forget this happened."

"The city isn't mine until you're dead." He lifted his gun again, this time toward me.

"I know."

Isaiah's head was shaking. "Emma won't go. She wants New Orleans now too, and it's your fault. We should have left her out of this."

I moved close enough to touch her hair. I imagined the way her hair created a curtain around us as she rode me, the way her perfect breasts heaved with heavy breaths, and the way she looked as she came apart. Emma was the best damn thing that I'd ever found and I didn't want to lose her.

From my position, I saw her blouse and blue jeans. I was relieved to know she wasn't naked as she'd been the last time she was found.

My hands were still raised. "Let my men take her. She'll be safe with them."

Leon nodded. The older man's gun was still aimed at him.

"Let them take her and once she's out of here, it's you and I. We settle this once and for all. I'll even send my men away. You can do the same, or you can fucking outnumber me."

"Like you did at your house on your wedding day," Isaiah said.

I ran my fingers through Emma's hair before looking up. "Yes." I nodded to Leon. "Come take her."

"Stop," Isaiah yelled. "I don't trust you."

"Let her go," I repeated. "She doesn't deserve to be hurt anymore."

"By you. You're the one who did this."

I nodded. "You're right. I wanted her in New Orleans."

"Not because you love her."

"I didn't when I had her brought here. I lured her here. I admit it. But now" —I turned back to Emma— "I love her."

Isaiah aimed his gun.

The next few seconds happened too quickly to think.

He spoke, "She can't live either and if you really love her, then you can watch her die."

I rushed toward Isaiah.

His gun fired.

The room echoed with the deafening explosions as other guns fired.

Isaiah was down, wounded but alive.

Kicking his gun away, I ran toward Emma as blood began to pool near her chair.

My men had entered. Leon now had a gun on the old man. If others of Isaiah's people were present, I wasn't sure where. I didn't care as I rushed to my wife.

"I'm sorry, Emma." I sent prayers to the God my mother loved, to her, and even to Miss Guidry's spirits. There was no reason for any of them to listen to me. I was the self-proclaimed devil, and yet I begged them all for another chance to show Emma that I did love her. That in itself was a miracle. I asked for one more.

Please let her be alive.

Kneeling, I rushed to untie her hands.

Her wedding rings were gone.

The realizations probably happened in less than a

second, consecutive thoughts that reached an unbelievable conclusion. Such as watching a string of numbers being assembled on a computer screen as digit after digit made sense, that was my process.

I walked around to the front of my wife.

"Leon," I screamed.

He hurried to my side, reached down, and held the unconscious body, his hands covering with her blood.

With her head on his shoulder, he looked up at me. His dark eyes opened wide as he stared at me. "Where's Mrs. Ramses?"

EMMA

The shop, somewhere in the middle of the French Quarter, boasted futures told and palms read. The front of the store had shelves lined with jars filled with all sorts of things. There were candles and incense, oils, and books. There was a room with a crystal ball and another with sofas and soft chairs. Edmée and I had been dropped off at the back door and were currently in what was simply a break room with a microwave, coffee pot, refrigerator, and table. Compared to the rest of the shop, it was benign.

I poured myself another cup of coffee as I looked up at the clock. "Edmée, I have to get to Rett."

"Child, be patient."

"For what? I don't understand any of this."

"The spirits aren't wrong, they never are. You're in danger." She took a deep breath and smiled. Her gaze narrowed. "They are working and the battle is almost over."

"Where did my mother go?"

Edmée shook her head as her smile faded. "When you were inside of Miss Betsy—that's the name her momma gave her. She never much cared for it. Said people always thought it was short for Elizabeth, but it wasn't. Her given name was Betsy. Your grandmother didn't believe in the fanfare of a longer name. Your momma thought Betsy was too plain."

"Why would she choose Jezebel?"

"First, you should understand that before you were born, the battle began. You have been protected because you were meant to be here, Emma." She smiled. "It's so good to be with you."

I reached across the table and Edmée squeezed my hand. "Did you really deliver me?"

"I sure did. You and Kyle. He was stubborn and you, oh, child, you were loud and demanding."

I wrapped my fingers around the warm mug. "I never knew about any of this."

"You weren't supposed to, not until the time was right."

"Why would my mother choose the name of someone like Jezebel?"

"'Cause Jezebel was a strong, misunderstood woman of the Bible."

"A prostitute."

Edmée shook her head. "You know that isn't said; it's assumed."

Lifting my coffee mug to my lips, I tried to remember the story I'd learned in Sunday school, something the O'Briens insisted upon up until Kyle and

I were too old for the classes our church taught. "She was a harlot and a sorceress, as I recall."

Edmée smiled and leaned back in the chair across the table.

The sun had risen outside on St. Peter Street, yet no one else had entered the shop. We were alone as we'd been since Jezebel and Daniel dropped us here.

"Your mother is very much like the Jezebel you're referencing, child. The part you don't realize is that like your mother, the Jezebel in First and Second Kings was terribly misrepresented. Have you noticed that the writers of the Deuteronomy through 2 Kings failed to give any information from Jezebel's point of view? She was a priestess, the daughter of a king, sent to Israel to marry King Ahab. Did she want to go? Was she happy? Did anyone care? We're never told those things. Instead, the writers concentrate on her lack of acceptance of Baal or Yahweh and the monotheistic beliefs of her husband's people. She was villainized as a foreigner and made into the embodiment of everything that should be eliminated from Israel."

"Didn't she have worshippers killed for praying to Yahweh?"

Edmée nodded. "She did. That incited the battle on Mount Carmel to determine the greater supreme deity."

"Elijah won."

"Good for you. However, it wasn't a fair battle. First, Jezebel wasn't allowed to attend. You see, she was a woman. The meeting occurred on Mount Carmel to vilify and degrade Jezebel, and when Elijah won, do you recall what he did?"

I shook my head.

"He had the four hundred prophets of Asherah, Jezebel's men, murdered." She bowed her head and looked back up at me. "And the writers of the Scriptures don't criticize him as they did Jezebel because it was all right for him to commit mass murder but not all right for a woman."

My thoughts went back to Jezebel's question of whether I knew what Rett did to maintain power. The same principles from centuries ago seemed to apply today. "I'm not trying to argue, but if Mother wanted a name, it seems like she chose one that was a target."

"She chose to make a statement of strength. She chose a name that has been misunderstood, like her. You see, Jezebel, unlike most women named in the Old Testament, showed her resilience by maintaining her beliefs. There's no record of her being unfaithful to her husband. She encouraged him. They called her a sorceress simply because she worshipped differently. It wasn't until King Ahab and their eldest son were both dead that the defamation occurred. There was a battle for Israel. Jezebel's second son was the reigning king. One day he met his opponent on the battlefield and called out, 'Is all well?' The response from his aggressor was the source of all ill connotations related to Jezebel."

"What did he say?"

"He replied, 'How can all be well as long as your mother, Jezebel, carries on her countless harlotries and sorceries?' There is absolutely nothing to substantiate his declaration, just the word of a man, the one who then killed Jezebel's son. She isn't mentioned again until her death scene. Even there she demonstrates her strength by preparing for death. Some interpret her preparation as a form of seduction. When in reality, the cosmetics she applied could be closer equated to her donning a female version of armor, preparing for battle as only a woman can. When her son's murderer approaches, she speaks to him and taunts him. Again, demonstrating that she actually had a voice. Jezebel was a strong woman in the time of men. It was easy to blame her for all the wrongs of the world. Do you see the similarities?"

"I do. I also heard," I said, "that my mother changed her name before...Kyle and I were conceived. So she didn't do it to spite Isaiah."

"You're right. She didn't. He doesn't deserve credit. It was all her. Your momma chose her name to demonstrate her voice and strength to the world." Edmée sighed. "She was already calling herself Jezebel when the spirits directed me to her." She lifted her coffee mug, wrapping her fingers around it. "I too questioned the spirits, why they would choose a woman with that name and the reputation your father gave her."

"What did the spirits tell you?"

A smile came to Edmée's lips. "They didn't. The spirits don't need to explain themselves, and listening to them doesn't eliminate other deities. Spirits don't replace a supreme being; they often work in unison, much like the saints who some people worship. The spirits are often souls who either can't or won't cross over."

"Why wouldn't they?"

"Their work isn't complete."

"Miss Guidry speaks of Miss Marilyn all the time as if she's with her. She never mentions Rett's father."

"It sounds like Mr. Abraham didn't stay. He crossed over. His work was done."

My head tilted to the side. "People in New Orleans were really saying prayers for my safety?"

Edmée nodded.

"Why do they care?"

"Because you are the prophecy." She grinned. "But I'm not telling you anything you don't know."

Setting my coffee mug on the table, I looked down at the caramel-colored liquid. "They told me, I think." When I looked up, Edmée's smile had grown as a mixture of love and pride radiated from her dark eyes. "The spirits, I mean."

"Keep listening, child."

"Rett told me too."

She took a deep breath. "Over seven years ago, your mother took an opportunity to help the spirits." Her smile disappeared. "Afterward, she knew she'd overstepped. She'd fast forwarded the spirits' schedule because she wanted you and Kyle in her life. It was the mistake she mentioned. Today, she's doing what she can to right that wrong."

"What did she do?"

"Miss Jezebel can be very convincing."

It was the first time I'd heard Edmée call her by that name.

She continued, "Your mother had many friends and a thriving business."

I nodded. "I heard about that."

"I'm sure you have. The thing is that while her business sold sex, they collected more than money. They collected secrets. You can't blame her bitterness regarding Mr. Boudreau."

I shook my head.

"When she realized the precariousness of the state of affairs in New Orleans, she set up what she thought would be his downfall. It was meant to ruin him."

I thought for a moment. "Seven years ago? That's when Rett took over New Orleans."

"Yes, child. The city was supposed to all go to his father." She shrugged. "Maybe Abraham's work was done and he was ready for his son to reign. No matter, your husband's triumph was a surprise to many of us. Today, your momma is doing what she can do to give the control back to the spirits, allow them to choose."

"Choose what?"

"New Orleans's leader."

"I don't understand. You said I'm the fulfillment of the prophecy. I should rule with Rett."

Edmée took a deep breath. "I pray that we're right with the spirits. We'll know soon. I feel it."

As she spoke, the back door to the shop opened.

EMMA

*J*n the time it took for the door to open, the world stopped spinning. Standing with the sunlight streaming around him was Leon. He stepped closer, his shoulders stooped forward and his expression blank. Blood colored his shirt and suit coat in patches of crimson.

My stomach sank as I held my breath, waiting for the world to spin, for time to pass and give me the answers that were hidden. My trembling began nearing full-blown convulsions as I fought to stand. "Rett?" I finally managed the one name.

Leon turned to the side, looking outside of the shop. When he stepped back, the world again spun. The Earth's axis was righted as the dark stare I'd seen in my dream was once again upon me.

Our bodies crashed together somewhere between the table and the door as Rett's arms surrounded me, pulling me against him. His lips unapologetically found mine and everything and everyone around us melted away.

With my cheeks sandwiched between his palms, Rett's brown orbs stared into mine. "I was so fucking scared, Emma. I thought I lost you."

I took a step back, realizing that Leon wasn't the only one with blood on his clothes. "What happened? Are you hurt?"

"It's over."

Leon had stepped inside, closing the door behind him.

"Mr. Ramses," Edmée said, "please tell me about Ms. North."

Rett turned to Leon.

Leon's solemn expression morphed into a smile. "You must be Edmée."

"Yes, sir, I am." She stood, her frail shoulders straightening. "Now I asked a question."

I placed my hand on Rett's chest, feeling the beat of his heart and relishing the knowledge that he was safe. "Was my mother there?"

Rett nodded as he took both my hands in his. "She was. Kyle and William Ingalls too."

"But you're safe. You won?"

He tilted his forehead until it rested on mine. "I succeeded. I don't know if winning is the right word. I maintained what was mine."

"The city."

He shook his head. "Something fucking more important than that."

"What?"

"You, Emma."

"Where is Jezebel?" Edmée said louder than before.

Leon lifted his hand. "Ms. North is probably in her home. Come with me. She asked that you be brought to her."

Edmée bent forward as she stumbled backward. One hand went to the table to steady her while the other went into the air. "Praise be." Her gaze narrowed. "Why didn't she and Daniel come to get me?"

Leon pointed to his shirt. "She sustained an injury."

Edmée gasped as she fell backward into the chair.

"It's not life threatening," Leon said. "The bullet grazed her arm. There was a lot of blood, but as far as healing...'cording to her, she's almost there. The spirits protected her."

Edmée nodded. "They do. I pray for that every day." She turned to Rett. "Bullet, whose bullet?"

"Mr. Boudreau's," Leon said.

My volume rose. "Kyle?"

"He shot his mother?" Edmée asked.

"It's a long story," Leon said. "Come with me. I'll take you to her."

"Ms. Jezebel told you where she lives?" she asked as she stood.

"She told us quite a bit," Rett said, holding tightly to my hand. He gave it a tug, turning me to him. "She loves you very much."

As Edmée and Leon walked beyond the door, I thought about what Rett said. My eyes filled with tears and my chest tightened. "I barely know her." The dam broke as the tears cascaded down my cheeks. "I love her too. I can't explain it, what she's like, but she's calm. She was in the back seat of the car when they took me. I was never scared with her. I felt..." I searched for the right word. "...home."

"Your home is New Orleans, Emma. But it's not in the middle of the bayou. Your home is with me."

One thought led to another. "Liam said Kyle would take your house and he—Liam—wanted something else."

"I know what he wanted—who he wanted." Rett stood taller, his shoulders squaring. "There's no easy way to say this. William Ingalls is dead."

"You killed him." I didn't ask. I guess I was looking for confirmation.

"No. I wanted to. I would have and when I did, it wouldn't have been as quick."

"If not you, who?"

"The layers of deceit were becoming clearer, but the gist of the story is that there were two coups underway. There was Isaiah's quest to overthrow me, and Ingalls's plan to come out on top over both of us. This time when two people walked into that warehouse presuming to be working together, the one ready to betray his partner was the one killed. The clues were coming in, but it came to a head...this" —he looked at his watch— "morning."

"And Kyle figured it out?"

Rett nodded. "It appears so but not until after your mother did."

My head shook. "This is all so much." I ran the palms of my hands over Rett's sleeves, relishing the feeling of his muscular build beneath. The night without sleep was catching up to me. "You're safe. My mother is safe?"

"Yes. Like Leon said, the bullet grazed her arm. She'll be fine."

"William is dead."

Rett nodded. "He planned to take control of New Orleans. From what Jezebel and we were able to piece together, his plan was to do it with you. Then he realized you were taken." Rett smiled.

"I am. I'm taken. Very taken."

"His plan then changed to do it alone."

"Kyle killed him? But wait, you said he shot Mother —Jezebel too?"

"He thought she was you."

"Me?" I shook my head. "Is he...?"

"He's currently alive."

"Currently?"

"I'll explain, but first..." Rett's finger curled under my chin as he wiped the tears from my cheek with his thumb. "I know we've been through an ordeal, but we've been asked to make a public statement."

"A public statement?"

"To tell the world that you're safe and above all that you're mine." He smiled. "From what I've heard, New Orleans is anxious to see and hear from their queen."

I let my forehead fall to his chest and sighed. "I don't know."

Rett lifted my chin. "While I'm not always up to taking advice from Richard Michelson and the

NOPD...regarding this statement, I believe they're right."

My eyes opened wide. "Michelson arranged our adoptions. He changed the dates of Kyle's and my birth. He helped Mother hide us."

Rett's brow wrinkled as his eyes opened wider. "So he's known all along that both you and Kyle were Isaiah's children."

"He has."

Rett looked again at his watch. "We should go home and clean up. The news crew will be at our house in two hours."

I turned to the clock on the wall, the one that had been moving painstakingly slow. It was nearly nine and we were still the only two in the shop. "I don't know who owns this shop."

"Your mother."

"She does?"

"Since before I took over New Orleans, she'd become more of a myth than reality. Come to find out, she's been a vital part of the city." He smiled. "From what little she shared, she has a knack for understanding business. It seems that she's behind a slew of well-known establishments."

It was her dream.

My tears were back. "Is that true?"

"I'm having some of my people try to verify what she told me, but I've already learned that Betsy North began her entrepreneurial journey by utilizing shell companies. Leon had told me that she had a way of learning people's secrets. Apparently, at first, she used capital to invest in struggling businesses. Some of those businesses she rescued and retained part ownership. Others, she took over."

"She did it," I said.

Rett took my hand. "Let's go home, Mrs. Ramses. Your public awaits."

"Leon left. How are we getting home?"

"There's a car waiting."

As we left the shop, Rett entered a code into the security system. After a few beeps, the door locked.

"Jezebel?" I asked.

My husband nodded and opened the door to the back seat of another black SUV. I wondered how many he had in the underground garage. It wasn't until we had made it to that garage and climbed the concrete steps, hand in hand, that I realized the magnitude of a word: home.

As the door opened to the back entry and I stepped onto the marble floors, I heard them. Instead of heading straight upstairs, I dropped Rett's hand and made my way to the front sitting room, the one with the large fireplace.

He was a step behind me, stopping when I stopped.

I couldn't testify under oath that the images in my mind were real. Perhaps I was delusional or dreaming or maybe I'd been manipulated, not by Rett but by Jezebel. Either way, as tears filled my eyes, I longed to touch them, to hug them.

I nodded. "I promise," I whispered.

There was more that I wanted to tell them. I

wanted to say that I would keep the promise Miss Guidry had asked for on the night of our wedding.

I would do what I could to keep their son and grandson safe.

As Miss Marilyn smiled at me from her portrait over the fireplace and Miss Delphine smiled from her smaller picture in a frame on top of the mantel, I felt their relief, their gratitude, and their love.

"Talk to me," Rett said as his arms circled my waist and he tugged my back to his chest. His chin landed on top of my head. "What's happening behind those beautiful eyes?"

My body quaked as tears washed away the smiling faces, no longer contained to the portrait or the frame but of the two women standing before the fireplace, holding hands, and smiling at us.

Rett spun me around. "Hey, hey, it's okay. We're home and safe."

Spinning toward him, my arms went around his neck as I stared into the black holes of his gaze. Similar to the real place in space, I was drawn to him in a way I couldn't fight, not even if I wanted to. I wiped my tears on my sleeve and smiled. "I want to tell you something."

"Before the statement?"

"Yes. I don't want another minute to pass without you knowing."

"I'm intrigued, Mrs. Ramses."

"I meant what I said when you first spoke about marriage. I would agree to your stipulations as long as you agreed to mine." I swallowed. "My stipulation is gone, Rett. I don't know the moment when it happened, but it happened. Jezebel asked me and there was no hesitation on my part. I love you. My heart is yours."

Pushing up on my tiptoes, my lips met his.

Before he could speak, I added, "I don't need to hear you say it. I don't want to hear it unless it's true. And like the one requirement of me to be ready for you anytime, you said you weren't capable of love." I nodded as I inhaled. "And I'm all right with that. Because, Rett Ramses, I love you enough for both of us."

There was something in his smile. A gleam as he stared down at me.

"What?"

"You told Jezebel?"

"Yes, she asked."

"I told Jezebel too."

I took a step back. "What did you tell her?"

"Well, you see, I thought she was you."

"I don't understand."

"Give me time, Emma. I'll explain it all." He reached for my hand. "Let's get ready for the statement so the reporters will come and go."

The Ramses family crest glowed from the morning sun as we climbed the front steps. I turned to the man holding my hand. "What did you tell Jezebel?"

"The same thing you did."

RETT

*A*s Emma was adding finishing touches to her makeup, I leaned down and kissed her neck. Her stunning blue stare met mine in the lighted mirror. "I'm headed downstairs," I said. "The people from the local station have arrived and there seem to be uninvited guests outside."

"Uninvited?"

"National syndicates."

"Oh," she sighed, "this is...so much."

Dressed in a fresh suit, pressed shirt, and tie, I crouched near the makeup chair and spun my wife toward me. We said that we were conserving water when we chose to shower together, but that wasn't my motivation. I couldn't bear to let her out of my sight even for a short time. I ran my hand up her smooth calf and over her knee before my gaze met hers. "It's taking every ounce of self-control not to untie that robe and show you again how much I missed you."

Emma's eyes sparkled as she smiled. "I liked the way you showed me in the shower."

"That's good to know. We'll do that again."

"I hope so."

I gave her sash a quick tug.

Emma shook her head as her robe fell open just enough to see perfect half globes of each breast. I slowly ran my finger between them. Scanning down, I let my finger drag over her flat stomach and down further, stopping right before her warm pussy.

Unable to look away, I gently pressed on the inside of her knees, getting an even better view of what was mine.

"Rett, you were the one who said you needed to go downstairs."

I looked back up. "We could cancel. Send Miss Guidry to give our statement."

Her laugh echoed off the glass and tile. "Can you imagine the headlines?"

"You're right." I leaned down and delivered soft kisses to the inside of each thigh.

"Oh."

"Are you wet, Emma?"

"Only whenever you're around."

"So you're ready for me?"

She reached for my left hand and twisted the ring. When her gaze met mine, she smiled. "Yes, Rett, I'm ready for you anytime, anyplace. Are you ready for me?"

I winked. "I'll do my best to keep up." Standing, I left one last kiss on the top of her head.

As I was walking out of the bathroom, she called my

name. I turned back, again looking at her beautiful reflection within the mirror. Her similarities to Jezebel were truly remarkable. Everything Leon had warned me about was manifested in the woman I loved. I was hopelessly bewitched by my wife, and I no longer had any urge to fight it. "What?"

"What do I say...to the reporter?"

"We agreed to leave your mother out of the news."

Emma nodded. "And Kyle?"

"He was behind what appeared to be an abduction. He wanted to hide the truth, and the truth is that you're the daughter of Isaiah Boudreau. Don't let them question that information. Don't answer about him. There's no need to lie. Simply state the fact: you are the daughter of Jezebel North and Isaiah Boudreau. If anyone pushes for more, I'll interrupt and tell them we have proof."

"Okay. What about Liam?"

I refused to give him the space in my thoughts after what he'd told Johnny. "I see no reason to ever mention his name again, do you?"

Emma's head shook. "No, I really don't." She took a deep breath. "I'll be down in a few minutes."

"Hurry," I said, "The sooner we speak, the sooner they leave us."

Exiting her suite, I stepped into the hallway and closed the door.

"Sir."

I spun toward the voice. "You are supposed to be resting."

"I hoped I could see Mrs. Ramses before her interview."

I nodded and opened the door again. "Emma, can you come here a minute?" I took a step inside to be certain she'd secured her robe before allowing Ian to enter.

As she stepped into the bedroom, the sash was again tied. I was awed at her simple ability to take my breath away. Even wearing a robe, she was every bit the queen she was born to be.

"What?"

I took a step to the side and allowed Ian to enter.

Emma's shriek was probably heard all the way downstairs.

"Ian." She ran toward him, stopping just short. "I was so afraid. I asked but no one would tell me." She scanned him up and down. "Are you...? Can I hug you?"

"If Mr. Ramses doesn't mind, I'd like that."

She gently wrapped her arms around his torso and squeezed before stepping back. "Tell me what happened."

I answered, "Ian was shot as was Noah."

Emma's hand went to her bright red lips. "Noah?"

Ian grinned. "Mr. Ramses is a stickler about certain things. One is not leaving the house without wearing Kevlar."

"Kevlar?" Her eyes opened wide. "Oh, thank God, you were wearing a bulletproof vest."

"I'm sore, but don't you worry, I'll be as good as new. I wanted you to know if I could have, I would have gone after you."

She shook her head. "I was safe but worried." Her eyes came to me and back to Ian. "I was concerned about all the people I care about."

"We're all happy you're home."

"Thank you, Ian. Are you going to get to do real work for my husband now or is he keeping you on babysitting duty?"

Ian's lips curled. "He offered me the most important job in his realm."

"Oh." She straightened her neck. "Well, that's great. I'll miss you, but you deserve that."

He nodded. "I took it, for now anyway."

"May I ask what it entails?" She looked at me and back to him. "Or is it some kind of Ramses secret?"

"I believe the secret is out, Mrs. Ram—Miss Emma," he grinned. "You see, the position was very covert at first, but in a few minutes, my special assignment will be speaking to the press."

My wife's expression softened. "You want to stay with me? Aren't there more important jobs?"

Ian shook his head. "No one is more important to Mr. Ramses. Not only him, ma'am, you're important to New Orleans."

Pink climbed from Emma's neck to her cheeks. If Ian weren't here, I'd be willing to see if her blush went lower to her...

Ian spoke, "Besides, who else will know what shoes you should wear with what dress?"

Emma reached for his hand. "Let me show you what I planned for the media statement."

As I walked away, I had a sense of peace that was a

welcome emotion. If I believed Miss Guidry, I'd say the spirits were pleased. I knew my wife was in good hands. I also knew that she was where she wanted to be. It was time to make it all public.

By the time I turned on the landing midway to the bottom of the staircase, I could not only hear but also see the people gathering. One set of gray eyes met mine.

Fuck.

It was eleven o'clock.

Taking a deep breath, I made my way down the remaining stairs.

"Mr. Ramses, if you don't mind," Miss Guidry said, "I'll be happy to get the camera crew settled in your front office. They said it takes some time for lights and sound equipment."

"Thank you, Miss Guidry." I didn't give a fuck about any of that. "Mrs. Ramses," I added, "will be down shortly. I need a minute with Mr. Michelson."

Ms. Lynch stepped forward. "Mr. Ramses, Boyd and I have gone through the questions. I wanted you to know."

"Thank you, if you'll excuse me for a moment."

As Miss Guidry gathered Boyd Clark, Sophie Lynch, and the others and ushered them into the front office, Richard Michelson and I went the opposite direction, to the front sitting room. Closing the doors behind us, I didn't offer him a seat. "I obviously forgot about our meeting."

He nodded. "I heard you were giving the statement. I assume that means no one is missing."

"No one would include a great number of people. I'm sure someone is missing."

Michelson took a deep breath. "Will the missing person or persons be missed?"

"Not by me."

"You have a great deal of support at NOPD," Richard said. "News is already spreading that Boudreau's claims were false, and Mrs. Ramses is the true Boudreau heir."

"That sounds reasonable."

He took a step back. "You know, don't you?"

"That my wife is a twin and her birth certificate was altered? Yes, Richard, that came to our attention."

"There's no reason for that information to be shared."

Scoffing, I took a seat on one of the velvet loveseats, leaned back, and brought my ankle to my knee. "Yes, I can see how sharing that information would bring about questions. You see, I wondered how it all worked until Emma told me what Jezebel said."

"Jezebel?"

I nodded.

"She's alive?"

"Very much so." I lowered my foot and leaned forward. "Here's the thing, Richard, she's done with people. So don't ask anything more."

"Is she still...?" He shook his head.

"The rumors are correct. My wife looks very much like her mother. So much so, they could be mistaken one for the other."

"What I did," he said, "it can't come out."

"What did you do?"

Michelson's Adam's apple bobbed. "The Underwood stuff will go away. I'll make sure of it."

I nodded. "William Ingalls left town. If you ever have the opportunity, I'm sure you can corroborate that."

"Did he go far enough that he won't be found?"

I looked at the watch on my wrist and grinned. "Have you ever figured out the digestive cycle of gators? I know they prefer to eat at night." I shrugged. "Give us twenty-four hours."

"Boudreau?" he asked.

"My wife will be down shortly."

"Kyle O'Brien?"

"I heard he died in an automobile accident."

"Everett, I don't need surprises. I'm getting too fucking old for them."

"I don't know his future." I stood. "It's not in my hands."

"Who would you let make that...? Your wife?"

I grinned. "No, my wife isn't ready for life-or-death decisions. I entrusted him to someone more experienced."

"Mr. Ramses," Miss Guidry interrupted as she opened the doors. "They're ready."

"Mrs. Ramses?" I asked.

Miss Guidry nodded.

I turned to Richard. "I'd like to limit our visits in the future."

He offered me his hand. "I'm around when you need me."

We shook.

Leading the way, I stepped into the foyer. Across the hallway through the opened double doors, I watched as Emma greeted each person. Cameraperson or reporter, she shook each hand and smiled as they introduced themselves. She was striking, wearing a blue dress with a small jacket. The color matched her eyes.

"Fuck," I mumbled, unaware anyone heard.

"She'll make a fine queen," Miss Guidry said.

I nodded. "You're right."

"The spirits believed in her."

I looked down at the old lady who had spent my whole life making such statements. "Were they worried?"

"They were but not about her." Miss Guidry smiled. "She kept her promise, sir." She pushed on my arm. "Now go, and be nice."

Who knew that was a possibility?

Emma's blue eyes lit up as I came closer. "And you all know my husband—"

I took her hand, sat at her side, and squinted into the bright lights. The two chairs normally separated by a table had been moved together. I nodded at the reporter. "Hello, I'm Emma Ramses's husband."

After agreeing to the terms Mr. Clark and Ms. Lynch had come to with the news crew, the cameras began to roll. With Emma's hand in mine, we waited.

"Mrs. Ramses," the reporter began, "what do you want to tell the people of New Orleans?"

We hadn't planned for such an open-ended question. Nevertheless, I knew my wife was capable.

Emma smiled at me and back to the reporter. "I want to personally thank the people of New Orleans. I have no doubt that their actions and prayers worked for the greater good." She squeezed my hand. "I'm safe and" —she looked around— "home and exactly where I belong."

"Can you tell us what brought you to New Orleans?"

"I was offered a deal that I couldn't resist."

A deal with the devil.

EMMA

*R*ett and I traveled in the back seat as Leon drove and Ian sat beside him. Rett knew our destination—he'd arranged this gathering. However, only Ian, Leon, and I knew a particular stipulation. I asked the men that Rett not know the details until it was necessary.

I squeezed my husband's hand.

It had been over a month since our television interview. And although we refused to talk to the syndicated reporters on the street in front of our home, our interview was picked up by all the cable news networks all over the world, appearing not only on television but also on social media, and living forever on sites such as YouTube.

During the last month, we'd settled into a comfortable routine. At least once a week, we made our way out in public. Of course, Ian, Leon, or Noah was nearby and more of Rett's men were on the perimeter. I'd even made one trip without Rett to the city library. They had a reading program that they wanted to expand. Their website had a way to give donations.

Their goal was to add on to their building as an outreach program for New Orleans's children of all backgrounds. Ian called and set up an appointment with the president of the library board. When Ian and I entered the meeting, the board president wasn't alone. His assistant was present.

For only a moment, I imagined the horror of what happened to my mother, to enter a room with hopes and expectations only to have them crushed. Of course, my meeting was different. I'd been the one, through Ian, to call it.

As I handed them a check for $750,000 to begin the first phase of construction with a promise to double the donation once construction was started, no one present wanted to dash my dreams. The board president gushed and thanked me profusely.

That donation was only a small part of the money that came my way from Ross's electronic currency. It seemed, with some persuasion on Ross's parents' part, his death was changed from suicide to accidental. I offered them the cryptocurrency, but they refused, saying they wanted me to use it to keep Ross's dream alive. After all, we'd both gone to the University of Pittsburgh to be great writers. By investing in libraries and literary programs, I believed that his funds would open the world of literature and writing to the next generation.

"Mrs. Ramses," Leon said. We were still on the

highway, but from what little I could remember, the secret part of our journey was about to begin.

Ian grinned my direction as I opened my purse and removed two blindfolds. I handed one to my husband.

"What the hell?" Rett asked as he took the strip of material.

I tried to contain my smile. "It's your turn."

By Rett's expression, he was obviously confused.

"Do you remember the morning you came to get me in the back of the shop on St. Peter?"

"Yes, that day is etched forever in my mind." He lowered his voice. "I especially remember after the reporters left."

My eyelids fluttered as warmth crept up my neck and cheeks.

After the reporters and our attorneys left, we retired to our suites. Neither of us had slept the night before, and yet once we were alone, sleeping wasn't our goal.

I cleared my throat. "Yes, well that day, Edmée questioned Leon because my mother is very private. She only allows a select few to know where she lives."

Rett looked up from the blindfold in his grasp. "It's the bayou. I'll never remember."

"Boss," Leon said, "Ms. Edmée made me promise. If I upset her, I'll upset the spirits."

Rett rolled his eyes and exhaled. "Only me?"

Ian and I both held up a blindfold. "She said it was all right for Leon to see since he's been there once before."

"And he's driving," Rett added. He tied a knot with both ends of the fabric. "May I help you, Mrs. Ramses?"

"As long as you promise to put yours on too."

"I promise."

I turned away as he fitted the soft material over my eyes. Securing the tie, he leaned close and lowered his voice. Warm breaths skirted my neck, leaving goose bumps. "I'd forgotten how sexy you are in a blindfold."

My smile grew as I turned to him. Even though he was obscured from my vision, I pictured him, every inch, every muscle and crevice. I reached out until I found his eyes, also covered. "Thank you."

The tires bounced as the terrain became less refined.

I wasn't sure how long it took. With my hand in Rett's and my head on his shoulder, I didn't care. I was with the man I loved, surrounded by others I knew would protect me, and on my way to see my mother.

The SUV came to a stop.

"We're here," Leon announced.

I tugged on the knot in time to see Rett's eyes covered. Leaning closer, I kissed his cheek. "You can take that off now."

His handsome features morphed to a grin as he removed the fabric and the sexiest brown stare came my way. "This gave me a few ideas."

I shook my head as Ian opened the door beside Rett and we both stepped out onto the hard-packed ground.

"Wow," Rett said. "This house is..." His sentence trailed away.

"It's nicer than you expected," I said, finishing his sentence. I tugged on his suit coat. "I'd leave that in the car if I were you. I warned you about the lack of air conditioning."

Before he had the jacket off, Jezebel stepped onto the porch, her presence announced by the slamming of the screen door.

"You came."

Leaving my husband, I hurried up the steps and we embraced. If it were to be a quick hug, neither of us got the memo. There weren't words to describe my feelings at being in her arms. When the hug ended, she reached for my hand and with her other, she reached out to Rett.

I knew they'd spoken at the warehouse. He'd told me about it, yet as he stepped forward and offered a bow before taking her hand, I was certain my chest would explode. It was everything I'd never imagined.

"Mr. Ramses, welcome to my home."

"Rett, please," he said with a dashing smile. "Your home is lovely."

She spoke to Leon and Ian, "Please join us."

Leon shook his head. "We're fine, ma'am. If it's all right with you, we'll sit out here on the porch."

"You're welcome inside anytime."

I took in the surroundings as Rett and I followed my mother inside and walked back to the kitchen. Nothing had changed since I was there before, but this was the first time I was able to admire all that she had.

"Edmée made us supper," Jezebel said as we entered the kitchen, "but first, I have some lemonade if you'd like a glass."

"May I help?" I asked.

Jezebel smiled. "I'm so happy you're here. Let me enjoy having guests."

Before Rett and I took a seat at the table, he finished removing his suit coat, unlatched his cuff links, and rolled up his sleeves.

Mother smiled as she set two glasses of lemonade on the table. "I apologize for the heat. I'm not a fan of cold air."

After we all had our lemonade in front of us, Mother sat across from us. She turned to Rett. "I never properly thanked you."

Rett shook his head. "It's not—"

My curiosity was piqued. "For what?"

Mother's lips curled as she looked at my husband. "Didn't he tell you what happened?"

"Yes."

She nodded. "He saved my life."

I sat straight before turning toward Rett and back to my mother. "I must have missed that part of the story."

Jezebel reached across the table. I offered her my hands. Similar to what she'd worn when I first met her, each finger had a ring with a different colored stone. Looking at our union, she turned our hands one way and the next. Her blue eyes met mine. "I think my hands were the first clue."

Rett nodded.

"Clue?"

"I didn't know how much your mother wanted you to know. That's why I agreed to come here today, to bring you," Rett was speaking to me. "This way you know exactly what happened."

Jezebel released my hands and sat back. "Don't let him be modest. Mr. Ramses did save me even if it wasn't his intention."

"You didn't want to save her?"

Jezebel continued, "I left you and Edmée at the shop because" —she grinned at Rett— "I didn't know who to trust. I'd made misjudgments and well, I wasn't sure about Mr. Ramses. The shop was safe, and Daniel knew to bring you back here if I didn't survive or if here was the safest option for you." She exhaled. "You see, I had a plan. The spirits were loud, angry. The turmoil was not just in this realm. The answer was supposed to be clear, but I didn't want to see it. I wanted the prophecy to be for both you and Kyle. Once you were with me, I knew I'd been wrong. I'd hoped if I worked with him... And then Damas came to me." She paused. "He lives here. He and his wife have been here as long as I can remember. I think you spoke to them when you were here, on the back porch."

I nodded. "I remember."

"When someone doesn't even try to communicate, to learn a language or understand it, they become arrogant."

"Kyle?" I asked.

"William. He became careless about what he said in front of Damas and Cleo. Damas used William's carelessness. He later told me the spirits told him to listen." She smiled. "Even so, he apologized for eavesdropping. I'm grateful. What he did saved my children." She took a breath. "William was working to take over what I'd prepared. He knew about my money, my investments, and he wanted control of everything."

"What was your plan when you dropped us off?" I asked.

"I lured William, Kyle, and" —she lifted her chin toward Rett— "Mr. Ramses. I lured them to a warehouse outside of Baton Rouge. They all thought they were coming because of you. I had to learn the truth."

"Why *that* warehouse?" Rett asked.

"Sentimental reasons."

He tilted his head before asking, "How did you get the picture? The one you sent to me."

Jezebel sat taller. "I didn't take it if that's what you're asking."

The man beside me tensed. "I wasn't, but how?"

"It was shown to me. When I learned the men had been killed, I was relieved."

"Did you send them?"

She shook her head. "Sadly, I did; however, not for them to do what they did. William later explained that he gave the orders. He believed if Emma was scared, she'd go to him."

It was as if I was watching a tennis match as one spoke and then the other. I turned to my mother. "Liam was responsible for what the men did who...?" I didn't finish the sentence.

"They hurt you, Emma. I'm sorry. Claim it and it will never be used against you. I didn't know what they had been told to do until it was too late. Mr. Ramses had already found you. William wasn't far behind. He planned to save you as he did when you two were young, and then you two would be reunited. I didn't understand it all as part of his plan, but it was. When that didn't work, he had other ideas."

I stared down at my hands, seeing my wedding rings.

What would have happened if Liam had been the one to save me?

"So that morning," she said, "I lured all three men individually to the warehouse. They all thought they were coming for you, Emma." She sighed. "Daniel helped me."

"Helped you what?"

"He tied me to a chair."

"Not naked," I exclaimed.

"No, dear. He tied me facing away with my hair hanging down my back."

I turned to Rett. "Now I remember you saying Kyle thought Mother was me, but with everything that's happened, I'd forgotten."

He nodded. "I didn't bring it back up."

Jezebel nodded. "I kept my face down. From behind with our hair...I hoped that they'd all believe I was you, unconscious."

"Did they?" I turned to Rett. "You didn't."

He nodded. "I did. I saw her and I remembered when you were taken from me the first time. By the time I arrived to where I thought you were, William was already dead. I'd heard shouting so..." He looked at Jezebel. "You will have to tell us—if you want to—what they said. When I entered, a man surprised me.

My guard was down." He turned to me. "I only saw you."

"Mr. Ramses." She took a breath. "Rett. You'll have to forgive me. Old habits die hard and well, the Mr. and Mrs. Ramses I knew wouldn't be keen on me calling them by their first names."

Rett reached for my hand. "This Mr. and Mrs. Ramses would be honored if you'd forget our last name and only call us by our first."

"Rett," she said, "have you told Emma what you said?"

He shook his head. "Not in so many words."

Jezebel grinned. "So you haven't."

"I wasn't sure how to say it without explaining the entire episode."

"What did you say?" I asked.

Rett squeezed my hand. "Emma, I could claim temporary insanity. You see, my wife was missing, and then I thought I found her, but Isaiah was there with a gun pointed at her and..."

"And," I prompted.

"I told your brother the city was his. He could kill me if he wanted to as long as he let you go. I told him to let you go back to Pittsburgh, to let you forget you knew any of what was happening."

"And." This time the encouraging came from Jezebel.

Rett grinned my way. "The first time you said you loved me, who did you tell?"

"I told my..." —my eyes opened wide— "mother. Did you?"

"He did, Emma. It was beautiful and heartfelt. I knew at that moment that you were right, that you had the discernment I'd lacked. You married a good man. All of the things you'd said about him weren't manipulation or deceit. I knew then that he loved you, just as I knew you loved him."

I leaned over and kissed Rett's cheek. "I know that too." I turned to Jezebel. "Whatever happened to Emily?"

Mother shrugged.

"What about Kyle?"

She shook her head. "He won't be bothering you, I promise."

Rett sat taller. "Are you confident?"

"Yes, I am. He tried to kill Emma. If you hadn't rushed him, he would have killed me."

I shook my head. "Please don't tell me more."

Jezebel and Rett may be able to see lives as expendable, but I wasn't there yet. I didn't know if I'd ever be. Nevertheless, my mother had been right. Sometimes decisions had to be made.

Jezebel smiled. "More what, dear? Oh, I saw your interview."

My smile returned. "It's crazy."

"No, it's exactly what was meant to be. I heard you were trending."

A giggle bubbled within me. "Do you know what that means?"

"I'm sure she does," Rett said. "Your mother here has prompted me to learn the world of cryptocurrency. I'm certain that someone who can navigate that complicated and ever-changing world understands hashtags." He turned to her. "My people have done some digging. You're an accomplished businesswoman. Your assets are impressive, and you've done more than any of us realized for New Orleans's family-owned businesses."

"Thank you," she said modestly. "I've had things happen, but along the way I've been blessed with good people. If I could help in any way to repay the kindness they showed me, I've tried."

"Would you like to help us?"

Jezebel smiled. "Help you?"

"Ramses is a family business," Rett said. "I believe that means you."

Jezebel's blue eyes shone as she shook her head. "I'm good, but I can't tell you what the offer means."

"Mother, are you all right out here?" I asked. "Our house is big, and Rett and I have considered that maybe you'd like to live there."

Jezebel shook her head. "Maybe one day I can visit. But currently, I'm where I want to be. The city is loud. I enjoy the simple melody of the bayou." She grinned. "I would like it if you came around now and then."

"I can do that."

She tilted her chin toward the necklace I was wearing. "You're wearing the jade."

I reached for it and rolled the pendant between my fingers. "I am." I smiled. "I hoped you'd notice."

"It's right that you should have it."

"Emma said it belonged to her grandmother...Boudreau?" Rett asked.

Jezebel nodded with a grin. "The fire that took their home was tragic." She shrugged. "Not as tragic as it could have been. You see, I was there. Perhaps it was wrong of me, but I believed that after he was gone, my children were entitled to...things."

I turned to my husband trying to read his expression.

His spoke his question slowly. "You were there?"

She nodded. "In Baton Rouge too."

"What are you two talking about?" I asked.

Rett's stare was on my mother. His lips were still. It was as if for the first time since I'd met him, Everett Ramses was speechless.

Jezebel smiled. "Mr. Ramses, it seems the spirits have been crossing our paths for years as we unwittingly strove for many of the same goals. I didn't fully understand until recently. You see, I thought I knew what was meant to be, but I didn't. I never dreamt their plan would bring us to where we are today."

My husband sighed as he reached for my hand. "I can honestly say the same thing."

"Now," Jezebel said as she stood, "shall we eat?"

EPILOGUE - CHAPTER ONE

A year later

Emma

Warm rays of sun shone down from the open skylight. Alternating between pacing and practically bouncing on my toes, I waited for Miss Guidry to finish reading.

Content with my suite on the second floor, I'd decided to make the third-floor suite my writing room, my office. While I loved my suite on the second floor, and more importantly, the connection it shared with Rett's, there was something about this third floor, the library, and the sunshine. I felt at peace in this suite.

Finally, Miss Guidry wiped her tears as she turned away from the manuscript and smiled at me. "It's wonderful, Miss Emma."

"I know it's not one hundred percent accurate." I shrugged. "That's why they call it fiction."

She shook her head. "It's more accurate than I expected. Tell me how you knew."

"Knew what?"

I'd finished the story I began when I first arrived.

While I'd written short stories and novellas in college, this was my first full-length novel. The sense of accomplishment was greater than I expected. The story was women's fiction, the story of two friends. One was promised in marriage, the other was a modern-day lady in waiting. Through the years they shared their love for one another as only best friends can do. They celebrated and cried, rejoiced and mourned. They lived life devoted to one another, as well as the family the first woman bore, and the family the second woman adored. Even death couldn't stop their connection.

Miss Guidry stood, remaining unusually quiet, and looked out the window no longer obscured by shutters. The street below was lined with wrought-iron fences and beautiful hedges filled with flowers. The lawns were maintained to perfection as if ready to be featured on the Garden District tour.

"Is there something that I should change?" I asked.

"No." She wrapped her arms around her midsection. "I think that it's hard to explain choosing a life like mine. I'm sure there are people who believe it was wasted, not marrying or having my own family." She turned as silent tears streamed from her hazel eyes. "In your story, you don't call Miss Marilyn or me by name, but your story is about us, and you make it seem significant. It's beautiful."

I reached for Miss Guidry's hands. "You have a

family, us. And I believe friendship is both significant and beautiful."

"It's as if you saw or heard us, two scared young women on a journey that would change both of our lives. I've only spoken to Miss Marilyn about some things that my character sees and feels." Her eyes opened wider. "Did she tell you?"

I shrugged. "I'm trying to listen. Maybe I am. Sometimes when I was up here" —I turned a full circle taking in the beauty of the bookcases and the delight of the skylight— "I would just write. I can't explain it. No one was speaking, yet my fingers knew what to type."

Her smile grew. "Miss Marilyn loves you very much. She also wishes she could hug you."

"Also?" I took a step back. It was what I'd thought when I imagined her and Miss Delphine in the sitting room. I couldn't remember saying the words aloud.

"Don't be afraid, Miss Emma. Spirits mean no harm —well, most of them. Miss Marilyn knows she needs to go and she's trying to hold on."

"Go? Go where?"

"Beyond with Mr. Abraham. You understand, she couldn't leave, not when Mr. Ramses was alone. That's why I stayed when he offered me my own home and all the money I could spend. If I'd left, I'd be leaving her and him." Miss Guidry smiled at the manuscript on the desk. "Few people are as blessed as I've been. And in there, in your words, you show that."

I sat on the long chair. "I never thought about her leaving." There was an ache in my chest that was as real as if we were discussing a living being. "I don't want her to leave."

"That's kind."

"No, it's not." I looked up. "It's egocentric. I've lost people in my life, and then Rett found me when I didn't know that I was lost. I had forgotten what life could be and how I'd missed being loved and being around others who care about me and who I care for. The parents who raised us loved us. I'm certain of that. But they died. And now I have Rett, you, and my mother." I sighed. "There is also Ian and Leon, so many people." I tilted my head. "And included in that mix is Miss Marilyn. I started trying to talk to her when I was taken to Jezebel's house. I asked her to tell Rett I wasn't scared and that I was safe. I was more worried about what he might do to try to save me."

Miss Guidry nodded. "She heard you, child."

"And she told you and you told Rett." It wasn't really a question.

"I did." Her head shook. "He doesn't believe."

"I don't know about that. I'm not sure he believes or not. Rett's just...a man. What can we do to keep Miss Marilyn here?"

"She isn't sad about leaving," Miss Guidry said. "She knows Mr. Ramses is in good hands. She trusts you." She looked back at the manuscript. "What are you going to do with that?"

"Publish. It's always been my dream."

"Does Mr. Ramses share that dream?"

"He asked me to use a pseudonym."

"And are you all right with that?"

"I am. Emma Ramses's place is here with Rett, doing what I can do for New Orleans." I shrugged. "The writing can be a separate part of my life. When I first met Rett, he told me I could pursue my dream to write and that there's no better place to do it than in this city. I believe he was right."

"Have you decided on a name?" she asked.

"Betsy O'Brien." I grinned. "It's my way of honoring both of my mothers."

Miss Guidry smiled as she looked down. "I'm not supposed to tell you this."

"Is that going to stop you?"

She looked up through her lashes. "Miss Marilyn is concerned about Mr. Ramses's age. You see, before she leaves, she hopes she'll see at least one of her grandchildren."

My hand went to my stomach as my eyes opened wide. "You better tell her to hold off on crossing for a while. Rett and I haven't discussed children."

"Oh, child, talking doesn't make children."

I nodded with a grin. "Thank you. I'm aware of what makes children."

EPILOGUE - CHAPTER TWO

A few days later

Emma

Standing at the window of my suite, I lifted my long hair from my neck and stared down at the courtyard. It was a beautiful time of night as stars peppered the sky and the Ramses family crest glistened in the color-changing lights from the fountain. While the days remained steamy as only Louisiana weather can, I mostly enjoyed the open windows in the evenings. Even the warmth radiating in the night air was getting more comfortable. Maybe it was Jezebel's influence though I was quite certain that banning all air conditioning would never be on my agenda.

I turned as footsteps echoed from Rett's suite.

With my hands on the window's ledge, a smile curled my lips and lifted my cheeks as I waited for Rett to enter. I don't recall dreaming about marriage or predicting what it would entail, but as my husband's dark stare met mine and my body reacted, I believed that our marriage was something special.

We were two people who knew nothing about one another—okay, Rett had researched me—and yet despite our lack of knowledge and completely diverse childhoods and life choices, fate intervened. Our union didn't simply happen. No, fate demanded it. The spirits and the people of New Orleans approved.

As he came closer, I remembered seeing him the first night in the crowded courtyard. Even without knowing him, I felt his stare, a pull from across the crowded space. He'd been leaning against the stone archway. His white shirt strained at the seams beneath his broad shoulders. His sleeves were rolled to his elbows and his hair was combed back in soft waves.

That night as now, Everett Ramses radiated power. Crowds parted as he walked.

And yet as I'd mused when with my brother, Rett didn't need to say a word or prove his significance. His confidence was innate, his power resounded in his voice, and his sincerity manifested in his concern, not only for me but for New Orleans.

"I thought you said you'd be late," I said with a grin.

Flames of desire flickered in his gaze as he scanned me from my blonde hair to my toes. After over a year, I couldn't understand how Rett was still capable of melting my insides with only a look or a phrase.

"Are you ready for me?"

It was one of his favorite questions. Mine too.

I could answer, but there was no doubt that he knew.

My nipples hardened, noticeable beneath my satin camisole. And if I were to be asked, the satin shorts would probably show the telltale sign of my need.

His strong hands came to my waist. As if I weighed nothing, Rett lifted me to the window sill with a grin, spread my knees, and stepped between my legs. "Are you going to make me wait for your answer?" He tried to sound stern. "You should know, I don't like to wait."

"My answer is the same as it was yesterday and will be tomorrow." I framed his cheeks with my palms. His day-long beard growth ignited a flicker within me that was already poised to start a raging blaze as I imagined that roughness on my sensitive skin.

His strong lips met mine, taking what was his as I willingly gave in return. Our tongues found one another's and his fingers splayed on my lower back, pulling me to him. My breasts flattened against his solid chest. When he leaned away, Rett answered my earlier question. "I cut one meeting short and canceled the other."

I lifted his chin, returning his gaze from my breasts to my eyes. "Any reason?"

"I couldn't stand the idea of you up here all alone."

"My hero."

"No, Emma. I'm no hero. My motivation wasn't as chivalrous as I made it sound."

"Then what could your motivation possibly be?"

Scooping me from the window sill, Rett carried me

to my bed and laid me on sheets where I'd pulled back the covers. "Take off your clothes."

There was no hesitation as I pulled the camisole over my head and lowered the shorts. Not to be outdone, Rett's shirt, belt, pants, socks, and shoes were scattered over the floor. I stared as each muscle within him was defined as he moved, from his powerful thighs, to his tight abs and his broad shoulders. I found myself obsessed with everything about him.

Like a predator stalking its prey, Rett came closer. A tug of my ankles and my ass was on the edge of the mattress. "Lift your feet to the bed and spread your legs."

There was a quality in his demand, a tone and timbre that set me on edge. I could try to hold out, to not be affected, but each time I failed miserably.

One of his large hands came to my stomach, pushing me back.

"Lift your arms."

As I obeyed, two fingers plunged inside me. My back arched as I sucked in a breath.

"I love how wet you are."

Closing my eyes, I became lost in his touch, his rhythm, and his skill. Bending over me, he coated my flesh in kisses and nips. His plan was to attack on multiple fronts. My mind was scattered as I tried to keep up.

First, each nipple was adored and then his thumb found my clit. Somehow Rett understood my body more than I as he'd work me to the edge of ecstasy only to pull me back.

Each time I felt so close, so ready, only to have him tease me more.

Reaching for his cheeks, I pulled his lips to mine. Once the kiss ended, I asked, "Did you cut your meeting short to drive me insane?"

Rett's lips curled as his stare glistened. "Is that what I'm doing?"

"You know you are."

He lifted his chin toward the headboard and followed me onto the bed. "On your hands and knees, beautiful."

The suite filled with my sounds of pleasure as he held onto my hips and thrust deep inside. My body contracted around him as he filled me completely. The friction consumed my thoughts as his rhythm and speed increased. Faster and faster. I was aboard a high-speed locomotive and there was no way to stop, no brakes, or even the ability to slow.

I called out his name as every muscle tightened and every nerve synapsed. Like electrical wires in an ice storm, explosion after explosion detonated. I fought to maintain my position but the orgasm was too intense. Maybe it was because he'd denied me as my need grew or it was simply the man I'd married.

Rett pulled out, rolled me to my back, and we joined again as one.

His handsome face was before me as his muscles strained and he continued his drive. My second release was near as his lips opened and he found his own. Before Rett, I'd never known the stunning beauty and connection that occurred when watching a man come apart. The way his features contorted and his body tensed was raw and primitive and absolutely breathtaking.

My release came, quivering my muscles and holding him tight, not wanting our connection to end. Rett's lips met mine before he rolled and we were no longer one.

I rolled too, until we were face-to-face.

His molten stare was all I could see. "I'm glad you cut your meetings short."

He teased a stray strand of my hair away from my face before kissing my nose. "You were quiet at dinner. I couldn't stop thinking about it."

A smile lifted my cheeks. "Are you saying I talk a lot?"

"No, I'm saying you didn't talk. I know that look of yours. You're thinking or overthinking. What's happening behind those beautiful eyes?"

I shook my head, not willing to spoil our moment.

Rett lifted my chin. "I could demand you tell me."

"I'm not scared of you, Everett Ramses."

After a kiss to my hair, he sat up against the headboard. "Good."

I scooted until my head rested upon his wide chest. The tapping of his heart sounded a soft drum against my ear, giving me courage. Taking a breath, I spoke, "Miss Guidry said something the other day that has me thinking."

He laid his head back. "Oh God. I wish I hadn't mentioned it."

Grinning, I looked up. "No, you're getting more observant. That's a good thing."

Rett placed a finger under my chin. "I'm almost afraid to ask, but what did she say?"

"Your mom is ready to go."

From Rett's expression, that wasn't what he expected. "Go? On a trip? Is that a thing?"

I shook my head. "Edmée explained that spirits stay in this realm when they can't or don't want to cross over. Your mom didn't want to leave you, but now she believes you're in good hands."

Lifting one of my hands, Rett kissed the tips of my fingers and grinned. "I like being in your hands."

"Edmée said that spirits freely cross over when they believe their work here is done."

"So my mother thinks her work is done."

"Kind of," I said, hedging whether I would continue.

"Now you have me curious."

"She is concerned about your age and would like to see a grandchild."

Rett's eyes opened wide. "I'm old, am I? And a grandchild? She would. Or is it Miss Guidry or you?"

"It's not me," I answered too fast. "I mean, maybe one day." I turned away. "This sounds selfish."

"Emma, look at me."

I turned back.

"Talk to me."

"I want children someday, but right now, I want to be us. I'm excited about the book, and the construction at the library is progressing. My mother recently told me about a homeless shelter and food distribution center in the Lower Ninth that needs help..." I sat up. "I'm sorry if I'm not what you want."

"You are every fucking thing I want. Don't apologize for being the queen New Orleans loves." Rett wrapped his arms around me and pulled me closer until our lips touched. When we separated, he was smiling. "I love you. I never thought that would happen. I didn't know I was capable of feeling it, much less saying it. But fuck, you're..." He inhaled as his chest inflated. "I want time for us too, Emma. And I'm relatively certain that while I am older than you, I'm not too old to father a child. Besides, my mother knows I've always been a bit stubborn. Children can be on *our* schedule. She can go or she can stay. I hope she stays."

"You do? You believe Miss Guidry?"

"I believe Miss Guidry believes my mother is here."

I nodded. "You don't think waiting is selfish?"

"No, Emma. I asked you to marry me, to be beside me, to rule New Orleans with me, and to be the queen you were born to be. I didn't marry you for children." He shrugged. "Maybe one day." His grin grew.

"What are you thinking?"

"I was thinking about a little you. After all, you look so much like Jezebel; our daughter could be another carbon copy."

"How about a little you?" I asked.

"Oh, then my mother will definitely leave. She went through that once." He exhaled. "I guess that I'm not against children, but I want some time too. I mean, how can you be ready for me anytime, anyplace if your attention is divided?"

"But someday?" I asked, surprised I was pushing this.

Rett nodded. "When you're ready and I'm ready. Our schedule, not my mother's." He kissed my nose. "As long as I have you, I'm content. Are you?"

"More than I ever imagined."

"Are you sure, angel?" he asked.

"I promise."

And They Lived Happily Ever After

Thank you for reading Everett and Emma's story. For a glimpse into the honeymoon Rett promised Emma, click this link: Honeymoon Extra, sign up for Aleatha's newsletter (you can unsubscribe in the future), stay informed, and enjoy one more peek into the world of the Devil's Series.

If you enjoyed Rett and Emma and you like sexy alphas and strong, smart heroines, be sure to pre-order Aleatha's upcoming dark and dangerous and oh, so steamy story **RED SIN** . Donavan and Julia will be here soon.

If you're looking for more of Aleatha's signature stories, alphas you love, and heroines you'll admire, check out these already released series:

Web of Sin trilogy
SECRETS - free
LIES
PROMISES

Tangled Web trilogy
TWISTED
OBSESSED
BOUND

Web of Desire trilogy
SPARK
FLAME
ASHES

Dangerous Web trilogy
Prequel: "Danger's First Kiss" – free
DUSK
DARK
DAWN

Infidelity Series (Not about cheating)
BETRAYAL- free
CUNNING
DECEPTION
ENTRAPMENT
FIDELITY

Consequences Series
CONSEQUENCES - free
TRUTH

CONVICTED
REVEALED
BEYOND THE CONSEQUENCES
RIPPLES

Light Duet
INTO THE LIGHT
AWAY FROM THE DARK

For a complete list of all of Aleatha's books, please go to
BOOKS BY NY TIMES AUTHOR -ALEATHA
ROMIG in the back of this book.

WHAT TO DO NOW

LEND IT: Did you enjoy ANGEL'S PROMISE? Do you have a friend who'd enjoy ANGEL'S PROMISE? ANGEL'S PROMISE may be lent one time. Sharing is caring!

RECOMMEND IT: Do you have multiple friends who'd enjoy my dark romance with twists and turns and an all new sexy and infuriating anti-hero? Tell them about it! Call, text, post, tweet...your recommendation is the nicest gift you can give to an author!

REVIEW IT: Tell the world. Please go to the retailer where you purchased this book, as well as Goodreads, and write a review. Please share your thoughts about ANGEL'S PROMISE on:

*Amazon, ANGEL'S PROMISE Customer Reviews

*Barnes & Noble, ANGEL'S PROMISE, Customer Reviews

*iBooks, ANGEL'S PROMISE Customer Reviews

* BookBub, ANGEL'S PROMISE Customer Reviews

*Goodreads.com/Aleatha Romig

BOOKS BY NEW YORK TIMES BESTSELLING AUTHOR
ALEATHA ROMIG

RIBBON SERIES:

WHITE RIBBON

August 2021

RED SIN

October 2021

DEVIL'S SERIES (Duet):

Prequel: **"FATES DEMAND"**

March 18

DEVIL'S DEAL

May 2021

ANGEL'S PROMISE

June 2021

WEB OF SIN:

SECRETS

October 2018

LIES

December 2018

PROMISES

January 2019

TANGLED WEB:

TWISTED

May 2019

OBSESSED

July 2019

BOUND

August 2019

WEB OF DESIRE:

SPARK

Jan. 14, 2020

FLAME

February 25, 2020

ASHES

April 7, 2020

DANGEROUS WEB:

Prequel: "Danger's First Kiss"

DUSK

November 2020

DARK

January 2021

DAWN

February 2021

THE INFIDELITY SERIES:

BETRAYAL

Book #1

October 2015

CUNNING

Book #2

January 2016

DECEPTION

Book #3

May 2016

ENTRAPMENT

Book #4

September 2016

FIDELITY

Book #5

January 2017

~

CONSEQUENCES COMPANION READS:

BEHIND HIS EYES-CONSEQUENCES

January 2014

BEHIND HIS EYES-TRUTH

March 2014

∿

STAND ALONE MAFIA THRILLER:

PRICE OF HONOR

Available Now

∿

THE LIGHT DUET:

Published through Thomas and Mercer Amazon exclusive

INTO THE LIGHT

June 2016

AWAY FROM THE DARK

October 2016

∿

TALES FROM THE DARK SIDE SERIES:

INSIDIOUS

(All books in this series are stand-alone erotic thrillers)

Released October 2014

ALEATHA'S LIGHTER ONES:

PLUS ONE

Stand-alone fun, sexy romance

May 2017

ANOTHER ONE

Stand-alone fun, sexy romance

May 2018

ONE NIGHT

Stand-alone, sexy contemporary romance

September 2017

A SECRET ONE

April 2018

ABOUT THE AUTHOR

Aleatha Romig is a New York Times, Wall Street Journal, and USA Today bestselling author who lives in Indiana, USA. She has raised three children with her high school sweetheart and husband of over thirty years. Before she became a full-time author, she worked days as a dental hygienist and spent her nights writing. Now, when she's not imagining mind-blowing twists and turns, she likes to spend her time with her family and friends. Her other pastimes include reading and creating heroes/anti-heroes who haunt your dreams!

Aleatha impresses with her versatility in writing. She released her first novel, CONSEQUENCES, in August of 2011. CONSEQUENCES, a dark romance, became a bestselling series with five novels and two companions released from 2011 through 2015. The compelling and epic story of Anthony and Claire Rawlings has graced more than half a million e-readers. Her first stand-alone smart, sexy thriller INSIDIOUS was next. Then Aleatha released the five-novel INFIDELITY series, a romantic suspense saga, that took the reading world by storm, the final book landing on three of the top bestseller lists. She ventured into traditional publishing with Thomas and Mercer. Her books INTO THE

LIGHT and AWAY FROM THE DARK were published through this mystery/thriller publisher in 2016. In the spring of 2017, Aleatha again ventured into a different genre with her first fun and sexy stand-alone romantic comedy with the USA Today bestseller PLUS ONE. She continued with ONE NIGHT and ANOTHER ONE. If you like fun, sexy, novellas that make your heart pound, try her INDULGENCE SERIES. In 2018 Aleatha returned to her dark romance roots with SPARROW WEBS.

Aleatha is a "Published Author's Network" member of the Romance Writers of America and PEN America. She is represented by Kevan Lyon of Marsal Lyon Literary Agency and Dani Sanchez with Wildfire Marketing.

facebook.com/aleatharomig
twitter.com/aleatharomig
instagram.com/aleatharomig

Made in the USA
Monee, IL
29 July 2021